DEEP WOODS

HELENA NEWBURY

FOSTER & BLACK

For Isabelle, who sparkles

ISBN: 978-1-914526-01-5

PROLOGUE

THIS IS A STORY about people.

It's about a smoking hot guy called Cal, a guy so big and intimidating, so much part of the forest that they nicknamed him *Bigfoot*. A guy who turned out to be the most loving, most protective guy in the world. And it's about me, Bethany, a very normal, pale, curvy girl who never thought she'd leave the city, or even why she'd want to.

But this is also a story about *people* and what happens when they're treated like a commodity. And it's about the huge, wild places where there *are* no people, where you can walk and walk and never see another living soul, where you can be totally alone with the person you love.

We need to start at the beginning, though. And before the stars and the sunrises and the rivers, before campfires crackling and a cow nuzzling my palm and being carried in Cal's strong arms and before I was running barefoot through the forest, terrified for my life...I met Rufus.

This is a story about people, but it begins with a dog.

1

BETHANY

IF I HADN'T been moving slowly, I'd never have heard him. A shift had just ended and most people were running through the cold March rain to their cars. I was left far behind as I trudged across the parking lot, exhausted. I'd just pulled a double shift and my neck and back were in agony from hunching over my computer, my ears ringing from twenty-four hours of being yelled at. Everything seemed gray. Slate-gray sky overhead, newspaper-gray buildings all around me...even the fumes from the factory next door smelled gray: a bland chemical tang that got inside your nostrils and blocked out anything pleasant. All I wanted to do was get home and cocoon myself in bed with a movie—

I froze. *What was that?*

There'd been a sound. Faint, almost covered by the hissing rain. But it resonated deep in my chest, waking a chain of instincts and setting them ringing like silvery bells. My mom had had those same instincts, and her mom before her. None of us could ignore them.

It was the sound of someone in pain.

I looked around. Everyone else was getting into their cars. The next shift were already inside. I was the only one who'd heard it.

The sound again: high and ragged, a kind of wail. I moved slowly towards it. In the alley between two buildings, I could just barely make out a dark shape on the ground. A drunk, passed out? Or was it a trap, was the guy going to leap up and grab me when I got close? I looked back at the parking lot and cursed. Everyone else was driving away.

I took a tentative step into the alley. I could hear him breathing, now. Slow. Labored. And there was something off about it: each out-breath was a throaty rasp.

I took another step and the shape twisted and lunged, teeth snapping. I screamed and jumped back, going down on my ass on the soaked concrete.

I dug out my phone and switched on the flashlight. Tan fur and a shining black nose. Big brown eyes. A dog. It was stretched out on its side, but it had twisted and raised its head to snap at me. I traced the light over its tall, silky ears and the black patch that covered its back. A German Shepherd, almost as big as me.

We stared at each other. The dog gave a warning growl, a rumble that made my insides turn to water. *Stay back.* But as I retreated down the alley, the growl became a whimper.

I lifted my phone higher and traced it over the dog again, lighting up the rest of it. Metal strands gleamed bright, tangled around two of the dog's legs. Barbed wire. The ugly little spikes had sunk into its flesh and the more it struggled, the more it hurt itself.

That feeling in my chest again, the one I couldn't ignore. I needed to help it but as soon as I inched forward, it barked, loud enough to make my ears ring. I froze, my heart hammering. I'd gotten a glimpse of its teeth, this time, teeth designed to rip and tear flesh. It was only aggressive because it was scared, but it could still injure me. Maybe even kill me if it went for my throat.

I had no idea what to do. I'd never been around a dog before, at least not a big one. The only ones I saw around my apartment building were tiny little pugs. "It's okay," I told the dog. I crawled forward and, on instinct, I held out my hand.

The dog stared at it and then sniffed suspiciously, its nose twitching. It growled again, but less certainly.

I crawled closer, one inch at a time, hand still extended. The dog tensed, ready to attack. I could see the muscles coiling under its coat. "It's okay," I said in a strangled voice.

We stared at one another, neither of us daring to move. I held my breath...and moved my hand close enough for it to reach. Images flashed through my head: teeth snapping, severed fingers falling—

The dog sniffed at my hand. It was so big, I could feel the suck of air against my fingertips. "It's okay," I whispered.

The dog drew its head back and relaxed, flopping back onto its side. I crawled right up to it. God, it was enormous! *How big would it be, if it was standing?* Past my waist, at least.

How do you calm dogs? I hesitantly reached out and put my hand on its side. My fingers sank into deep, soft fur. I thought of German Shepherds as having short, bristly coats, but this one didn't. I stroked and it was so soft...I felt both of us relax. "Good dog," I breathed.

I shone the flashlight over its legs. *Shit.* It was really tangled. It must have gotten wrapped up in the wire and then struggled, unable to escape, and made it worse and worse. It would have been trapped there until it died of thirst if I hadn't heard it.

I reached for one of the loops of wire, and the dog lifted its head and growled again. There was a metal jangle right next to my head and I looked round...and stopped dead.

There was a coil of barbed wire an inch from my face. I leaned back out of the way and shone the flashlight around, lighting up the dark parts of the alley I'd ignored until now. The wire led up to the top of the fence at the end of the alley. The dog must have scrambled over the fence, gotten tangled in the barbed wire, and pulled half of it down with him. It lay in sharp, springy coils all around us. When the dog moved, it moved. If the dog struggled, I could lose an eye. If it panicked and tried to get away, I could wind up with wire wrapped around my neck.

I looked back towards the mouth of the alley. I could just walk away, and I'd be safe. But if I didn't help it, no one would.

Barely daring to breathe, I took hold of a loop that had dug deep into the dog's leg. The dog raised its head and let out a whimper. The coils jangled and moved around us. "Shh," I told it desperately. "Shh, I know, I know it hurts. But you have to stay still." *Idiot. Like it's going to understand you.*

But the dog looked at me with big, sorrowful eyes and then slowly laid its head back down as if it *did* understand.

I loosened the wire, wincing as I teased the barbs from the dog's flesh. Its breathing tightened and it trembled in pain...but it didn't move. I ran a hand over its big, furry flank. "*Shh, shh.* You're doing great."

Barb by barb, loop by loop, I slowly freed the dog. I didn't have anything to cut the wire with, so I had to just pull it out of the way and use my elbows and legs to hold it clear so it didn't spring back. I picked up a few scrapes and cuts even through my jeans and hooded top, and my hands were scratched to hell. But finally, I got the last leg free. "*There,*" I said triumphantly. The dog scrambled free and rose up: God, it was even bigger than I'd thought, looming over me as I knelt. I expected it to run away but it waited for me as if wanting to make sure I was safe, too.

At the mouth of the alley, I crouched down and ruffled its fur. A big, wet tongue licked my cheek and I yelped in surprise and then laughed, relief washing over me. *We did it.* When I stood up, the dog immediately pressed close to me. It felt like we'd bonded for life.

I stood up, ruffled its fur again and waited, expecting it to run off home. But it looked around, sniffed the air and then moved over to me, limping a little. Either it didn't have a home, or it didn't know the way. I looked for a collar but there wasn't one. *Shit. Now what?* It needed a vet, but even if I could find one at this time of night, I had no money to pay. I couldn't just leave it like this. Its wounds would get infected if they weren't dressed.

The dog looked at me and cocked its head to the side, then snuffled its wet nose into my hand.

I sighed. "Okay," I said aloud. "Looks like you're coming home with me."

It limped alongside me, pressing tight against my legs as I crossed the parking lot. As soon as I opened the back door of my aging

Toyota, it jumped inside and curled up, taking up the entire back seat.

When we arrived at my apartment building, I sneaked the dog into the elevator and up to my floor. My apartment was silent: I share it with three other women, but we're all on different shifts at the call center so we barely see each other, and because people don't stay at this sort of job long, there's no time to get to know them. Some of my flatmates I see literally once every few weeks: if it wasn't for notes on the refrigerator, they wouldn't know I was still there.

I fetched the first aid kit, then sat down cross-legged on the kitchen floor and went to work on the dog's wounds, gently cleaning and bandaging them. The dog seemed to trust me now, and let me work, occasionally pushing its head at me so I could scratch behind its silky ears. When I'd finished, I dug in the refrigerator and found it some raw steak I'd been saving for the weekend, which it wolfed down, and gave it a bowl full of water which it noisily drank. Then I laid some towels on the couch to make a bed. "You can sleep there," I told it, yawning.

I stumbled into my room, stripped off my clothes, and fell into bed, exhausted. I'm sure I remember sleep being pleasant when I was a kid, a slow drift into warm peace. But ever since things went south, I don't so much sleep as pass out when my body runs out of energy. I wake up exhausted, like I've slept with one eye open, afraid that something bad might happen if I sleep too heavily. Maybe it's the shift work or maybe it's something deeper, something to do with everything in my life being so temporary. Maybe I don't sleep well because I never feel truly safe.

Just as my eyes closed, I heard a pattering and the creak of my door opening, and then the whole bed bounced as something warm and heavy landed on it.

"Oh...no," I told it half-heartedly. "No, wait, you can't sleep—"

The dog turned around three times and then sank down and curled up in a determined warm croissant against my legs.

I sighed and relented. It was a cold night and the warmth of it was very comforting. "Okay," I said. "Just for tonight."

~

I had the next day off and I'd been planning to spend it catching up on sleep. But I needed to find the dog's owner and I figured the alley was a good place to start. Maybe in the daylight, the dog would be able to retrace its steps.

But I'd barely pulled up and let the dog out of the back door when it pricked up its ears, sniffed the air and bolted off, a furry missile. Its wounds didn't seem to slow it down at all: it raced down the street and disappeared around the corner. I sprinted after it, rounded the corner, and *whumped* straight into someone.

A flash of impressions. The huge size of him: a wall of warm, hard muscle. A red and black plaid shirt. The scent of him: pine needles and freshly-chopped wood, dark earth and clean air.

I fell on my ass for the second time in twenty-four hours and looked up....

And *up.*

He was taller than me by a full head. What was he, 6'8"?! But he wasn't lanky, he was *big.* His biceps stretched out his plaid shirt like boulders. Lower down, the fabric was rolled up to reveal caramel-tanned forearms loaded with muscle and they led down to huge, powerful hands with fingers twice the size of mine. His legs, in faded black jeans and muddy boots, were as sturdy as giant redwoods. He looked like he could wrestle a freakin' bear. But it wasn't his size that made me gaze up in wonder. It was his spirit, his attitude: it affected everything, from his clothes to the way he stood.

He was *wild.* The polar opposite of everything I was. He didn't sit in an office, or commute by car, or worry about customer satisfaction surveys. He lived *out there,* someplace far from the city, where you had to hunt and kill to survive. It throbbed from his soul and when it hit me, I could feel my whole body reacting in a way I didn't understand. It was like running your hand over rough tree bark when you've only ever felt smooth plastic. It was like mountain air when you've only ever breathed air conditioning.

Then I became aware of the dog, up on its hind legs and

frantically trying to lick the man's face. Its big, furry tail was wagging so hard I could feel the breeze. It was ecstatic. And the relief in the man's eyes as he ruffled the dog's fur and scratched behind his ears made my throat close up. *This* was who the dog had been running to. This was its owner.

God, he was hot as hell. Not in a Hollywood movie star, smoothly perfect way. In a rough, whiskey-and-nails way. He was tanned from a life spent outdoors and his hair was thick and untamed, the color of a wheat field. His beard was just as richly gold and framed a hard upper lip and a gorgeously soft, full lower one. Then he turned to me and—

Cornflower-blue eyes that lit up as they stared at me. They pinned me, held me as securely as if he'd used those massive hands to push me up against a tree. I couldn't move, couldn't fight. Didn't want to. A hot ripple went right through my body—

And when that ripple hit my soul, it vibrated like a guitar string plucked just right. For a second, I forgot how to breathe.

He stared down at me, transfixed, those deep blue eyes gobbling me up in huge, hungry chunks. And it made no sense because this was *me*. I'm not some tanned, willowy blonde with abs you can bounce a quarter off. My hair's black and curly and won't behave. I was pale even *before* I started working in the call center and I'm curvy, all hips and ass and boobs. My German great-grandmother used to proudly say that our family came from *good healthy peasant stock*. We're dependable, not remarkable. I never transfixed anyone.

And yet he was looking at me like I was the best thing he'd ever seen.

Then he looked away for a second, and when he looked back at me, his brows had lowered and his jaw was set. Those blue eyes had frozen hard and the combination of that glare, and his monstrous size, almost made me back away.

But then, as he looked into my eyes, I saw the lust flash again for a second, scalding hot and primal. In an instant, it was buried again and the glare was back.

I thought of his dog, growling at me in the alley, trying to scare me away.

He reached down and offered me his hand. I stared at it stupidly, then reached up and took it. I was hoisted upright, so fast and effortlessly it was like being in an express elevator. *God,* he was strong. And his hand was so big, engulfing mine in its warmth, his skin rough and calloused. When he released my hand, I could feel my skin tingling. I couldn't explain it, but I wanted more of that touch, more of that roughness against me. I wanted to mold myself to him and have him crush my softness against him. *What the hell is the matter with me?*

He looked at his dog again, at the bandages on its legs. Then he looked at me. "That was you?" Just the bare minimum of words and even they came out haltingly. Like he hadn't spoken in a really long time.

I nodded and explained how I'd found his dog and treated it. And he just stood there, staring down at me, listening. *Really* listening, like he didn't want to miss a word. And the longer it went on, the more I saw those cornflower-blue eyes soften. He started to lean in, millimeter by millimeter.

I finished my story but he said nothing, just kept staring down at me. The dog bounded over to me and circled around and around my legs, pushing up against me so hard it almost knocked me over. I put a hand down and let it trail through the dog's thick fur, but I couldn't look away from those blue eyes. Every time I looked into them, I felt that slow, aching vibration. Like he had one of those big, calloused fingers resting right on that guitar string inside me and he was just caressing it, both of us unsure but both of us feeling how loaded with tension it was.

He finally looked away. He glanced at the street, the passing cars, the skyscrapers, as if suddenly remembering where he was, and I saw his body tense. I thought of some huge animal, prowling its concrete cell at the zoo. He didn't belong here.

"Thanks," he said gruffly. He turned to go and a sudden, cold panic washed through me. *I'll never see him again!* I blinked. What the hell was wrong with me? I'd only just met him!

The dog, I told myself. I'd miss the big fluffball. That was all it was. He took a step away.

"I'm Bethany." It was out before I realized my mouth was moving. I cringed. *Idiot!* What if he just ignored me and walked on? *He's way out of your league.*

But he turned back to me. And the shock I saw in his eyes was the good kind. Like he was surprised *I'd* be into *him.* Something in my chest lifted and bobbed like a balloon.

For a second, it was like he was battling with himself. Something powerful was trying to make him turn away and march off: he'd glance away from me and those big shoulders would tense as if he was about to turn...then he'd catch my eye again and it was like he...melted.

"Cal," he said at last. He nodded at the dog. "That's Rufus."

Cal? Short for...Caleb? It made me think of log cabins and covered wagons. I liked it. And I liked his voice. Big, like him, and low...I didn't just hear it, I felt it in my chest. The men I met in Seattle used their voices as weapons, sweet and cajoling and then, if you dared to say *no* to them, bitter and vicious. And all the while, they stared at my chest. But Cal looked me right in the eye and although he still spoke slowly, like he was out of practice, he talked straight. Each word was like a rough-hewn hunk of sandstone that he chiseled out of the ground and slammed down on the ground between us. *There. That's what I said. Take it or leave it.*

"How'd you lose him?" I asked.

The man frowned at Rufus. "He ran after a cat." Rufus did his best to look innocent. "He'd never seen one before."

I stared at Rufus. "He'd never seen a *cat* before?!"

His words seemed to be coming a little easier, now, like he was loosening up. He looked east, towards the edge of the city and beyond. "We live...a long way out. Just here for a day."

How far into the country did you have to live to never see a cat? Even people on farms had cats, right? Who *was* this guy? His clothes weren't shabby but they were faded from the sunlight, patched and repatched where they'd been torn. I looked down at my sweater and jeans. I'd bought both on the internet just a few months ago. They were dirt cheap, but I only gave them another week before they started to fall apart.

Cal looked again at the bandages on Rufus's legs. "How'd you learn to do that?"

"Med school."

"You're a doctor?"

I looked away, shame heating my face. "I was going to be." I caught sight of the call center behind me, reflected in a puddle. I nodded over my shoulder at it. "I work there, now."

He kept looking at me and I could feel the concern, the questions he wanted to ask. But I wouldn't meet his eyes and, at last, he dutifully looked at the call center. "No windows?"

"Yeah, they just keep the lights on inside 24/7. You don't know what time of day it is. Stops people getting sleepy on the night shift."

He took a half step forward. With his size, it should have felt scary but it didn't. He loomed over me almost protectively and I felt an unexpected rush of warmth. "Ain't right, them cooping people up like that," he said. "What do you do in there?"

"It's a call center. You know when you call the helpdesk because there's something wrong with your computer? That's us."

He just blinked at me.

He doesn't use a computer?! "We help people fix the problem." I grimaced. "There's a lot of yelling."

His whole body stiffened and if it was possible, he seemed to grow even bigger. Those deep blue eyes flashed, like he wanted to personally hunt down every last person who'd ever yelled at me.

And I got a hint, just for a split second, of what it might be like to feel safe. And it felt so good, my chest went tight and I got a lump in my throat.

Don't be stupid. He was a complete stranger and he lived hundreds of miles away, probably in a different state. I made my voice cheery and light. "It was good to meet you, Cal." I scratched Rufus behind the ears and he pushed up against me, his tail thumping the sidewalk happily. "You too, Rufus."

But when I looked up at Cal, he was still staring at me. And as soon as our eyes locked, I felt that string inside me pull tight, ready to sing. My fake lightness fell away. I swallowed.

He leaned an inch closer, looming over me again—

Then he looked away. And whatever he wanted to say, instead he muttered, "Don't let 'em use you, Bethany."

He turned on his heel and strode off, his long legs eating up the distance. Rufus looked between us uncertainly. He trotted after Cal, then stopped and looked back again. He kept doing it, all the way down the street.

Then they turned the corner and were gone. And I became aware of an ache inside, one I'd had for years but hadn't ever acknowledged.

I'd glimpsed what I didn't even know I'd been searching for.

And now I'd never see him again.

2

CAL

A S WE WALKED AWAY, I could see Rufus looking back over his shoulder at her. I had to force myself not to do the same.

When I was a teenager, growing up in the country, the posters on my wall were all from TV shows and movies set in cities. Cities were almost mythical places, all towering skyscrapers and cocktail parties, and the most fascinating part of them, for a teenage boy, was the women: sexy and sophisticated, gentle and refined. They were so different to the women around me, women who'd been raised to shuck wheat and milk cows. I knew a city woman wouldn't last a week in the world I lived in, but that didn't stop me from constructing a million teenage fantasies about bedding one.

Bethany brought back all those teenage longings. She was from a world so different to mine, it might as well have been Mars: WiFi and electric cars and ordering things on a computer and having it delivered to your door in a couple of hours. She was soft and delicate in a way I found hypnotic. Every part of her: the sneakers with the blindingly white rubber, like they'd never seen mud. The jeans that hadn't been made for toughness, but to hug that wonderful ass and curving hips. The sweater that wasn't just a practical layer, for warmth, but had little gold threads woven into the cranberry-colored wool, creating little sparkling tracks that arched like contour lines as they reached the hills and valleys of her breasts.

She had hair as jet black and glossy as a stretch limousine and it fell in thick, glossy waves halfway down her back. When she'd crashed into me, the tumbling locks had brushed my chin and it had been so silky soft, and smelled so good, that all I'd wanted to do was bury my nose in it. Her eyes were a warm, rich hazel, and her mouth...hypnotically soft, wide lips. And when she smiled, it was with one of these lopsided, shy little grins that was goddamn adorable.

The best thing about Bethany, though? Her curves. If I hadn't been so held by those big brown eyes, I wouldn't have been able to stop my gaze rolling down the sweet slopes of her body. Those full, lush breasts pushing out the front of that cranberry sweater...the sweep of her waist that I wanted to follow with my palm, *in* and then gloriously *out* to a mouthwatering bounty of hips and an ass I needed to grab hold of *right now.* She looked old-fashioned, in a way I couldn't put into words.

Her skin was milky-pale, like she'd never spent a day outside in the sun. And when I'd taken her hand to pull her up, her fingers had been so amazingly soft and soothing on my big, calloused paws. I couldn't get enough of that smooth softness. I kept thinking back to the glimpses her sweater had revealed: the elegant curve of her throat, down to her collarbone; the top of the soft valley between her breasts. I wanted to start just below her jaw and kiss downwards, exploring her with my lips, feeling her writhe against me. I wanted to see all of her, wanted to hook my hands under that sweater and drag it up and off her, run my hands all over her. I couldn't help but have visions of her nipples, imagining them darkly pink against the whiteness, rising into peaks beneath my thumbs. Dammit, I wanted to push her up against a tree and...I gave a little growl of lust, just imagining it.

She was the most feminine woman I'd ever met. Not *girly,* not giggly and look-at-me, but soft and sweet and sexual, a femininity that was completely intoxicating. There was this word I couldn't get out of my head, from some book my mom read to me as a kid: *entranced.* I was entranced by her. I felt like Rufus when he chases after a butterfly.

When she told me what they had her doing, being a chew-toy for customers to savage, I'd felt something rise up inside me I hadn't felt for a long time. A deep, protective urge. There'd been a second, as I looked down into those big brown eyes, when I just wanted to scoop her up into my arms.

And there was something else. Beyond the need to run my hands over those fine curves. Beyond the urge to protect her.

I'd felt myself react to her in a way I didn't think I could, anymore. In a way I hadn't for a long time. I'd felt this *pull,* way down deep and stronger than any river's current.

But then reality returned and I scowled and marched faster down the street, Rufus trotting by my side. I didn't deserve someone like her, after what I'd done.

I was a monster. And monsters belong in the woods.

We'd only come to Seattle for the funeral. The idea was to be in the city for less than an hour. We'd found the cemetery and stood there in the rain as the casket was lowered. Only a few other people had been there: his relatives, I guess. They'd glanced curiously at the giant in the plaid shirt with his dog, but no one had plucked up the courage to talk to me and as soon as I'd paid my respects, we headed home. I didn't want to go to some reception or wake and try to make small talk, or, worse, have to lie to Shawn's folks about what he and I used to do for a living.

Except I never could navigate in cities, with their artificial grid of streets that all look the same. On the way out of Seattle, I'd gotten lost in an industrial area and then, while I was stuck at a stoplight, Rufus had seen a stray cat and scrambled out of the window to chase after it. Even after searching for him all night, I hadn't been able to find him. I'd been worried sick.

But thanks to Bethany, we'd been reunited. Now we could go home and we never needed to come to the city again.

A guy in a suit appeared from around the corner and strolled towards us. He did a double-take at my size. Then he looked me in the eyes and—

I don't mean to glare. It just sort of happens. I don't want to talk to people, don't want to be around people. People, and society: roads and cars and schools and adverts, *normal life*...all that stuff just reminds me of what I am. Reminds me that I don't belong in that normal, polite world anymore...and why.

The guy's eyes went wide with fear and he looked away, then crossed the street. Most people did the same.

But not Bethany. She hadn't been scared of me. Even when I'd tried to scare her away.

Maybe because, deep down, I hadn't wanted to.

I pushed the thought away as we reached the borrowed pickup. I climbed in and Rufus leapt into the passenger seat and put his head out of the window. I threw it into gear and we sped off towards the interstate.

But as I sped past the city limits sign, I felt that pull again, stronger than ever. I glanced at the glittering skyscrapers in the rearview mirror. *Bethany....*

I crushed the feelings down inside.

Monsters belong in the woods.

I'd never see Bethany again.

3

BETHANY

Six Months Later

"Bethany," whispered Rachel, "Will you take this one?"
I looked across and saw her eyes shining with tears. I nodded quickly. And then, before I'd even had time to mentally brace, he was in my ear in crystal-clear clarity. Male, forties, East Coast. I could almost feel the spittle hitting my cheek. *"You make this fucking thing work, NOW! I'm losing money, standing here, don't you understand? What the fuck are you people doing? Answer me, you bitch!"*

The others know that I'm good at calming people. So when they get a really angry call and they just can't deal with it, they pass it to me. And that's okay. I'd rather take the call than see Rachel reduced to tears by the guy.

But it means that I spend my day as a verbal punching bag. And there's only so many times you can be told you're worthless before it begins to soak into your psyche, like rain leaching into concrete and weakening it. Weirdly, it wouldn't be so bad if we were face-to-face with the customers. Then they'd have to look us in the eye as they yell and most people aren't that brave. But when we're just an anonymous voice at the end of the phone, they get to take all their frustrations out on us: their cheating wife, their money problems, their sports team losing.

And we can't answer back. We can't get mad. The callers hold our jobs in their hands because if our average customer satisfaction rating drops too low, we're fired. So when they yell at us, or tell us they hope we die, or heavy-breathe and ask us what sort of panties we have on, we count to three and ask, "Is there anything else I can help you with, today?"

This is my life, for twelve hours each day. Two two minute bathroom breaks. A fifteen-minute lunch break. If you're late back it's a warning. A second offense and you're fired. If I pull a double shift, it's twenty-four hours straight. Sometimes, I stumble out into the parking lot and I'm not sure if it's 8 am or 8 pm.

After ten minutes of soaking up his rage, I finally managed to get the caller to calm down enough to reset his system: a five-second process. As soon as it booted back up, he hung up on me. I let out a sigh of exhaustion and put my forehead in my hands. Ten seconds. I'd give myself ten seconds before I answered another call.

And I knew just how I wanted to spend those ten seconds. I inhaled slowly, imagining I could still smell the clean, outdoor scent of him. Six months on, I still couldn't get Cal out of my mind. He was so different from any man I'd ever met. *Wild,* like a white-water river, ready to suck you in and carry you off, or a mountain so huge and steep it's said to be unscalable, its peak disappearing into the clouds. That voice, the words heavy and solid as rocks, their edges rough and unpolished. But with that glorious country warmth, like the sun had been soaking into the stone all day and all you wanted to do was press up against them.

I'd reacted to him in a way I never had with anyone else, his physical presence so intense that it seemed to reach inside me and touch my soul, making my whole body quiver and sing.

I didn't understand it because there was something deeply intimidating about him. It wasn't just his size or the way he glared. He felt...*dangerous*. Not in the way some guys are dangerous, all loud and angry and spoiling for a fight, a firework that can go off at any time. Cal was more like a gun you know is loaded or a knife you know is razor-sharp. He just stood there, calm and quiet. But something in his eyes hinted that he could take on an army, if he needed to.

I should have been scared, but I wasn't. Because when he'd looked at me, the hardness in his eyes had just melted away. He might be big, might even be dangerous...but it didn't feel as if he'd ever hurt me, or anyone who didn't deserve it. And when I told him about the call center and his eyes had flared with anger... at that moment, I'd felt protected in a way I never had before. I wished he was there now. I imagined pressing my cheek against soft plaid and warm, hard muscle, sliding my arms around him and snuggling close—

My computer beeped and I reluctantly opened my eyes. A message edged in red had popped up on my screen: Bob Tanner, the head of the call center, wanted to see me. *Shit!*

His office was on the opposite side of the main floor, a space the size of a football field. They'd packed almost a thousand of us into the room in long rows of desks, our elbows almost touching as we worked our computers. Only a few heads lifted as I passed. They make it deliberately difficult to make friends: we're assigned a different desk each day, to discourage wasting time on fraternizing.

I knocked and waited, my heart thumping. I'd never been called to Tanner's office before. What had I done? I'd worked my ass off, I'd hit every quota, I'd only ever been late from lunch *once* and that was because Angela had gotten her period a day early and I'd run out to get her tampons—

Mr. Tanner called me in. He was slumped in an office chair and on the computer screen in front of him were hundreds of tiny windows. As I got closer, I saw that each one was live video of a call center operator. A waist-up image shot from the cameras in our monitors: I'd noticed the little black pinholes but I'd never really thought about the fact we were being filmed. Why did they even need video: to make sure we weren't eating at our desks?

Mr. Tanner picked up a pen from his desk and started tapping it against his other hand. His thinning brown hair was sticking to his forehead with sweat, despite the air conditioning. "I'm sorry," he said, "But I've got to move you."

"Move me?"

"To San Francisco."

It took a second for that to sink in. *"What?* Why?! Did I do something wrong?"

He shook his head and shrugged as if it was no big deal. "Excess capacity here. Not enough in San Fran. You already know the ropes, you can slot right in."

I stared at him, incredulous. "But...." I didn't know where to start. *But I don't want to work in San Francisco. But I don't know anyone there. But you can't just move me like I'm cattle.*

"Unfortunately, I can't justify your position here," he told me. "You can have the job in San Fran, otherwise today is your last shift."

My jaw dropped. But then, before I could plead with him, he hit me with the sweetener. "The company's willing to pay you five thousand dollars relocation costs. We'll even drive you down to San Fran and pay for a hotel for the first week."

That stopped me dead. If I said no, I was out of work. I was only just making ends meet as it was. My pay from the call center only just covered the interest on my med school debts, with just enough left for my room in the shared apartment and groceries. If I said yes, that five thousand dollars would really help to get my head back above water.

My boss kept tapping the pen, faster, now. I noticed he was sweating more, his forehead glistening. "What's it going to be, Bethany?"

It should have been a hard decision but it really wasn't. I couldn't afford to lose my job and I couldn't turn down the money. And of course, he knew that.

I nodded.

～

Three hours later, I was in the back of a black Mercedes, heading out of the city. My possessions were in a small suitcase and a box in the trunk. Because I'd left in the middle of a shift, there'd been no time to say goodbye: a quick hug from Angela and Rachel between calls. A scribbled note to the women I shared the apartment with, telling them not to worry and that I had a new job. The five thousand dollars, less what I'd left to cover the last few weeks of rent, was in a thick brown envelope in my purse.

I'd never felt so insignificant. I was a tiny, anonymous cog, to be moved however the company saw fit.

I watched the city flash past the window for the first few miles, sipping from a bottle of water the limo driver had given me. I could feel myself slumping. My shift had started at eight that morning and I'd done four hours of it before everything had gone crazy. My head nodded and the leather seat became marshmallow-soft beneath me, taking me down to a warm, dark place. Before we'd even reached the city limits, I was asleep.

And I dreamed.

4

BETHANY

I FELT HIM FIRST, each heavy footstep shaking the ground. Then the outdoor scent of him: the smell of trees lush and thick around you, the sharp hit of freshly-split wood and just a subtle curl of woodsmoke. I filled my lungs, getting drunk on it: I wanted to breathe nothing but his smell. Finally, I heard him, his breathing getting closer and closer until I knew he was right in front of me, his pecs just shy of brushing my breasts as he inhaled.

I opened my eyes.

A rich golden sun was beating down on us from an unbroken blue sky, the heat soaking into my bones and making my skin tingle and come alive after so long indoors. I blinked up at his silhouette for a second and then my eyes adjusted. That gorgeous, brooding face came closer as he leaned down towards me. I stared into cornflower-blue eyes as his hands found my shoulders, palms smoothing over the bare skin and the thin straps of my sundress. Then down over my arms, down to my hands, his big fingers lacing with my slender ones and gently squeezing. Then his hands moved around behind me and—

I yelped as he grabbed my ass in both hands and hoisted me into the air. My legs swung up and suddenly I was against him, breathless, the hard ridges of his abs stroking against my groin, my thighs spread either side of his torso. My legs kicked for a second and then I got them hooked around him, my bare heels pressed up against the sun-warmed denim that covered his ass. I grabbed onto his shoulders and went a little heady at the sheer size of him, walking my fingers out along the solid muscle, wanting to feel all of him.

I'm not delicate or fragile or small...but in his arms, I felt all those things.

He held me there as if I weighed nothing and just gazed at me like he'd never get tired of looking. Those blue eyes narrowed and heated, and his hands squeezed my ass.

I melted.

He leaned down. I took a shuddering breath, my heartbeat racing. A lock of his golden hair fell forward, stroking my dark curls. I closed my eyes.

The rough scrape of his beard. Then the first warm brush of his full lower lip against my own—

I opened my eyes, confused because surely they were *already* open. And instead of getting lighter, it got darker. I was in a dark, moving room and there was soft leather beneath me. *What?!*

For several seconds, I sat there confused and frustrated, my heart still pounding. Then my cheeks went hot with embarrassment. The car. I was in the car. I looked at the back of the limo driver's head. *Please don't let me have moaned in my sleep.*

We were still moving but the sky was black outside. *How long was I asleep for?!* We must be nearly in San Francisco. But when I looked out of the window, it was just a featureless highway. A streetlight flashed past and I winced at the sudden brightness, my head throbbing. I felt like I had a hangover.

Then I looked out of the windshield and froze. We were turning off the highway and ahead of us, the world just...stopped. The lights that marked houses and roads went from long strings to isolated little clusters and then to nothing at all. Just infinite, cold blackness. *The sea. That must be the sea.* But wouldn't there at least be a boat with its lights on, out there in the blackness? "What is that?" I mumbled to the driver.

"The woods." he said.

The woods? But it stretched all the way to the horizon. There weren't areas of wilderness that big anymore, were there? At least not anywhere close to San Francisco. "Where are we?" I asked.

I waited, but he didn't answer. *Maybe he didn't hear.* A moment later, we turned again, skirting the edge of the blackness. I waited politely until he'd made the turn and then spoke up again, louder, this time. "Where are we, please?"

His shoulders rose just a little. He'd heard, but he still didn't answer. I went cold inside.

Tall metal gates opened silently in front of us. A long, winding driveway. Manicured hedges and, just visible behind them, fences topped with razor wire. There were security guards, too, serious-looking guys all dressed in black. I leaned forward between the seats. "Where the hell are we?" I demanded, my voice ragged.

We rounded a corner and pulled up. "We're here," he told me.

I stared. It was a mansion, three stories high and built of snow-white stone. Huge pillars flanked the doors and golden light spilled from ornate windows. There were flower beds and gardens. A sign pointed to a golf course.

The driver opened my door and I stumbled out. My head still felt woolly and thick and confusion held my fear back. *It must be a mistake. A screw up at the limo company. They were meant to take me to the San Francisco call center and they took me here.* Maybe this was some other place the company owned. A luxury spa or something. "I think I'm in the wrong place," I said.

The driver shook his head and nodded me towards the house. "I'll take care of your bags."

The fear started to build again. I walked up the steps and through the huge wooden doors...and stopped.

I was in a double-height hall big enough for a softball game, with a marble floor and a chandelier the size of a small car overhead. A grand piano stood in one corner and a massive, ornate staircase led to the upper floors. The place had been set up for a party: there was a bar in one corner where a barman was mixing drinks and a long table was loaded with platters of bread, cheese, and meat. Men in suits—ten or more—stood around talking and drinking. They were a mixture of ages, twenties all the way to sixties, but most were towards the older end and all had that easy confidence that comes with money. A fancy poker club, maybe, or one of those members' clubs for people who've been to Harvard or Yale. But what the hell was *I* doing there?

As they noticed me, the conversations died away. They began to move closer, spreading out to surround me. I thought of wolves, stalking a deer. I turned to the nearest man, a guy in his fifties with a round, moon-like face and black hair that had thinned on top. "I'm sorry, I'm in the wrong place," I told him.

"No, sweetie." His voice was fatherly and just a little patronizing. "You're in the *right* place." Everywhere I looked, men were grinning. I felt like I was back in high school with a *kick me* sign taped to my back. *Tell me what's going on!*

There was a creak from above. All of us looked up to see a man descending the stairs, the antique wood complaining with each unhurried step. The chandelier blocked our view of him but the men must have known who it was because the entire room fell silent.

His feet came into view first: polished black loafers twice the size of my feet. Then thick legs under expensive suit pants. A bulky torso, massively strong but running to fat. He wasn't wearing a tie and his open shirt collar revealed dark tattoos across his upper chest. A flabby neck like a bull's. And then, at last, we saw his face and—

My stomach flipped over. There was something horribly wrong with his face. It was as if the bones had been broken and the surgeons hadn't been able to put them back together quite right, the result just *off* enough to be terrifying. But worse than the face were the eyes. He looked at me with absolute hatred. As if I was responsible for everything wrong in his life. As if all women were.

He walked over to me, the men parting to let him through.

"*Bethany,*" he said with great satisfaction. He had a heavy, Eastern European accent. *Russian?* "Even better than your videos."

What videos?! I was starting to panic breathe. He reached out and nudged a lock of my hair with one of his sausage-like fingers and I flinched. "What is this place?" I asked, my voice quavering.

A newcomer walked towards us. A tall, thin man in his sixties, bald, with just a little gray hair above his ears. "It's a club, Miss Meier. A very exclusive club. One that my family has run for a very long time." He was American, his voice as rich and refined as vintage bourbon. "These men are members." He looked at the tattooed man. "Mr. Ralavich is our newest member." He said it warmly but I saw the way his lip curled, the way he looked disparagingly at the Russian's suit. Ralavich had money but no class.

I took a step backward, shaking my head. "I don't—Why am I here?"

Ralavich grinned. "Because I bought you."

The words bounced off my brain, refusing to go in. When I did process them, it seemed like a joke. It *had* to be a joke. "B—"

"Bought," confirmed Ralavich, enjoying my reaction. "I own you, now."

The other men were leaning forward expectantly, eager to see what happened next. Like tourists at the zoo, waiting for the lion to be fed.

"This is all a mistake," I said, my voice cracking. "I'm going to a *call center! In San Francisco!*"

They all laughed. And just as the laughter died away, a noise split the air from upstairs. A woman's scream. It was followed by the crack of a violent slap, and then whimpering.

Oh Jesus Christ. Raw fear pushed away the last of the fogginess in my brain. For the first time, I saw everything clearly.

When people thought of kidnapping, they imagined women grabbed off the street and pulled into a van. What these men had created was much more insidious.

I thought of my boss at the call center, watching all those little video windows of the call center workers. Almost all of us were young women. We all lived in cheap, shared apartments, moving jobs frequently, with no time to make connections. The call center was even set up to discourage making friends. We were women no one would miss.

I imagined the videos of us flowing over the internet to some website, where members of the club could browse workers: watching us, listening to our voices before making their selection. And then my boss would make the offer he'd made me and the woman would be taken here. I felt ill. How many times had this already happened, since I'd been working there? There were close to a thousand workers. One a month could be disappearing, their jobs instantly filled, and no one would ever question it.

And...God, this was probably happening in the San Francisco call center, too: they were telling those women they were being sent to Seattle. And in how many other call centers, and warehouses, and other places with high turnovers of staff? All legitimate businesses whose bosses were paid a fat bribe each month to let the club skim off a few women.

I thought of the bottle of water in the limo. Drugged, to make sure I slept for the journey. *I don't even know what state I'm in!*

"I take it you're satisfied?" the owner of the club asked Ralavich.

Ralavich grunted. He turned to a man I hadn't noticed before: he had the same suit and tattoos as Ralavich but looked to be in better shape: a bodyguard, perhaps. "Get the others ready for transport. We'll leave tomorrow." Ralavich turned back to me. "Tonight, I'm going to enjoy this one."

He grabbed my hand, his fingers clammy and flabby, nothing like Cal's warm grip. He jerked on my arm with terrifying strength, pulling me towards the stairs. The other men were nodding approvingly and some even slapped his back. My stomach churned. They were waiting to hear *my* screams.

Upstairs, he pushed me into a bedroom and stood there gazing at me, his face flushed red with excitement. "Where are you taking me?" I asked. "You said *others,* there are others?" I thought that if I kept him talking, maybe I could escape.

"Back to Russia. The other nine, to brothels. American women are our most popular."

It all slotted together in my head, now: the tattoos, the bodyguard, the way the other men feared him. Ralavich was Russian Mafia.

He leaned forward and cupped my chin. I shrank from his grasp. "But *you*, Bethany," he continued. "You, I keep for myself."

Me? Why me? There's nothing special about me!

He pointed to an ivory dress on the bed. "Put that on. And make-up. Shoes." His English was fracturing as his excitement increased. "Be quick. I have to smoke." He went into the hall and slammed the door, trapping me inside.

I pictured him watching me as I worked in the call center, fantasizing about this night for weeks or months. I looked at the clothes on the bed and my nausea rose. He wanted to dress me like a doll, have everything *just right* before he—*This is not happening. This cannot be happening.* I dug in my purse for my phone. It had been taken while I slept. *Shit!*

I didn't want to give him an excuse to hurt me so I changed into the dress, my hands shaking. It was made up of lots of thin, gauzy layers and looked expensive. It had a square, low cut neckline, an ankle-length hem and splits up the sides of the skirt. There were fancy white heels, too, and a panties and bra set made of silk and lace.

As I pulled on the clothes, I looked frantically around the room for a way out. The window looked like it opened but below it was a paved driveway and we were on the third floor: I'd never survive the fall. I was taking huge panicked gulps of air, now, imagining what would happen when Ralavich came back in. There was something wrong with this man. I could feel the hatred oozing out of him, and he wanted to take it all out on me. I thought of him raping me every night...and then, when he got bored of me, I'd join the others in one of his brothels. My legs went shaky with fear. *Think of something! Think!*

"Are you ready?" asked Ralavich from outside the door.

"Just doing my make-up!" I checked the bathroom. The door had a lock but he'd just break it down. *Think!*

"Hurry up!" ordered Ralavich.

"One second!" I was hysterical, now. The room began to swim behind hot tears. *It wasn't meant to be like this.* Just a year ago, I'd been following my dream. Then one day changed everything. Suddenly, I was out of medical school, my future gone. Then came the call center and the daily screaming in my ear. And now....

I'd been wrong, in the car. I wasn't a cog in a corporate machine. I was an asset, a thing to be bought and sold.

I hiccoughed and sobbed, my chest heaving. *I might as well give up. Maybe he won't hurt me as much if I don't fight.* The tears began to run down my cheeks.

But as I stood there sobbing, something happened. With everything stripped away from me, every hope gone, I found something deep inside me, something I'd never known I had. All those months of being yelled at in the call center had worn down the rest of me, but there was something right at my core, something tiny, that had hardened, instead. Hardened until it was like diamond.

I wasn't going to let him have me. And once I decided that, there was only one way out.

I opened the window wide and looked down. Three floors onto paving stones. A quick death. Better than being his slave.

I stepped up onto the sill.

Ralavich banged on the door. "What are you doing in there?"

I took a long, deep breath—

And then, in that last moment of calm, I saw another way. I jumped down off the sill and slid under the bed.

I heard the door fly open and crash against the wall. I closed my eyes tight, trying to keep perfectly still. I imagined his gaze sweeping the room, then locking on the wide-open window. *Please—*

He raced to the window, his footsteps shaking the floor, and cursed in Russian. Then he ran back to the door and bellowed. *"Alik!"*

Feet pounded up the stairs. *Alik.* That must be the bodyguard I'd seen downstairs. I lay motionless, barely daring to breathe. I saw

Alik's feet run to the window and there was a hurried conversation in Russian. I could guess at the content, just from the amazement in Alik's voice. *She jumped?! And she survived?* He ran off, Ralavich close behind him. There was shouting downstairs and an alarm started to wail.

I slowly let out my breath and slid from under the bed. I could hear shouted orders, running footsteps. I crept out into the hallway and peeked down the stairs. The club members were ushered into another room, out of the way. Security guards dressed in black flooded from a doorway and ran outside. In just a few moments, the main hall was deserted.

I had no time to change clothes. I knew I wouldn't be able to run in the heels so I kicked them off and crept along the hallway barefoot. As I passed bedroom doors, I could hear sounds from inside. Wailing. Sobbing. My chest contracted. There were at least nine other women here, destined for Ralavich's brothels in Russia. Maybe many more, if the other members had all bought women, too. *I can't just leave them here!*

But I couldn't help them now. I needed to escape and bring the cops. I forced myself to keep walking. Down the stairs. Across the massive hall, the marble ice-cold on my bare feet—

Footsteps. I ducked behind the grand piano.

"Why weren't the windows locked?!" yelled Ralavich as he stormed in.

The head of the club walked alongside him, placating and just a little patronizing. "Mr. Ralavich, please. In all the years this club has been open, do you know how many escapes we've had? *Zero.* She probably broke both her legs in the fall and she's crawled under some bush somewhere. It's over a mile to the edge of the property and then she'd have to climb a ten-foot fence. We'll have her back here in a few minutes."

They passed into the next room. I crept over to the door and peeked outside. I could see flashlight beams sweeping back and forth as men searched the grounds. None of them were looking towards the mansion.

For now. Sooner or later, they'd figure out I wasn't out there. Then someone would think to search the house and it would all be over.

Several cars were parked in the driveway. *Keys.* I needed keys. Heart thumping, I hurried to the room the security guards had run out of and peeked around the door. Empty. My stomach knotted when I saw a rack of guns: shotguns, rifles, handguns, all secured behind wire mesh. They were prepared for this. They'd kill me if they had to. Then I saw the little cupboard on the wall. *Please don't be locked—*

It wasn't. And it was full of chunky black keyfobs. I grabbed one at random and hurried back through the hall. I pressed the button on the keyfob and one of the cars outside flashed its lights. A few of the guards turned to look. I raced across the gravel driveway to the car, stones cutting into my bare feet, wrenched open the door, and threw myself into the driver's seat.

A shout went up. *Shit!* I groped for the start button and the car came to life. But now guards were running across the gravel towards me. I stared frantically at the unfamiliar controls and tried to figure out how to shift into drive.

A guard wrenched the driver's door open.

I shifted, stamped on the gas, and the car shot forward. I sped down the twisting driveway with the door still open and swinging wildly. Then the gates were looming up ahead of me, much bigger and sturdier than I remembered them. I suddenly remembered I wasn't wearing a safety belt and yanked it into place.

I closed my eyes as I hit the gates. There was a sickening crunch and a jolt that rattled up through every vertebra of my spine, but then I was through and speeding along the road. Some weird sounds were coming from under the hood but for now, I was still going.

I reached the next junction and slowed to a stop, leaning forward over the steering wheel, panting in fear. *Which way?* Left led back to the highway and civilization...but it was late at night and there was nowhere to hide on the empty road. They'd run me down in minutes.

I looked the other way, into the blackness. *The woods.*

Headlights behind me: they were coming. I turned right and sped into the ocean of black. I took each turn I came to, driving down smaller and smaller roads until I was thoroughly lost, deep in the forest. But the headlights behind me kept creeping closer.

I rounded a corner and eyes gleamed in the darkness ahead of me. Before my brain had even fully registered *deer,* I'd wrenched the wheel to the side. Enormous pine trees loomed up to meet me.

This time, it wasn't a crunch. It was a bang as the car slammed into a tree and stopped dead.

I must have blacked out for a second because the next thing I remember is lifting my face from the soft pillow of the airbag and hearing a car pulling up behind me.

I pushed open the driver's door and ran into the woods, gasping as the chill night air breezed straight through my thin dress. Twigs and stones dug into my bare feet. Branches scratched at my arms. There was no path to follow. This was wild land, littered with fallen trees and loose branches, and the only light was from the moon.

I stumbled, went down, and scrambled to my feet, fear lending me speed. I ran until the air in my lungs felt like liquid fire, until my muscles screamed. But it was no good. I could hear the men crashing through the trees behind me, gaining fast.

They were going to catch me.

And way out here, there was no one to help me.

5

CAL

WE WERE maybe ten miles from home. We'd been hunting for the last couple of days, sleeping under the stars at night, and I was just thinking about finally heading back.

I should have been pleased. We'd done well on this trip, getting plenty of meat we could smoke and store. We wouldn't starve, this winter.

But I had a gnawing, empty feeling inside: something was missing.

Stupid. I had everything I could need: food, a roof over my head, a dog for company.

But *she* slid into my mind, the memory seductive and irresistible. A lock of hair, soft as silk, brushing my chin. Big hazel eyes, a soft valley of pale cleavage peeking from beneath a cranberry sweater—

Goddammit! Every day. Every. Damn. Day. And even worse, every night, those pale curves haunting me until I was hard and frustrated as a teenager.

I'd lived out here a long time. This was my life, now, all I deserved. So why couldn't I get her out of my head, when I knew damn well I couldn't have her? I'd been doing fine until—

Until I realized what I was missing.

Don't think that way!

And the truth was, I *hadn't* been doing fine. Sure, being out here, away from people, helped keep the memories buried. But they were finding new ways of surfacing. The nightmares were back, and getting worse.

Rufus was snuffling in the grass, fluffy tail swishing. Suddenly, he went stock still and lifted his head to stare at the trees.

"What?" I asked. I followed his gaze but couldn't see anything.

Rufus cocked his head to the side and sniffed the air, then gave a sudden, sharp *woof!*

"What? What is it?" I walked over to him and put a gentle hand on his back. He'd got the scent of something. A deer?

He inhaled noisily, nose twitching, and then suddenly he bolted. I lurched forward to grab him but he was gone, moving as fast as I'd ever seen him go. "Rufus!" I yelled. "Get back here!"

But he plunged into the trees. *Goddammit!* What was the matter with him? He knew better than to run off after a rabbit or a squirrel. "Rufus!"

He didn't stop. I could hear him crashing through the undergrowth, going flat out. What the hell had he smelled?

I cursed and sprinted after him.

6

BETHANY

I STAGGERED into a clearing and looked around wildly as I heaved for air. Everything looked the same! I couldn't tell if I was following a straight line or running in circles and where was I going, anyway? I was deep in the woods, far from any roads, and even if I did find one, the chances of seeing a car I could flag down was practically zero.

A noise behind me made me spin around. Flashlight beams swept and lanced between the trees. I ran for the far side of the clearing but before I reached it, my legs finally buckled from exhaustion and I stumbled and went down. I clawed at the ground, fingers sinking into soft soil, and managed to get to my knees and crawl. But then I heard someone burst out of the trees behind me and suddenly I was pinned by a flashlight beam. I gave a choking, desperate sob and turned around. Three guards were running across the clearing towards me.

I slumped, panting. It was over.

Something sprang out of the trees behind me, charged across the clearing and stopped between the guards and me. And then it gave an almighty bark.

What?!

The flashlight beam found it. I caught a glimpse of black and tan fur and a powerful body. A dog. A German Shepherd, like Rufus—

Then I saw the faint scars on its legs. *That is Rufus!*

The guards started toward me. Rufus lowered his head, hackles rising. I'd never seen him in guard mode before. He bared his teeth, showing off just how long they were. His muscles coiled, ready to spring, and a noise came from his throat that I wouldn't have believed he was capable of making, a growl that was like a knife being drawn slowly over the teeth of a chainsaw.

The guards cursed and stopped moving.

How is this possible? What was Rufus doing, all the way out here?

The guards were muttering to each other, discussing what to do. "Just shoot the fucking thing," one of them said at last. Another reached for his gun.

I lurched forward, frantic, and threw my arms around Rufus. "No! Don't hurt him!" My mind was still spinning, trying to catch up. How could Rufus be here?

Unless...

A voice filled the clearing. A voice heavy and rough as rock and filled with such raw, protective fury that the three guards froze instantly.

"Get the hell away from her!" growled Cal as he stepped from the trees.

7

BETHANY

H E MARCHED across the clearing, unafraid and unhurried, each big stride taking him closer to the guards. As he passed me, he glanced down and the concern in his eyes made me catch my breath.

Then he looked at the guards and his jaw tightened. He kept marching towards them, putting himself between them and Rufus and me.

The flashlight beam moved to Cal and I saw the guards size him up. They looked at his plaid shirt and muddy jeans and I saw them roll their eyes. *A local.* Sure, he was big and he had a rifle, but it was slung on his back, and it was one against three. "This is nothing to do with you," said one of the guards. His city accent sounded out of place, here.

"Get away from her," Cal repeated, as if the guard hadn't spoken. His voice was low, but it had an authority the guard could only dream of. He kept walking.

"You don't want to get involved in this," the guard told him. He sounded nervous, now. Cal wasn't stopping and the closer he got, the more intimidating his size was. "So just turn around and wa—"

"*Get away from her,*" snapped Cal, cutting him off. "That's three times I've told you." He finally stopped, no more than ten feet from the guards, and just stood there in the flashlight beam. He was outnumbered three to one and yet while the guards shifted nervously from foot to foot, he stood there like a rock.

"You don't know what you're doing. You don't know who we work for," the guard told him.

"Don't especially care," rumbled Cal.

And then the guard made a mistake: he reached towards his holster.

It was like a magic trick. One second, Cal was just standing there, hands by his sides. The next, his rifle was up to his shoulder, leveled right at the guard's head. The blood drained from the guard's face. I gaped. *Where did he learn to do that?*

"Guns at my feet," Cal said quietly. The barrel of his rifle didn't waver even a millimeter as he spoke.

The guards looked at one another. Then, one by one, they pulled out their handguns and tossed them towards Cal's feet.

"Take your boots off and walk back the way you came," Cal told them.

The three guards pulled off their boots and backed up into the trees. "You got no idea what you've started," said one of them. "The people we work for, they'll come for her."

Cal's voice was like iron. "You give them a message. These are my woods and she's under my protection. Anyone comes here and tries to take her, they'll regret it."

He kept the rifle pointed at them until they'd retreated into the darkness...and then he slowly lowered it and turned to me.

8

BETHANY

HE SLUNG his rifle over his shoulder and squatted down so that he was almost at my eye level. "You okay?"

That voice again. Words you could cling to, like huge, heavy rocks. And then he extended his hand, and I slipped my freezing fingers around his big, warm ones and was hoisted up, just like the first time. And I felt it: that feeling I'd gotten just a hint of when I first met him, like something solid under my feet after hours of treading water. I felt *safe*, and it felt so good I almost cried. I nodded. "Thank you," I said.

He looked away as if embarrassed and gave a quick, dismissive shake of his head. As if it was nothing, as if he would have done it for anyone. But when he met my eyes again, there was a protective heat there that warmed my entire body. "What happened?" he asked. "Why were they after you?"

I swallowed. "They were holding me. I escaped. This guy was going to—" My throat closed up and I couldn't say it. "I need to call the cops. Can I use your phone?"

He shook his head. "Don't have one. No signal out here, anyhow."

I blinked at him. Who doesn't have a phone? "Is there one around here I can use?"

He considered. "Nearest phone's at Tucker's Gas Station. But that's about five hours' hike."

"How can we be *five hours* from a phone?!"

"This is the deep woods. Nothing out here but wild forest."

I thought of the vast blackness I'd seen from the limo and my stomach flipped over. Rufus butted up against my legs, comforting and warm, and I stroked his head. "What are you two doing out here?"

"We live here."

In the wilderness? Why would anyone choose to live *here?* "And the nearest phone is *five hours'* walk?"

Cal nodded. "It's that or go back to the road, but...."

I followed his gaze towards where the guards had disappeared. *But that's where they are.* "Where are we?" I asked. "What state is this?"

He moved closer, looming over me, his eyes widening with concern. "You don't know which *state* you're in?!" He stared at me and his voice became gentle. "Idaho. You're in Idaho."

Idaho. My head spun. The limo had taken me east, not south. This was a part of the country I'd never been to. The few times I'd left Seattle, it had been to visit other cities. I looked around, turning a slow circle, and my brain went numb. It was just forest in every direction. There were no signs, no buildings arranged in neat, sensible grids. Even if I knew which direction to head, if I veered off course even a little, I could wander out here for days or weeks. *I could actually starve to death out here.*

I wasn't in my world, anymore. I was in his.

I turned back to Cal. "Could you please...show me the way?"

9

CAL

I STARED at her, unable to speak. Then I looked away: at the trees, at the ground, anywhere except those big brown eyes. A war was going on in my mind.

It's fate. If she hadn't saved Rufus in Seattle, he'd never have recognized her scent.

Bullshit. I didn't believe in fate. And the last thing I wanted was for her to think I was some sort of hero.

I had no choice, though. I couldn't leave her out here. But, dammit, why did it have to be *her?* I'd spent years putting myself as far from people as I could and now I'd have to spend five solid hours with a woman I already couldn't stop thinking about.

A woman I could never have.

I opened my eyes. Goddamn, she was beautiful. The moonlight was lighting up her dress, making it almost glow. It was like something a medieval princess would wear, all gauzy, thin enough that when the breeze flattened it against her legs, I could make out the lush curves of her thighs and ass. And up top, it had a square neckline that made me hold my breath every time I looked at it. The upper slopes of her breasts were revealed almost down to the nipples, the soft flesh pressed together and lifted as if I was cupping them in my hands....

I looked away. *Just five hours,* I told myself. *Get her to a phone and then we can part ways. Five hours. You can do five hours.* I'd just have to harden myself and be gruff with her. Keep her at arm's length. I could do that..., right?

I risked looking at her again. She was barefoot and that made her seem even smaller and more helpless as she looked up at me. That protective urge I was fighting came rushing back.

Dammit!

"Yeah," I told her. "I can show you the way."

10

RALAVICH

I HURLED the decanter across the room. It shattered, glittering shards spraying across the marble floor as the rich stink of bourbon filled the air. "*How could you let this happen?*" I bellowed. "You let her steal a car and just *drive off?!*" I pointed at the three guards who'd chased Bethany down. "And then your men, they just let her waltz off with some *yokel?!*"

"You didn't see this guy," one of the guards muttered. "He was fucking *huge*. Knew how to handle a gun, too."

I scoffed and, behind me, Alik gave a grunt of agreement. He's former *Spetsnaz,* Russian special forces, and he didn't think much of the mansion's guards.

The head of the club, a bald man called Preston Cairns, was unfazed. "Mr. Ralavich. I understand your frustration. While you wait for this to be resolved, perhaps you'd like to spend some time with one of the others you purchased? I could have one of them brought to your room, along with some vodka."

I glared at him. I'd disliked him right from the start. I knew he thought I was beneath him, that I wasn't good enough to be in his fucking club. But he needed my money and I needed him. There were powerful Russian men who would pay dearly to fuck unwilling

American women. With the supply chain Cairns had set up, I could make a fortune.

But for myself, I wanted Bethany. It wasn't just that she had a body made to give pleasure and a perfect, sweet face. There was something about her I found fascinating. Back in St. Petersburg, I'd sat for hours, watching her in the call center. At first, it had just been about her innocence, her *goodness*. The way she helped her colleagues, taking the calls they didn't want to. The way she looked truly pained, as callers called her a bitch or a whore. That was intoxicating. Few women were innocent, anymore. Defiling a woman like that would be fun.

But then I discovered something else about her. As I watched her take call after call, hours of abuse that would break any other person, I saw an inner strength in her. Deep down, she was made of rock.

Breaking a woman like that, seeing her fight and fight and finally snap and become my personal whore...*that* would be an experience. One I wasn't going to miss out on. "I don't want the others," I snapped. "I want *her*."

Cairns sighed. "We have procedures in place, Mr. Ralavich. We'll get her back. And we'll kill the man who's helping her."

11

CAL

WE WERE WALKING. I wanted to make as much progress as we could before the clouds moved in and we lost the moonlight. Bethany was keeping up a respectable pace, considering she was in bare feet and wearing a dress.

The dress. With the moonlight shining through it and the breeze shifting and flattening the thin layers, it looked ghostly and insubstantial, like those gorgeous curves were cloaked in nothing but mist. When she took a step, I could see it pull tight across her ass. When she lifted one knee to climb over a fallen tree, the dress fell away from her leg and I glimpsed her smooth, pale thigh.

I forced myself to look away.

"So you live out here?" she asked.

I went to answer but nothing came. It had been so long since I'd talked to anyone. When I'd first found her, the adrenaline had been flowing and we'd been talking about *things,* and that had helped. But now we were onto small talk, and the parts of my brain that were supposed to do that were jamming and snarling like rusty gears. It was all I could do to spit out a few words. "That way." I nodded east. "'Bout ten hours' walk."

She looked around her. "I can't imagine being so far from everyone."

She didn't understand that being far from everyone was exactly what I needed. What I deserved. I looked down at Rufus. We had each other. That was enough, right?

Rufus looked up at me, then trotted over to Bethany and pushed up against her legs as she walked. She reached down and tousled his coat. "I can't believe he found me, in all this."

I grunted. If it *was* fate, fate had a twisted sense of humor. I shouldn't be anyone's white knight.

I figured I'd just stay quiet: that would be best. But Bethany's voice was comforting, soaking into my mind like soothing oil. Slowly, grudgingly, I felt those jammed-up mechanisms start to ease and turn, just as they had when I met her in Seattle. And I was worried about her. "You want to tell me what happened?" I asked at last.

She lowered her head and the air filled with that heavy, aching silence you get when what's inside is too painful to let out. For a while, I wasn't sure she was going to be able to tell me. But one advantage of being not much of a talker: I'm a hell of a listener. We tramped through the undergrowth for a good mile in silence, the only sound being the snap of twigs and the rustle of leaves, and eventually, it started to come out. She told me about working at the call center and her boss, watching them all on cameras, and this Russian guy Ralavich and the secret club at the mansion.

The rage rose inside me, white-hot and vicious. I wanted to hunt this guy down, make him as scared and helpless as he'd made her.

She told me how she'd escaped. And as I listened, I started to realize just how out of her element she was in the woods. She kept glancing around us at the dark trees, as if afraid of what might come out of them. Every step she took was uncertain. She was as out of place here as—

As I'd been, in Seattle. My chest contracted in sympathy. *Aw, hell...*

"We need to help the others," she said.

I was thrown. "Others?"

"Ralavich bought nine other women. And there were other men

there, they must have bought women already, or theirs are on their way. We have to get them out!"

I just stared at her. She was exhausted and terrified, she'd been through hell and she was still worried about helping others. This woman had a core of steel. She didn't seem to realize how brave she was. I nodded dumbly.

Telling me about it must have brought it all back because her shoulders tensed and her breathing went tight. She marched quicker through the undergrowth, as if trying to put distance between her and the memories. "I'm sorry I involved you," she said. "They're going to come after us. They're going to come after us and find us—"

She was starting to panic and I had no idea what to do. I wasn't used to being around people, let alone a scared woman. "Hey..." I muttered awkwardly.

"They're going to find us, they'll find *you* and they'll kill you and they'll take me back—"

"Hey," I said, more urgently.

"Back to that place and to—to Ralavich and then—"—she gulped —" to *Russia* and—"

"*Hey!*" I grabbed her hand and hauled her to a stop. God, her hand felt so small in mine, her fingers slender and cool. "Now you listen. You listening?"

She blinked and I saw the wetness in her eyes. That need swelled up in me and my chest went tight. For a second, I couldn't speak. But when I did, the words came from somewhere deep inside, each one heavy and loaded with power. "He *will not get you*," I told her. "Do you know why?"

She shook her head.

The words spilled out before I could stop them. "Because I'm going to protect you."

She bit her lip and nodded. And I just—

I knew what I was. I knew I was as far from a hero as it was possible to get. But the way she looked at me...she believed me. She believed *in* me. It made me want to be that guy.

I gazed down into her eyes and the protective urge rose higher. All

I wanted to do was sweep her up in my arms and crush her against my chest. I still had hold of her hand...and I couldn't let go.

12

BETHANY

I WAS STANDING so close to him that I had my head tilted way back to look up at him. Those cornflower-blue eyes blazed down at me and the determination I saw there...it made me feel safer than I ever had in my life.

He was still holding my hand and I could feel the warmth of him throbbing into me in big, urgent pulses. He squeezed gently and I never wanted him to let go. That silver guitar string inside me was drawn *tight*.

And just for a second, he was open. *Vulnerable.* And I glimpsed something, buried beneath all the strength. Searing pain and heavy, brooding anger, trapped inside, like catching sight of a river of magma as a gap opened up between huge, heavy rocks. I squeezed *his* hand. *What is it? What's wrong?*

Then it was gone and there was only impenetrable rock again. He dropped my hand and looked up at the sky. "Cloud's nearly on us," he muttered. "We should get moving."

I blinked in surprise, then nodded, my mind spinning. He was in agony, inside, but he had it so well hidden, I hadn't seen it until now. *What happened to him?*

He marched on, stoic and silent, and I fell into step alongside him.

I missed the touch of his hand already. And then, as the wind picked up a little, I shivered. It wasn't just the cold, it was the endless blackness of the woods around us. I felt so small, in the middle of all this—

He noticed, cursed, and whipped off his thick, red-and-black plaid shirt. "Sorry. Didn't think. You must be frozen." Suddenly, the shirt was around me, big enough to be a coat. It was gloriously thick and still warm from his body and it smelled of sweet woodsmoke and pinecones. I cuddled into it. Cal pulled it closed and then kept his hands on the lapels for a moment as he stared down at me. He was still gruff, but I could hear the concern in his voice. "Better?"

I nodded dumbly, overcome by the look in his eyes: that fierce will to protect me and, beneath it, just a hint of that awful pain. *I have to help him!*

He removed his hands almost reluctantly and we walked on, Cal on one side of me and Rufus pushing up against my legs on the other.

Cal seemed to know exactly where he was going but I couldn't understand how: everything looked the same to me. We climbed carefully down steep banks and up rises, over a few small streams and through spooky, empty clearings where the moonlight lanced down in thick shafts through the trees.

We came to a gully as deep as I was tall and he had to lower me down by the hand until my feet touched bottom. On the far side, he put his hands together and motioned for me to put my foot in them, so he could boost me up. As I pushed off and climbed, I was very aware of just how thin the dress was, and how warm his cheek was as it nestled against my hip.

A little further on, he grabbed my shoulder to stop me. "Gorse bushes," he warned, nodding at a sea of undergrowth ahead of us. "They'll scratch your legs to pieces."

We looked at each other. Then he held his arms out and nodded. *I'll carry you.*

I swallowed. He bent down and I tentatively put my hands on his shoulders and...*jumped*—

My breasts pillowed against his chest and I went heady. His arms folded around my back and pressed me closer. God, he was so big: it was like hugging a bear. My legs slid either side of his body and I closed my eyes as his hard abs mashed against my groin. It was just like my dream.

"Okay?" he asked.

"*Mmm-hmm,*" I replied, trying to keep my voice level.

He straightened up and I gasped as we lifted into the air. The wind blew my hair across his face for a second and I felt him sway. "You okay?" I asked, worried.

Now it almost sounded like *he* was trying to keep his voice level. "Mm-hmm."

Then he was marching through the gorse bushes, the rough denim of his jeans battering the thorns aside. Rufus expertly threaded his way between and under the tangled stems and waited for us on the far side, tail wagging.

When we were through, Cal put me gently down. My whole front was deliciously warm from where it had pressed against him. The feel of him—the huge, solid bulges of his pecs, the washboard of his abs—was imprinted on my mind, never to be forgotten. It had felt so right, like that was my natural place, and all I wanted to do was nestle in again. I looked at a tree in the distance, unable to meet his eyes, and hoped he couldn't see how red my cheeks had gone. He pulled a few gorse stems from his jeans, freeing the thorns that had stabbed through the fabric. I was sure he must have picked up a few painful scratches but he made no mention of it.

A little further on, we came to a clearing and he stopped. "We should stop here for the night," he said.

Spend the night out here?! "Why?"

He pointed at the moon. "Cloud's just about to hit. Once it does, there'll be no light at all. Remember that gully we crossed? We could step right into the next one and break our legs."

I stared at the thick bank of cloud that seemed to stretch all the way to the horizon. It was already nibbling at the moon. I nodded, completely thrown. In the city, the night just means the sky changes color. The idea that darkness could trap you somewhere until morning was alien and chilling.

He found a spot, took a blanket from his small backpack, and laid it out on the ground. "Stay here with her," he told Rufus. Rufus immediately sat down on the blanket. I knelt next to him and watched as Cal walked off into the trees, getting smaller and smaller and then—

It came as suddenly as if someone had thrown a switch. One second, I was watching Cal through the trees; the next, I couldn't even see Rufus next to me. It was *black,* the sort of darkness I'd never known. I looked around in panic but there was nothing, not the soft, glowing square of a window with a streetlight outside, not the bright rectangle of a phone screen, not even the tiny, cold sapphire of a laptop power LED. I couldn't even tell if I still had my eyes open. I heard myself begin to panic breathe—

And then I heard the slow panting of Rufus next to me. I groped in the darkness and found him, then flung my arms around his big, furry neck, cuddling close. "Good boy," I whispered to him, relieved. "Good boy."

I strained my ears but couldn't hear anything. How far had Cal gone? Would he be able to find his way back? I petted Rufus, stroking his head and then scratching behind his ears. He pushed his head into my hand in ecstasy and thumped the ground with his hind leg.

It was the first time I'd really stopped since this whole thing began. Reality caught up with me and my stomach lurched. Only that morning, I'd been starting my shift at the call center. I should be tucked up in bed, now, asleep, ready for another shift tomorrow morning, and instead I was...I looked around at the impenetrable blackness. I was *out here,* in the middle of nowhere. And somewhere out there, the men from the club were looking for us. Just knowing that things like the club existed was terrifying.

And what about Cal? He'd saved me from the guards, he was taking care of me...but I still barely knew him. And I was out here alone with him, about to sleep out under the stars. About the only thing I knew about him was that he lived way out here on his own. Didn't that make him a little...strange?

Suddenly, I heard footsteps, right in front of me. I sat bolt upright, but then Rufus gave a happy woof and leaned forward to lick a hand and I knew it was Cal. I heard him clearing a patch of ground, then the rattle of dry twigs and the clack of branches as he built a fire. Then the flare of a match, dazzlingly bright after the darkness. For a second, it lit him up as he hunkered down in front of me, his face only a few feet from mine. It threw dancing shadows under those heavy, brooding brows. It turned the gold of his hair and beard to warm amber. The flame danced in his eyes as he watched me and I realized it must be lighting me up for him, too.

I felt myself relax. Yes, he was a stranger. Yes, he was intimidatingly big. But there was something in the way he looked at me that told me he'd never, ever hurt me.

He put the match to the fire he'd built and the flame caught and slowly rose. I'd never *heard* fire, before. I'd never been in a place quiet enough. Out here, it was like a living thing, a fourth person who'd joined us, filling the air with snaps and creaks, sticks shifting and tumbling as it devoured them. An orange glow filled the clearing.

Cal sat down close to the fire. "Let me see your feet."

I scooched around on the blanket and extended my feet towards him. Rufus pressed close to my shoulder, curious about this new game. I'd almost forgotten about my feet hurting: I'd been walking on them for so many hours, the pain had just become normal and the numbing cold had helped a little, too. But now, as Cal's big hands warmed them and the blood flow returned, I winced at all the cuts and scrapes I'd picked up.

"Nothing too bad," Cal muttered. "But you can't keep walking around like that or they'll get infected." He took a first aid kit from his backpack and cleaned and dressed the wounds, his hands gentle despite their size. I had to push my feet almost into his lap so that he could get to my heels and when he lifted them, the dress slithered down my legs. I pushed it back into place. It slithered down again and I felt Cal's eyes following it.

When he finished, he sat back and considered. "My boots won't fit you."

I blinked, my heart unexpectedly lifting and bobbing. *He would have given me his boots?!*

"But I've got something that might work," he said. He dug in his backpack again and brought out a pair of dry, thick socks, then gently slid them onto my feet. They felt so good I nearly wept. Then he brought out some waterproof bags and put one over each foot, tying them in place with a cord around the bottom of my ankle and again at the top.

I tried a few experimental steps and they were great: warm and so much more comfortable than walking barefoot. "Thank you," I said with feeling. Then I looked down at myself and laughed. I was in a billowing ivory dress, torn in places and stained with dirt, topped off with a plaid shirt that was far too big for me. There were pine needles in my hair, my calves were muddy and I had plastic bags on my feet. "I look ridiculous."

And then I looked up and caught my breath, because I saw the way he was looking at me.

His gaze started on my face and traveled slowly down my body. As it rose again, I could feel the heat of it, as surely as if he was running his hand over my flesh. I felt it going all the way up my bare leg, where it was revealed by the split in the dress. Then higher, tracing the contours of my thigh where the thin ivory fabric was plastered to my leg by the breeze. Up and round and—my breath tightened— right up to my groin. Then up over my waist, up to the low-cut neckline and the pale valley it revealed, and finally back to my face, where it stayed.

The look said, very firmly, that I didn't look ridiculous at all.

13

CAL

ook away. I couldn't. *Look away.* My gaze wouldn't move, lost in those brown eyes. *Look away, goddammit!*

I finally broke the gaze and stared into the fire. "We should get some sleep," I muttered. Out of the corner of my eye, I saw her look startled for a moment, then look at the ground and nod.

I didn't want to keep pushing her away. God knows, all I wanted to do was pull her close. But she deserved better than the likes of me. The sooner I got her to Tucker's, the better. Those bastards in the mansion could go to jail, she could go back to the city and I could go back to being alone.

I lay down on my side of the blanket. The ground beneath us was mossy and springy and the fire made it pleasantly warm.

Bethany hesitantly sat down, then lay down on her side, her back towards my chest. Both of us were almost at the edges of the blanket, but it was really only designed for one. The gorgeous curves of her ass were maybe six inches from my groin. I could see strands of her hair move when I breathed and smell the exotic scent of her shampoo: some fancy city stuff, pomegranate and honeysuckle or some nonsense like that. It smelled amazing. And underneath there was another, subtler scent. *Her,* feminine and sweet. A scent that drove me crazy, that had my cock swelling in my jeans. I gave a silent sigh.

Rufus came and stood over me, then tilted his head, confused. Normally, when we sleep in the open, he cuddles up against me. He looked at Bethany, then at me, then at the cold, inefficient gap we'd left between us. *Why aren't you cuddling up together?* he seemed to be asking.

I silently shook my head. *That's not happening.*

Rufus hesitated, then stepped over me, over Bethany, and stopped in front of her. He turned around three times, then curled himself up and cuddled into her front. *Traitor,* I thought. But I was glad she'd be warm.

I lay there staring at her. I was rock-hard, now, and there was an even more maddening side to it, an ache in my chest that I didn't want to think about, a need that went way beyond sex.

I was sure I wouldn't be able to even doze. But it had been a long day of hunting, followed by hours of walking. As the fire died down, I slept.

14

BETHANY

I WOKE UP CONFUSED, opening my eyes and then screwing them shut again. Bright light was trying to force its way under my lids. *Did I forget to close the blinds?* I groped for my phone to check the time. When my hand found only leaves and twigs, I woke up fast.

The first thing that hit me was the silence. I hadn't realized how used I had gotten to the constant hum of traffic and the whir of air conditioning. It was just so...*still.* The fear I'd felt the night before crept back: I was so tiny, out here in the vast wilderness.

Then I looked up at the sky and my breath caught in my throat. It was dawn and through the gaps in the trees overhead, clouds like fluffy, soft-edged snowdrifts were lit up salmon pink, dusted with gold. I suddenly understood what all the fuss was about sunrises.

I couldn't remember the last time I'd been woken by the sun. Or when night and day even had meaning in my life: until today, my phone had always blared me awake with music and I opened my eyes to a room made dark by blackout blinds, whether I was waking up for a day shift or a night one.

I was a little stiff from sleeping on the ground but surprisingly cozy, despite the fire having burned down to embers. In front of me, Rufus was still asleep, a furry croissant. And behind me—

My eyes widened in shock: Cal was pressed against my back. I could feel him all the way from shoulder to ankle, big and powerful and gloriously warm. His arm was around me protectively—or maybe possessively—wrapped a few inches below my breasts.

It felt really, really good.

And as I explored the feel of him behind me, I became aware of something else: his cock was hard in his jeans and the length of it was nestled right between my ass cheeks. I was self-consciously aware of how good *that* felt, too.

I carefully turned my head. He was still asleep, his face relaxed and strangely vulnerable. I twisted more and watched him sleeping. And the longer I watched, the more I became aware of how right this felt: him and me and Rufus, peaceful and secure. Even though I knew that was nuts.

A frown creased Cal's brow. His arm tightened a little around me. I watched his eyes moving behind his closed lids. *He's dreaming.* And not a good dream. As the minutes passed, his breathing came faster and faster, building to a peak. *Should I wake him?* Before I could, his whole body tensed—

His eyes opened and the raw horror there was like nothing I'd ever seen. He was still half in the dream, staring at whatever haunted him, and it was beyond terrifying. His face went dead-white, his skin clammy.

I slid a hand through his tousled, gold hair, and said. "*Shh.* It's okay. It's okay."

He blinked at me and for just a second, he was open and unshielded. And I saw again the pain he was in, every day of his life.

Then he came fully awake and in a heartbeat, he was his gruff, stoic self. He realized where his arm was and pulled it back, so quickly that his hand brushed against my left breast: a brief, scalding contact we both felt. He jumped up as if trying to put as much distance between us as possible. "Sorry. Must have—"

"It's okay—" I started.

"—In my sleep—" He wouldn't look at me.

"Really, it's okay." I jumped to my feet. "Seemed like you were having a nightmare."

He met my eyes for a split second. Then he looked away and gave a quick shake of his head. *Subject closed.*

Rufus opened one eye to see what all the noise was, then reluctantly unwound himself and got up. He stretched, then shook himself and glared at both of us reproachfully. I ruffled the fur on his head and watched Cal as he stuffed the blanket viciously into his backpack and kicked soil over the embers of the fire.

We started walking and immediately, I was grateful for the makeshift shoes. I still had to be careful not to step on any sharp rocks but I was no longer wincing at every stone and twig, and my feet were dry and warm.

I noticed how silently Cal moved, slipping through the landscape like a panther, like he was part of it. Rufus was the same, trotting between us and bounding over tree trunks and branches without a sound. I felt clumsy by comparison: wherever I stepped, something cracked or rustled. And every noise was magnified because it was so quiet. I hadn't realized how loud the city was until I left it.

I still couldn't get over how isolated we were. It wasn't just that we hadn't seen another person, we hadn't seen any signs of civilization: not a power line or a fence or a plane overhead. It was eerie. Why would anyone choose to live all the way out here?

As we climbed a hill covered in thick, waist-high bushes, I blurted, "What were you doing in Seattle?"

Cal looked around at me, his face unreadable.

"I mean, it's a long drive, from all the way out here. If you just needed a city, Boise is way closer. So it must be something specific you could only do in Seattle. I was just wondering what it was."

He held my gaze for a long time, then turned to face front. "Personal errand." He closed his eyes for a second and something flashed across his face before he could control it: terrible, bitter loss.

Shit! I'd been trying to get to know him so I could help, not make things worse. "Cal—"

He just shook his head.

But I didn't want to leave it like that. I ran forward through the bushes and got in front of him, then walked backward so he had to look at me. "Cal—"

He suddenly grabbed my waist with both hands and pulled me to him. I yelped. My whole front was crushed against him, my breasts soft against his pecs. My eyes searched his face. He was panting, as shocked as I was. I saw his eyes go to my lips and I swallowed. I could feel his cock hardening against my thigh—

He broke the gaze, then nodded over my shoulder...and down.

I shuffled around...and my stomach dropped to my feet. Just a couple of feet further on, the ground dropped suddenly away. The rise we were climbing had made it invisible until we were right on it and the bushes had hidden the edge, actually overhanging it in places. Walking backward, I wouldn't have known it was there until my feet came down on air.

I shuffled closer and looked, very glad that Cal still had his hands on my waist. It was a canyon. The far side sloped gently down but our side was a vertical wall of smooth, dark slate. It dropped straight down at least forty feet. At the bottom, a wide river rushed and foamed over rocks, throwing up spray that made the canyon walls shine.

"The gas station's about two miles from here," said Cal, nodding towards the far side.

"How do we get across *that?!*"

"We climb," he said. And finally—almost reluctantly—he let go of my waist and pointed at something on the rock wall. I frowned and squinted, not seeing what he was seeing. Wait—He didn't mean—*Oh Jesus....*

There were steps...sort of. A series of rocks that stuck out from the sheer wall and that would let you climb down, if you were some sort of mountain goat. I wasn't. I looked down at the rocky bottom, so far away. If I slipped, there'd be a horribly long time before I hit.

I looked around for another way. This couldn't be *it,* we couldn't have no other choice, just to reach a phone! But the canyon extended as far as I could see in either direction. I looked down at the drop again and gulped.

"You'll be fine," Cal told me, his voice a low, reassuring rumble in my ear. "I'll go first, so if you slip, I'll stop you."

I took the plastic bags and socks off my feet to give me more grip and then Cal led the way, picking his way easily down the side of the canyon. Each "step" was less than a foot wide, with absolutely nothing to stop you from falling off the edge to your right and nothing except the flat rock wall to hang onto on your left. I took a deep breath and followed. I made it to the fourth rock before I made the mistake of glancing down. The river seemed to spin and my stomach churned as vertigo hit. I tried to flatten myself against the cliff but there was no room, the rocks were too narrow—

"Hey!" said Cal sharply. "Look at me!"

I found those blue eyes and locked onto them for all I was worth. Gradually, my vision stabilized. I started breathing again.

"Just keep your eyes on me," he said, his voice worried but gentle. "Keep looking at me and you'll be fine."

I swallowed and nodded and we started to move again. This time, I kept my eyes firmly on his muscled back and shoulders. I couldn't forget about the drop but it started to recede a little in my mind. Soon, we were halfway down and I breathed a little easier. Behind us, I could hear Rufus pattering effortlessly down the rocks, probably wondering why humans were so slow.

But then it got harder, and we were still twenty feet up. The rocks here were slick from the spray and the rocks sucked all the warmth from my bare feet, leaving them numb just as I needed to feel when I had grip. My thighs were soon aching from tensing to stabilize myself. And then, without any warning, I put my left foot on a rock, lifted my right—

My left foot shot out from under me, I went down on my ass and slid, heading straight for Cal. I screamed a warning, scared I'd knock him off. He started to turn—

I bounced painfully off a rock and went sideways into space.

15

BETHANY

I TWISTED and flailed but grabbed nothing but air. I saw the river and rocks twenty feet below me and my stomach shot into my mouth.

A hand grabbed my wrist and I jerked to a stop, crying out in pain as all my weight tugged on my shoulder. I swung and hit the cliff—by sheer luck, with my hip and not my head. Then I looked down and saw the rocks and my brain shut down as panic took over. I scrabbled and kicked, frantically trying to find something to grab onto so that I wasn't just dangling over the drop. My fingernails scraped smooth slate and my feet skittered uselessly at wet rock. There was a noise above me but I was too terrified to pay attention. All my fighting had set me swinging like a pendulum and my shoulder screamed.

That noise again. It sounded like something I recognized. I forced myself to listen.

"Bethany!"

I looked up, wide-eyed and panting with fear. Cal was lying on the rocks, holding me by the wrist. "Stop moving," he ordered, "then I can pull you up!"

I kicked again and now I was twisting as well as swinging. I could hear what Cal was saying and it even made sense, but I couldn't stop: the panic had me.

"It's alright," he told me. Those blue eyes stared right into mine. "I won't let you go."

And I believed him. The words soaked into me, calmed me. I stopped kicking and flailing and my swinging slowed and then stopped. Cal hauled on my arm and lifted me and then got his other hand around my shoulder and pulled and finally he hauled me over the edge and onto the rocks. They weren't wide enough for two so we wound up with him lying on his back and me flopped on my stomach on top of him. Both of us were panting. Cal was gripping my upper arms and as I looked into his eyes from just a few inches away, he looked like....

Like he never wanted to let me go again. My heart gave this massive, double *th-thump*—

And then a big, wet tongue licked my ear. Rufus was there, nuzzling both of us, and we petted him and carefully got to our feet and continued down the cliff. We went more slowly, this time, with me shuffling instead of stepping and Cal ready to grab me if I slipped again.

When we reached the bottom, Cal sat me down on a rock beside the river and told me to just take a minute. I didn't argue: the adrenaline was draining out of me and I'd gone weak-kneed and heady, almost drunk with relief at being on flat ground again. *How does he live like this?!* He knew the route, he must come this way all the time, even when the rocks were covered in ice and snow. If he slipped, there was no one to grab *his* wrist. He'd be left lying at the bottom of the canyon with a broken leg or head injuries. And out here, there was no cell coverage, no ambulance or rescue unit he could call. He'd die, all alone. Who would choose this life?

When I'd recovered, he led the way over to the river. It was wider than it had looked from up above and the sound of the crashing water echoed around the steep walls, loud enough that he had to raise his voice. "You ever cross something like this before?"

I shook my head.

"You'll be fine," he said. "You're lucky, it's not too cold. Give it another few weeks, once we get into fall, and it'll be freezing. Just plant each foot good and firm before you lift off with the other, or the current will knock you right over. I'll have your hand the whole way."

He took my hand and we waded slowly out. Cal was right, the water wasn't too cold and in the shallows, it was easy going. But as we got farther out, the river bed dropped away and the current started to pick up. The water rose up my calves, then up to my thighs, and finally up over my waist. The river sucked at my feet as I lifted each one and it was hard work just to walk in a straight line. But Cal, standing upstream of me, was like an oak, shielding me from the worst of the current and hauling me up each time I stumbled.

The water got deeper and deeper, climbing steadily up my chest, the spray soaking my face and hair. Just as I thought we were going to have to turn back, we reached the halfway point and the river bed started to rise again. That was when Rufus jumped in, bounded through the shallows, and then doggy-paddled past us. He was waiting on the bank for us when we staggered ashore, our legs weak and shaky. The sun was getting high in the sky now and the warmth was blissful on my chilled body.

I looked back at the river and the cliff we'd climbed down, amazed and just a little proud. When I turned around, Cal was staring at me. "What?" I asked.

He just stared. His expression was torn. He *wanted* to look away, but—

I glanced down.

The fabric that covered my breasts was clinging damply and, given that my nipples had gone pebble-hard from the cold, everything was visible. Below my waist, the gauzy layers of the dress were stuck together and plastered to my hips and thighs, and the water had turned the ivory fabric almost transparent. You could see every curve of my legs and ass. I was wearing panties but they were the lacy, silky pair that Ralavich had made me wear and they had turned just as translucent as the dress. At the juncture of my thighs, there was just a hint of a dark shadow.

I looked up. Cal looked away. Then looked back, unable to stop himself. A wave of heat rippled down my body, making every inch of my skin throb, my groin tighten, and my breath catch. I'd always been self-conscious about my curves. I'd had my breasts ogled by men but I've never felt sexy, or alluring, or any of those things that seem to come so naturally to other women. I'd never felt *special.*

Until now. When he looked at me that way, I felt every one of those things.

That was when Rufus decided that now was the right time for a good shake. Both of us yelped and twisted away as we were sprayed. It broke the tension and when I looked at Cal again, he'd finally managed to avert his eyes. I dried my feet on the grass, put the socks and plastic bags back on and we set off.

The sun rose even higher and our clothes gradually dried. After another mile or so, I thought the trees were starting to thin out. And a mile after *that....*

I drew in my breath as we emerged onto a road. It was a dirt road and only two lanes but it was a *road...*and there was even a telephone line running alongside it. On the far side was a tiny, tumbledown garage with a faded hand-painted sign that read *Tucker's Garage.* There was even a car filling up at the pump.

I was shocked at how much my heart leaped, just at the tiny hint of civilization. A day ago, I would have thought of this place as backwoods: now it felt like we'd arrived in Times Square. *We made it!*

I started across the road, then realized that Cal wasn't with me. I looked back and saw him standing at the edge of the woods. He was looking at the road and the gas station with distaste, like an animal unwilling to venture out of its natural territory. *How long has it been, since he came to the edge of the woods? Weeks? Months?*

I hurried back, grabbed his hand, and squeezed it. "It's okay," I told him. "I'll be okay, now. You don't have to come any further."

He looked away as if embarrassed that I'd noticed. When he looked at me again, that protective gleam was back, stronger than ever. He squeezed *my* hand and that silver string went tight and strummed, sending a hot swell of emotion through me. Then he was marching me towards the gas station.

At the door, Cal pointed to the ground and Rufus sat down next to the *no animals* sign, looking disgruntled, then started noisily drinking from the water bowl the owner had put there.

The place was old enough that an actual bell tinkled when I pushed open the door. It was a small store: a rack of car parts, some shelves of candy, drinks and chips, and an aging TV up on the wall showing a news channel. Behind the counter, a man in his seventies with gold-rimmed glasses, a thick white beard, and an impressive potbelly looked up from his crossword. Tucker, I guessed.

For a second, he just blinked at me. I'd stopped thinking about what I looked like, but now I glanced down and took it in: loose hair full of bits of leaf and pine needles, a torn, muddy, old-fashioned dress stained with river water, Cal's huge plaid shirt and plastic bags on my feet. Tucker looked as if he had about a million questions. Then he looked behind me and they all vanished.

I frowned, confused. Then I turned and saw Cal. He'd had to duck to get through the door and now that he straightened up, he *loomed*. He was scowling and, combined with his size, it was intimidating as hell. I hadn't seen him like this since....

Since Seattle. Since he was last around people. He didn't *like* people, glaring and scowling to keep them at bay.

I looked at Tucker again. He gave Cal a shaky nod of recognition and swallowed nervously. So Cal had been here before...that made sense. And if every time, Cal had been like this, of course Tucker would be scared. He'd never gotten to know the gentle giant I knew. My chest ached. *That's so sad!* Why was he like this? Because he lived way out here in the wilderness and wasn't used to human contact? Or—

I froze. Or was it the other way around? Was it that he hated people so much that he'd isolated himself out here? But that made no sense: I'd seen pain in his eyes, not hate. And he'd gone out of his way to help me.

"Lady needs to use your phone," Cal muttered. He'd loosened up so much with me, during our journey, that it was jarring, hearing him be so gruff.

Tucker nodded and turned the phone on the counter to face me. I smiled my thanks. As I picked up the handset, it hit me that *this is goodbye.* Cal would go back into the woods, I'd go back to Seattle and we'd never see each other again. I looked at Cal in panic. He'd helped me but I hadn't had the chance to help him. I'd be leaving him in pain.

Cal nodded at me.

I dialed 911.

"911, please hold," said a recorded message. I couldn't look at Cal again: if I did, I was going to lose it completely. So I looked at the TV on the wall. A news anchor was talking about some hearing the attorney general had been involved in last week.

"911, what is your emergency?" asked the operator.

I opened my mouth...and nothing came out.

"911, what is the nature of your emergency?"

I was staring at the TV. The phone, Tucker's...everything except the screen had ceased to exist.

"911," said the operator more urgently, "do you require assistance?"

On the TV, a recording played of the attorney general addressing a senate hearing the week before. He was calling for stricter laws to fight international crime and—

I recognized him. I recognized the thinning black hair and the wide, moon-like face—

I recognized him because I'd seen him at the mansion.

16

BETHANY

I CLOSED MY EYES and I could see him in the mansion: every line of his crow's feet, every fold of his flabby neck. I recognized that patronizing voice: *No, sweetie. You're in the* right *place.*

The attorney general was a member of the club.

And then it got worse. I opened my eyes just as the camera cut to a shot of the senate panel and—

He was there, too. I was sure of it. An overweight guy with old-fashioned, aviator-style glasses: the caption on-screen told me he was a senator from Texas who sat on the foreign intelligence committee. And *him,* a senator from Oregon who was chair of the federal intelligence oversight panel. The man who oversaw the freakin' *FBI!*

The room felt like it was tipping and shifting under my feet. Now I understood why they'd all been so confident and self-assured. The club wasn't a collection of criminals: Ralavich was the exception, that's why they were so scared of him. The members were the elite of society: the rich and the very, very powerful. I looked again at the TV, at the men in their suits, and my stomach churned. This thing had been growing right at the heart of our society. These were men everyone trusted, men whose reputations were pristine. But maybe once a year, they'd jet off to their secret little clubhouse in Idaho, far

from the TV cameras, where scared young women would be waiting
for them

There'd been others at the mansion, too. Young men, too young to
be senators. CEOs? Tech billionaires? There was no telling who else
was involved.

I became aware of a voice in my ear. The 911 operator was still
asking if I needed help. "Sorry," I whispered, and hung up the phone.

"Bethany?" said Cal, concerned. But I couldn't answer him,
couldn't focus on anything. My mind was spinning too fast.

I couldn't go to the police.

No one would believe me. A secret club, for the political elite? In a
luxury mansion I wouldn't be able to find again? They'd think I was
crazy. And if by some miracle I managed to convince someone and
they looked into it, there was no way charges would ever be filed. The
attorney general was involved, and the man who oversaw the FBI.
Between the two of them, they knew everything that was going on in
law enforcement. They'd crush any investigation before it even got
started. I remembered the guns I'd seen at the mansion. These
people weren't afraid to kill to protect their secret. They'd make sure I
was silenced.

Cal's hands closed on my shoulders. "*Bethany?*"

This time, I looked up at him but I still couldn't speak. *I can't go
home.* They had my employment records. They knew where I lived.
They'd kill me, or take me back to Ralavich. Silent tears scalded my
eyes and started to spill down my cheeks. In less than twenty-four
hours, my life had come apart. I had no money, no job, no place to
live. I was being hunted by the most powerful men in the nation and
the police couldn't help me. *What the hell am I going to do?*

Cal's hands guided me out of the gas station. Rufus sprang to his
feet as we passed him and looked up at me, concerned. But I left
them both behind and stumbled across the road. I couldn't talk,
could barely process.

I sank to the ground at the edge of the woods and sat with my
arms on my knees and my face pressed against them. The despair
rose up inside me in huge, shuddering waves, hot tears streaming

down my cheeks and plopping into the dirt. I've never felt so utterly alone.

The scrape of boots and then denim in the dirt as Cal sat down next to me. A big, muscled arm encircled my shoulders, warming my shaking body. Then Rufus's furry head forced its way under my arm and a tongue started licking my tears away.

I wasn't alone.

"What happened?" asked Cal, his voice gentle. He held me, his big body pressed against my side, until my tears slowed. And then he listened as I told him.

17

CAL

WITH EACH WORD she spoke, I felt the rage rise inside me. Not the anger I was used to, that fiery black cloud of pain and guilt that seared me from the inside out. This was fiery and pure. Protective.

I was visualizing the smug bastards in suits and the sick club they'd built. A massive, shadowy machine, cloaked by money and power. No wonder they'd been able to hide it for so long: the people who were meant to protect us were the ones running it.

To them, we were just serfs, peasants to be exploited. We voted for them, we bought their products, followed their laws. And if one of the club members saw a woman they liked, they'd pluck her from her life and carry her off, like a king raiding a village, and there was nothing she or we could do about it—

I sucked in a long, shuddering breath, the blood pounding in my ears. *No. Not her.* I didn't care how goddamn powerful they were. They weren't having Bethany.

We'd protect her. Me and Rufus.

I looked into her eyes and my chest tightened. I couldn't kid myself anymore: I was crazy about this woman. But I couldn't let myself get close to her. She was good...*innocent*. And that meant she needed to be kept well away from someone like me.

I had to keep her at arm's length. That was already damn near impossible and it would get harder the longer I was with her. But the only other option was to abandon her, and that wasn't an option at all.

She shook her head. "I don't know what to do," she whispered, her voice ragged from crying. She looked at the ground. "I can't go to the police. I can't go home. There's nowhere I can go where they won't find me."

"No," I said. I stood and offered her my hand. "There's one place."

18

RALAVICH

"It's been almost twelve hours!" I yelled. "How can you not have them, yet?"

To his credit, Cairns, the head of the club, didn't flinch. "Mr. Ralavich, you've been up all night. Please, let my people bring you some breakfast."

That nearly pushed me over the edge. "I don't want fucking breakfast! I'm wanted by the FBI in this fucking country! What if she's talking to the authorities *right now?*" I swept my arm around at the mansion. "Everyone here, all of your members, are at risk!"

Carl Jammer, the attorney general, shook his head. He was lounging in an armchair with a girl on his knee. "I have people I trust in the state police and the FBI. If she'd popped up on their radar, I'd know about it." He turned and fondled the girl's breasts. She closed her eyes, as if trying to wish herself somewhere else.

Cairns saw me watching. "Why don't you let me get you another girl? Or you could try the golf course or the pool...we can even arrange a hunting trip for you, we have rifles and a helicopter that can take you right to the best spots for deer."

That did it. I grabbed him by the throat, lifting him so that I could snarl in his face. "Because I want *her!*"

Didn't any of them get it? Bethany was special. So good, so pure. In the few minutes of sleep I'd managed, I'd dreamed of defiling her in every possible way. The fact she'd escaped me made her even more irresistible. There'd been time for her fear of me to build. She'd be twice as scared, when I finally took her. Pale and sobbing and pleading, exactly as it should be.

The need has been with me since my first sexual experience: my father offered me the captured wife of one of our rivals, telling me it would make me a man. And it did. I suddenly realized there was a way I could get even with all the girls who'd rejected me in school as too fat, too unsophisticated. And later, when I was beaten so badly that my face was left ruined, and women shrank away from me, I knew exactly how to make them pay.

Cairns had finally lost his irritating cool and was struggling to breathe. "Find them," I ordered.

He nodded frantically and I let him fall to the floor, choking and gasping.

"Quickly," I added. "Otherwise..."—I looked at Alik—"I'll take matters into my own hands."

19

BETHANY

I TOOK A LAST look back at Tucker's before the branches closed behind us and cut off my view. The wilderness seemed even scarier, having had that little taste of civilization. And from what Cal had told me, we were going even deeper, this time: his smallholding was right in the heart of the woods. A place where I'd be safe...but also a place we'd be alone together, for who knew how long?

"Why are you doing this?" I asked.

He was walking ahead of me, forging a path through the undergrowth. He didn't turn around but I saw his shoulders rise in response. "'Cause it's the right thing to do," he said at last.

"Thank you," I told him.

This time, he stopped and turned around. I'd already taken a step, not expecting him to stop, and suddenly we were very close. He looked down at me and I saw that need, undeniable and soul-deep. My chest went tight.

But then he turned away and marched on. I stood there for a second, staring at his back. *He feels it, too.* And he wanted to protect me. But he wouldn't let me get close enough to help him, or even know him.

After an hour or so, we moved into an older part of the forest where the trees were so big, I wouldn't be able to encircle them with both arms and a canopy that was high overhead, tinting the sunlight green. There wasn't much undergrowth here and the going was easier, so Cal drifted back to walk alongside me and Rufus. I gazed around at the trees. "How do you know where we're going?"

He looked at me blankly.

I threw my arms out wide in confusion. "There are no landmarks. There's *nothing,* just trees. You can barely even see the sun through the leaves. How are you finding your way?"

He looked at me for a long moment, then looked ahead of us. "See the tree with the weird branch?"

I looked sideways at him. "They *all* have weird branches!"

He considered. "It has two thick knots, like...like a snake that's eaten a couple of melons."

I felt a smile tug at the corners of my lips. It was an oddly funny description, for Cal. And now I *did* see it. "Okay, yeah."

"And over there, do you see the stump that's worn down in the middle, so it's like a big dish?"

"...yeah," I said, finding it.

"If we aim for a point midway between them, we're on the right course."

He started to point out each marker as we passed it and slowly, it began to make sense. My brain was tuned for the city. It needed hard edges and bright colors: the green and white of a Starbucks sign, the red awning of a cafe. But there were landmarks here, too: you just had to see the forest as he saw it.

By now, it was past noon. My stomach rumbled to remind me that it was time to run across the street to the deli for a salad with smoked chicken, sundried tomatoes, and some parmesan shavings. With maybe a sugar-dusted donut, fresh from the fryer, and a big cup of coffee. In my defense, I hadn't eaten in over twenty-four hours. "Don't suppose you have anything to eat, do you?" I asked.

Cal dug in his backpack and passed me a water bottle and a plastic bag full of...something. They looked like bark chips but they were soft and squishy. "What is it?" I asked.

"Jerky."

I drank some water and then tried a piece. Salty and meaty and very, very chewy. So chewy I had a feeling I might still be chewing it in an hour's time. But I didn't care: it was food. "Thank you," I mumbled around the mouthful.

As we walked, I tried to move more like he moved, stealthy and silent. I'd had a lifetime of clumping obliviously along sidewalks. Here, it mattered where you put each foot. I learned to keep one eye on the ground, skirting around dry twigs and loose rocks. As the hours passed, the noise I was making gradually dropped away.

And as I got quieter, the forest came alive.

All of the animals I'd been unknowingly scaring away started to creep back. Bird song moved from off in the distance to right overhead. I saw a squirrel, then two, then a chipmunk.

Cal suddenly stopped and put his hand up: *Stop.*

I stopped. Rufus stopped too: I'd never seen a dog so well trained.

Very slowly, Cal motioned me forward. I crept to him in silence, until we were shoulder to shoulder. But I still couldn't see why he'd stopped.

He reached across and took my chin in his hand. I felt my whole body come to trembling attention, the touch of those big, warm fingers on my skin indescribable.

He turned my head gently to the left...and I saw. A deer, no more than ten feet from us, nibbling at something on the ground. Its coat was the color of buttery caramel, glossy and smooth, with creamy white spots. Its eyes were huge and dark and it was so peaceful, so completely at ease, that the tranquility of it just soaked into me, washing away everything else. I could have watched it for hours. We stood there until it finally trotted away into the trees.

I caught Cal's eye and for a second, before he turned away and moved on, I glimpsed the same peace there that I felt. He might be big and intimidating, but he'd loved that just as much as I had.

As he walked on, I stayed still for a moment, looking around at the woods with new eyes. Maybe they weren't so scary—

A long, low howl split the air, then another one answered it. I went stock still for a second, one of those caveman responses you just can't shake. Then I relaxed, the way I would in the city. *Don't be stupid. It's just dogs.*

Then I remembered I wasn't *in* the city, anymore. "Wait. Wait, was that—"

Cal turned and looked back at me.

I felt my eyes go big. "Was that *wolves?* Actual *wolves?*"

"They won't bother people," he said. "Not unless you're injured, and on your own." He said it like it was meant to be reassuring. We moved on, with me keeping closer to him.

In the early afternoon, we came to a clearing and Cal said it was a good place to rest and eat. He set his backpack down, told Rufus to wait with me, and then walked off into the trees, unslinging his rifle as he went. It took a few seconds for me to get it: he didn't carry food with him, beyond jerky. That's how he traveled so far with just a small backpack. When he wanted to eat, he hunted. My life back in Seattle, when I could grab a bagel or a pizza slice on any street corner, suddenly seemed ridiculously easy.

I didn't want to just sit there while he did all the work: he'd done so much for me already. He'd need a fire to cook whatever he brought home, right? I didn't know how to build one but I could sure as hell collect wood. I made my way around the clearing, grabbing any loose sticks I could find, only slightly delayed by Rufus thinking it was a game and grabbing the sticks in his teeth and refusing to let go until I threw one for him to fetch.

A shot rang out, echoing through the trees. *So fast?!* It had only been a couple of minutes. Then another shot. I moved faster, gathering armfuls of wood, and when Cal re-entered the clearing a few moments later, I had an impressive pile. He looked surprised, but nodded his thanks and showed me the two birds he'd shot.

I got him to show me how to build a fire, clearing away scrub so that we didn't burn down the whole forest, making a teepee with kindling underneath and then building a layer of thicker wood on top. He prepared the birds and we strung them on a makeshift spit so they could roast over the fire. It was lengthy and laborious and fascinating.

A gentle breeze tousled our hair and sent the smoke twisting and dancing. The sun had warmed the grass and it was luxuriantly soft to lounge on as we took turns turning the spit. The flames crackled and hissed as juices dripped and the air filled with the smell of roasting meat. I was still on the run...but right at that moment, I wouldn't have wanted to be anywhere else in the world.

We ate with Rufus lying flat on his belly and making big, mournful eyes at us, then springing up to catch chunks of meat in mid-air when one of us took pity on him. He probably got more of our birds than we did. Bellies full, we put out the fire and moved on.

We walked all day, descending into a valley and then up a long hill. The sun sank in the sky, outlining every tree in orange-gold fire and the forest grew thicker and thicker, until I couldn't see more than fifty yards ahead. By the time the sun turned red and eased below the horizon, I was exhausted: this was the furthest I'd walked in my life. I stumbled along with my eyes on the ground, focused on not tripping over a fallen branch in the dim light. So when Cal stopped, I almost walked into his back. "What is it?" I asked. "What's up?"

He stepped out of the way and pointed through the trees. "We're home."

20

BETHANY

R UFUS RAN FORWARD, barking excitedly and sniffing everything in sight. But I just stood at the edge of the clearing and stared.

It was a cabin, no bigger than thirty feet on a side. The walls were made of thick, dark logs, crisscrossing at the corners, like something out of the Old West. More logs made up a sloping roof. The windows had heavy wooden shutters and I noticed the door was sized for Cal —probably one of the few he wouldn't have to stoop to get through.

Cal led me forward and showed me around while there was still enough light to see by. There was a chicken coop where chickens were just settling in to roost for the night. There was a lean-to for tools and a woodshed piled high with firewood ready for winter. A couple of things I had no idea about: a tall, narrow hut with a chimney and smoke drifting from it, and something big, round, and metal that was half-hidden under a tarpaulin. But I recognized the vegetable garden, with plants growing in neat rows, the herb pots and the fruit canes.

Finally, he showed me the barn. As soon as the door creaked open, there was a loud, commanding *moo.* Cal took me over to a stall where a large, black-and-cream cow was waiting for attention. She pushed her wet, pink nose into Cal's hand and wouldn't stop mooing until he expertly scratched behind her ears. In the next stall, a goat with a snow-white coat and curving brown horns put his front hooves up on the slats of the door and stayed there until Cal petted it. Back outside, he showed me around the back of the barn, where a pig pen held three snorting, boisterous pigs. Running along the back of the entire smallholding was a field of wheat, the golden stalks turning silver as the sun sank and the moon rose.

I turned a slow circle, taking it all in. "What do you do for power?" I asked.

"No power. There's a wood stove for cooking, lanterns for light."

"Phone?"

"No phone."

"Water?"

He showed me the wooden doors that covered the well.

He was completely self-sufficient here, I realized. And utterly alone. "How far is the nearest person?"

"There's a town, Marten Valley. I go there every three, four months for stuff I can't grow myself." He pointed. "It's about six hours' walk that way."

"You don't have a car?"

He shook his head. "No roads, out here. When I went to Seattle I borrowed one."

It was beautiful, idyllic: a little home carved out right in the center of the forest. But...now that the animals had quietened down, it was so *silent!* Even a bird squawking, far off, seemed loud. I realized that I'd never been this far from people my entire life. It was achingly lonely and this was with Cal there. How must it be for him, not hearing another voice or seeing another face for months at a time? What the hell would drive someone to choose this kind of isolation?

He opened the door and, immediately, Rufus pushed past our legs and ran inside. He trotted to a corner where a blue blanket, tattered but soft with age, lay spread out on the floor. As he curled up and went to sleep, I looked around.

The inside of the cabin was one big room. The log walls had been stripped of bark and sanded down so they were glossy and smooth, and the cracks sealed up so that there were no drafts. There was a table and chair, handmade and as big and chunky as Cal himself. As much as possible, I realized, was made of wood. Because everything *not* made from wood—every nail, every pane of glass in the windows —would have had to have been brought from the nearest town, carried for six hours on Cal's back. Building this place on his own, so far from any roads, was a monumental achievement. "It's amazing," I said.

Cal didn't answer. When I looked at him, he was just looking around as if seeing the cabin for the first time: seeing it through my eyes. It slowly hit me that I was the first person, other than him, to ever see it. He'd had no one to share it with. The thought was heartbreaking.

One wall was dominated by a huge iron stove. "How did you get *that* here?" I asked.

"In the winter," he said. "Boat brought it up the river, then I dragged it on a sled. Until then, I just cooked on a campfire."

Nothing was electric, I realized. Nothing was even battery-powered. Everything was sturdy and easily repairable and probably wouldn't have looked much different two hundred years ago. There was a cast-iron skillet, a stove-top coffee pot and a big, hand-cranked mill for grinding. There were oil-fired lanterns for when it got dark and blankets for when it got cold. It was basic but cozy. And very, very remote. For the first time since I got into the limo in Seattle, I felt myself relax. Cal was right: Ralavich would never find me, here.

"Let me see if I can find you something to wear," said Cal. In the corner of the room, a chunk of wood had been nailed to the wall. He put his foot on it and used it to boost himself up to the rafters, then hauled himself up into the roof space. One end of the room had been boarded over and I realized he used it for storage. While he hunted for clothes, I checked in on Rufus. He was still asleep on his blanket, paws and tail occasionally twitching as he chased dream-rabbits. His blanket, I saw, hadn't started out as one. I could see button holes along one frayed edge. The sleeves were missing, but it had been one of Cal's shirts, once,

Cal threw things down from the roof space one by one: some boots, a blue plaid shirt, a t-shirt and a pair of jeans.

He swung himself down and dropped to the floor, graceful despite his size. "They won't fit," he warned as he walked towards me, "But I figure we can make it work."

I nodded and crouched down to gather up the clothes. Arms full, I glanced up...and swallowed.

He was right in front of me, no more than a foot away, and indoors, he seemed even bigger. He was gazing down at me and the look in his eyes took my breath away. He was looking at me, all disheveled and muddy and with twigs in my hair, as if I was the best thing he'd ever seen. I felt that silver string inside me pull tight and tremble. And there was something else in his eyes, fiery and primal. His eyes flicked to my breasts, to the bare thigh revealed by the dress. A wave of heat rippled down my body and slammed into my groin.

I stood up, very slowly. I was so close to him that I could feel the heat of his body and it was making me almost drunk. My eyes passed his muscled thighs and I thought about the way they'd spread me, thick and solid, if he pressed even one of them between my legs. I passed his hands, curled almost into fists with the tension, hands that could so easily grab me, lift me, position me just how he wanted. And then, it was impossible to avoid: the bulge at his crotch, the denim tight and straining right down to—*oh wow*.

I kept going, my eyes rising past his belt, past the taut flatness of his stomach and then up to the broad swells of his chest. My eyes roved left and right: he was so big, he filled my vision. The urge to step forward and rub myself full length against the hardness of his body was unbelievable. It was more than just lust. There was an indescribable feeling of rightness. As if, if I pressed myself to him, I'd fit exactly, his big body sheltering me from any storm.

I looked up and met his gaze. His eyes were blazing down at me and I swore I could feel the heat on my face. He was frowning. *Why are you doing this to me?*

I looked helplessly back at him. *I'm not doing anything!*

He finally looked away, breaking the spell. Flushing, I looked around for somewhere to change. Then I remembered that the cabin was one big room. *Oh.*

I saw realization cross Cal's face. "I need to get some meat from the smoker," he muttered, and left.

The smoker. That was what the weird chimney hut outside was. I stood there for a few seconds, my cheeks cooling. Then I hurried to get changed before he got back. But when I had the dress half undone, I noticed something that made me stop.

He'd taken time, maybe years, building this place and getting it exactly right. But there wasn't a single personal item here. Not a picture of him drunk with buddies or with his family, not a lumpy ceramic mug made by a nephew for his birthday. Memories didn't have a place here. He hadn't just isolated himself physically, he'd obliterated his past.

And the only reason he'd do that was if his past was too painful to remember.

21

CAL

I PULLED a couple of venison steaks from the hooks in the smoker and took a deliberately slow walk back to the house, checking on the chickens and making sure the barn door was closed tight. *That should be enough time, right?* I rounded the corner and—

Through the window, I saw her standing in just bra and panties, looking off to the side. She was reaching behind her and just as my brain registered what I was seeing, just as I was thinking *I shouldn't be watching this,* the bra came free and the breasts I'd spent the last few days—hell, the last *six months*—fantasizing about, were revealed. God, they were incredible, weighty and full, and topped with dark pink nipples.

I swallowed and stepped back around the corner of the house, the image of her burned into my mind. I counted to *ten Mississipi. Okay, now she's got to be dressed, right?* I took a deep breath. I'd walk in there and pretend nothing had happened. I rounded the corner again—

She had her back to me, now. The panties were just falling to the floor to reveal her perfect, curvy rump. I stood there transfixed as she pulled the jeans up her legs, the milky cheeks of her ass swaying this way and that.

Yes, I kept watching. I'm only human, dammit.

She pulled on the t-shirt and then the plaid shirt and then I finally marched out of the darkness and opened the door. Inside, I busied myself slicing up the venison and frying it with an onion, mixing in water and beans and spices.

"How did you learn all this stuff?" she asked. "Hunting. Crops. Building a cabin."

I shrugged. "It was just normal, for me. That's the way my folks raised me. I could handle a rifle by the time I was ten."

She stared at that. I guess city folk aren't used to guns.

"Our place was a lot like this," I told her. "But bigger, big enough for my folks and me. We had a little land and we scratched a living farming. And we weren't as far into the woods as we are here, just a mile or so outside a town. The sweet spot, my dad used to call it, close enough to have friends and neighbors, far enough out to be left alone."

"My dad was a former Marine. Struck matches on his stubble, didn't allow any cursing in his house and if I left the chicken coop open or forgot to put the milk pail away, he'd dress me down like a drill sergeant. But he was fair. Taught me how to shoot, how to hunt and skin, how to fell trees and build a house."

"My mom homeschooled me. She'd coach me on science and math and French verbs till my brain hurt, but she made these cookies with cherries and white chocolate that..." I shook my head, my mouth watering. "God, I can taste them now. She came from a family of farmers and she taught me about crops and soil and what to plant when. She was as tough as my dad: she wasn't afraid to get up on the roof to fix a leak, or pick up a gun to see off a cougar." I looked at the floor. "She died when I was twelve. Problem with her heart, no one saw it coming. After that, it was just my dad and me." I stopped for a second, thinking. "We weren't rich...I guess we were poor. But I never felt like I wanted for anything."

She nodded and looked thoughtful. I wondered how different it was to her own childhood. Very, I was guessing. "Sounds nice," she said at last.

The sincerity in her voice made something break free inside me and rise to the surface. Because she was right: it *had* been nice. A good childhood. A happy family. A gift I should have been able to pass on, one day. A family, maybe with someone like Bethany.

But then, in one night, everything changed. My life was put on a different path.

I turned away, pretending to check the food, as the memories broke free. The alley walls, so cold under my palms. His grunt of pain. The stink of blood.

I stared at the bubbling pot, knuckles going white on the spoon as I stirred. I tried to take a slow breath, but the pain made it ragged. I could hear Bethany's silence, behind me. She knew something was up and I was worried she was going to ask, but she didn't. That was one of the things I liked about her: she was sensitive, good with people in a way I could never be.

I stirred and stirred and finally managed to force the memories back down. Only when I had myself under control did I turn down the heat and go to help her with the clothes.

The plaid shirt was more like a coat on her and the t-shirt hung halfway to her knees, but with some rolling up of sleeves and tucking in, they worked.

The jeans were harder. We had to roll the cuffs up and use some cord to make a belt to keep them on her hips. I knelt in front of her, threading it through the loops and tying it off, and trying to forget about the fact that I knew she wasn't wearing any panties under the loose denim. They were still a little damp from the river, so she'd hung them near the stove to dry...along with the bra. Every time she moved, her breasts would bob and swing under the t-shirt and I lost the thread of what I was saying.

The boots were the hardest to make work. She had dainty little feet and even with three pairs of thick socks, they were nowhere close to as big as mine. But I had some newspaper I kept for kindling and by scrunching that into the toes, we managed to get something that would stay on her feet. She tried a few experimental steps, the huge things clumping around like clown shoes and she looked—

I swallowed. She looked adorable.

I was kneeling in front of her and for once it was *me* looking up at *her*, at those big brown eyes, so liquid and soft. She gave me one of those shy little lopsided grins.

Suddenly, I couldn't stop looking at her lips. The world seemed to stop.

Idiot. I stood and twisted away, breathing fast. It wasn't just the attraction. As I'd looked at her, just for a second, stupid fantasies had started playing in my head: her and me and Rufus, all together like—

Like a family.

Stupid. The monster doesn't get a happy ending.

I checked the pot. "Food's ready."

I passed her a bowl of stew and a hunk of bread and she thanked me. But she kept looking at me, her eyes full of concern. All she wanted was to help me.

I deliberately looked away and avoided her eyes until I felt her finally drop her gaze. People like me don't deserve help.

I only had one chair, so I gave that to her and leaned against the edge of the table. As we ate, my mind was turning. *How the hell am I going to make this work?* Already, she was getting too damn close. She trusted me...*liked* me even. Thought I was a hero. I couldn't let her get close enough to find out the truth.

I was picking up her empty dish when she said, "Cal? What are we going to do?"

I looked at her and, in a heartbeat, my own problems were forgotten. The fear in her eyes made me want to just grab her and pull her into my arms.

"They know my name," she continued. "They know where I live. *I can't go home.*"

My hands actually twitched, I wanted to hug her so much. "I don't know," I told her. "But I know you're safe here. And you can stay here as long as you want."

She bit her lip, her eyes going moist. She started to thank me and I just nodded quickly and looked away. Anymore looking into those big, brown eyes and I was going to fall right into them.

A little later, as I cleaned the dishes, I heard her yawn: the poor thing was exhausted. She'd probably never walked so far in one day in her life, and she'd done it all without complaining. For a city girl, she was tougher than I could have believed.

The yawn woke Rufus from his nap and he trotted over to Bethany and butted his head against her, then rolled on his side, demanding tummy tickles. As she obliged, she gazed out of the window, just...listening. For a while, I tried to figure out what she was listening to, because I couldn't hear anything. Then I realized she was listening to the silence. She'd never heard it before. God, she was so far out of her comfort zone, here. Was she going to be okay? City folk *need* people around them, they need to chatter. It's okay for people like me. I do just fine on my own.

Right?

Bethany yawned again and looked around...and then she just went still. I frowned, wondering what she'd seen...and then I followed her gaze to the bed.

The only bed.

She looked up at me and then back to the bed and then to me again and I saw the math going on in her head. *Is that why he took me in? Is it a deal? Room and board in return for—*

Her lips parted in shock. Before she could say anything, I stepped forward and put my hands up, dish suds dripping from them. "No! No."

We stared at each other. She nodded. She believed me, but....

But I could feel how hot my face had gone. Just the thought of the two of us...God, I was rock-hard in my jeans. "I'll sleep on the floor," I said firmly.

She swallowed. Held my gaze almost defiantly.

I caught my breath. Dammit, the temptation to just crush my lips down on hers and run my hands all over those fantastic curves....

A *woof* made both of us jump. We looked down to see Rufus looking up at us, concerned. Then he trotted across the room, jumped onto the bed, and sat down very firmly. *Okay, but whoever's sleeping in the bed, I'm sleeping with them.*

I started grabbing blankets to bed down on the floor. When I turned back to Bethany, she'd stripped down to the t-shirt—on her, it was more like a nightshirt—and was slipping between the covers. Rufus pushed up against her legs, snuggling in for the night.

I turned down the lantern and lay down on the floor. But even with my back turned and my eyes closed, I couldn't forget she was there. Her dark curls spilling across the pillow, her full breasts pushing out the front of the soft white t-shirt.... And I was going to have days, maybe weeks of this. Living in a one-room cabin with a woman I was crazy about and could never, ever have.

What the hell am I going to do?

22

BETHANY

I WOKE FROM SLEEP so deliciously deep, so silent and complete, that I had to haul myself up hand-over-hand through the layers of wakefulness until I finally opened my eyes, a big, goofy grin on my face. I couldn't remember *ever* having slept so well.

I was used to jumping out of bed as soon as my phone woke me, racing against time to get to my shift. Here, I'd woken naturally. I could hear Cal moving around but he didn't seem to be in any hurry to get me up. I could just stay there, warm and snuggled. The freedom of it was glorious.

I was going to get up, though. I was curious: I wanted to see the outside of the cabin in the daylight. I wanted to see what life here was like. And I wanted to help. But first: I sat up, lifted my arms overhead and gave a fantastically satisfying yawn and stretch, arching my back and looking up at the rafters.

When I looked down again, I saw Cal standing across the room, those blue eyes catching the light as they watched me. A hot throb spiraled down my body and detonated in my groin. I was suddenly very aware of my breasts, under the soft t-shirt, and how the stretch had made everything lift and move. My hair was tangled, I wasn't wearing any make-up...and from the look he was giving me, it didn't matter at all. I swallowed. "Good morning."

He just nodded, his eyes eating me up. "Breakfast's done," he said at last. "If you'd like some."

Breakfast was thick slices of salty bacon, carved off a slab and fried in the skillet. There were eggs, the yolks richly yellow and sticky, and hunks of his crusty homemade bread to mop them up with. We ate outdoors, sitting side-by-side on the front step of the cabin, looking out at the forest. I couldn't get over how clean the air tasted.

After breakfast, he collected the dishes, like the previous night. But I stopped him on the way to wash them. "I want to help," I said. "There must be stuff I can do. Chores."

He blinked at me, then looked down. I realized he was looking at my hands, so soft compared to his. Like he thought I was some sort of princess who shouldn't sully herself with such things. "I can do it," I insisted. "I *want* to do it. I need to...pay my way."

His eyes caught mine and for just a second, they sparkled and went molten with lust. My face flushed hot as a vision seared my mind: Cal's big body between my thighs, his hard ass rising and falling as he drove into me—

Both of us looked away. Of course he didn't expect me to pay with my body. Cal was the most honorable man I'd ever met. But underneath, I could tell he was thinking about it, fantasizing about it...just as I was.

"I can do chores," I said firmly, my face scarlet.

He nodded slowly. "You can feed the chickens. Toss them a handful of corn. Bucket's in the barn."

I found the tin bucket and walked over to the coop. There were six chickens, some rust-brown, some gray and cream and some a mixture, all with bright red crests on their heads. I unlatched the gate and slipped inside the coop. "Okay, now do you get some each or do you all—"

They swarmed me, clucking and squawking and circling my legs. "Wait! Okay, okay, it's coming—" I dug my hand into the bucket but before I could throw some, they were pecking it out of my hand.

Others had their heads in the bucket. Another one had thrust its head into the rolled-up cuff of my jeans and wasn't going to stop hunting until it found the piece of corn that had dropped there. Six chickens felt like fifty. I was being overrun! I panicked, tossed a handful of corn to the far side of the coop, and, as the chickens raced to get it, I made my escape.

Through the window, I could see Cal watching as he did the dishes. It looked like his shoulders were shaking with laughter. And I smiled too. I wondered how long it had been since he'd laughed.

There was a lot to do. He showed me how to haul water up from the well and then we spent the next few hours weeding and watering the vegetable garden. There were carrots and potatoes and cabbages, beets and squashes and pumpkins. Raspberries and blackberries grew on canes and there were bushes full of plump, succulent blueberries. "How long did all this take you?" I asked in wonder. "How long have you been here?"

"Six years."

Six years?! He'd been out here, living completely by himself, for six years? *Why?* My chest contracted in sympathy. But I didn't push. I had to hope he'd open up, given time. "What next?" I asked instead.

"We need some milk."

Still in city mode, I prepared to run to the store. Then I followed his gaze to the cow, who'd been let out to graze.

The cow looked at me suspiciously as we approached. I gave her a scratch behind her velvety ears and she snorted, dipped her head and nuzzled my palm. I felt myself grin. You can't have a cow nuzzle your palm and *not* grin: it's physically impossible.

We led her back to the barn and Cal set two short, thick logs down on their ends to serve as stools. From down there, the cow looked enormous. "She's a thousand pounds," said Cal. "She could break your foot if she stepped on it, so be careful."

"Gotcha," I said nervously. "What's her name?"

He frowned as if he didn't understand. "She...doesn't have one."

I stared at him. He'd stripped life down to just the practicalities, with no time for sentimentality. And yet he'd still gone out of his way to help me.

He shuffled our stools closer until we were shoulder-to-shoulder and almost underneath the cow. Then he showed me how to gently wash and dry the udders and nudge against them like a calf to get the cow to let down her milk. He taught me how to strip each teat, squirting the first few ounces onto the ground in case it was contaminated. Then he put a tin bucket underneath and started milking the front two teats, alternating his hands in a steady rhythm. Warm milk hissed into the bucket. He nodded towards the two rear teats. "Now you try."

I hesitantly wrapped my fingers around them and tried to squeeze the way he had. A few drops of milk fell, then nothing. The cow gave a moo that might have been despair.

"Almost," said Cal reassuringly. He leaned closer and then his big, warm hands were encircling mine, gently pressing to show me. I went a little heady. "Relax when you get up here," he said, "to let the milk in." His lips were right by my ear, his voice a warm rumble, and I could feel his beard brush my ear lobe, the hair softer than I'd imagined. "Then squeeze *down*," he said, doing it. "Then back *up....*"

I swallowed and nodded. Milk hissed into the bucket. "There," he murmured. "Good."

He slowly released my hands. I took a deep breath and tried to ignore my racing heart and the tingling, sensitive skin all the way down the side of my neck where his warm breath had blown. I focused on keeping a steady rhythm. After a few moments, I settled into it.

"There. You got it," he told me and I grinned, pleased.

When we were done, we took a mid-morning coffee break. The coffee beans were hand-ground in the all-purpose grinder in the kitchen, the water was from the well, heated on the stove, and the milk was rich and creamy, still warm from the cow. It was the best cup of coffee I'd ever had and drinking it outdoors, leaning against a tree, I felt like an actual farmer, ready to take on the world. What would I be doing, if I was back in the call center? I'd be on my twentieth call of the day, mentally and emotionally exhausted and counting the minutes until the end of my shift....

I sipped at my coffee and listened to the wind in the trees. *I could get used to this.*

The days fell into a routine. I'd start the day by feeding the chickens and milking the cow and goat. We'd tend the garden together, then he'd either go hunting or chop wood. It was peaceful. I couldn't forget about the men looking for me, but I was sure they wouldn't find me: we literally didn't even see another person.

I was amazed at how little went to waste. Every food scrap that could be composted went on the compost heap and the rest went to the pigs. Back in Seattle, I'd tried to save the planet by buying reusable coffee cups and tote bags...which I kept losing. My old life suddenly seemed crazily complicated and wasteful.

There were things I missed, like the internet. But there was plenty to make up for them. One night, I was just about to get into bed when I glanced out of the window...and then ducked down and craned my head so I could look up in amazement. "What?" asked Cal when he saw me.

I ran to the door and stumbled outside in just the t-shirt I'd been planning to sleep in. The night air was shockingly cold against my bare thighs but I barely noticed. I was looking at the sky.

The clouds had cleared and above was a midnight blue bowl dusted with a billion shining stars. I was used to seeing maybe one or two in Seattle. This was something else: clusters and constellations and the broad sweep of the Milky Way. Every star was so clear, so bright, that they felt like real places, not just abstract dots in the sky.

I became aware of Cal, beside me. "I never saw them before," I mumbled, still gazing upward. What I couldn't wrap my head around —what was heartbreaking—was that this had been there my entire life. It had just been hidden by the city's glow.

Cal said nothing. But a moment later, he returned with a blanket he wrapped around my shoulders and we sat together on the front step, looking up at the stars, for over an hour.

Two weeks passed, with no sign of the men from the club. Cal had been right: we were too deep in the woods for anyone to find us. But I was only safe as long as I stayed there and I couldn't stay there forever...however tempting that was becoming.

After the second week, the temperature started to drop as fall took hold. The nights became colder, the days shorter. But we were cozy and warm in our little burrow.

Cozy...and *close*. The cabin was small and Cal was big. However careful and polite we were, accidental touching was inevitable. And the more we brushed ass-to-groin while putting away dishes, or turned around and found ourselves chest-to-chest, or went to reach for something at the same time and touched hands, the more the tension rose. We were like two charged particles, bouncing around in a confined space, with every brief contact making us buzz louder and attract each other more.

Sometimes, we'd swap ends of the room, passing in the middle, and as we approached it got harder and harder to stay on course, as if I was caught in his gravity.. As we passed, at the second I got so close to him that I could smell his scent and feel his warmth in the air, the urge to veer off and just press myself up against that huge, hard body was almost overwhelming. It went beyond lust. It felt like I fitted there, like my head's natural resting place was between his pecs, the softness of my breasts pushed up against the hard muscle of his chest and his arms folded around me. At the last second, I'd control myself and walk on, my steps shaky, my heart thumping. *This is crazy,* I'd tell myself.

But he felt it, too: I saw the way his hands twitched when we touched, like he was having to force himself not to grab me. Heard how he inhaled, whenever my hair skimmed his face. Most of all, I felt his eyes on me, whenever my back was turned. I've never been someone men look at but whenever he got the chance, Cal's gaze would soak into me, heating and heating me, until I turned around...and then he'd quickly look away and I'd feel that silver guitar string drawn breathtakingly tight. After two weeks of this, the tension was almost unbearable.

I told myself the attraction made no sense: we were as different as two people could be. He lived in isolation; I lived in a city surrounded by millions of people.

And yet...both of us were lonely.

He gradually started to talk more. He still wasn't a big talker but the words started to come more easily. He still wouldn't talk about his past, though. All I knew was that something terrible must have happened, to make him want to isolate himself out here. Something that still caused him pain, something that sometimes made him wake in the middle of the night, sweating and wide-eyed. I'd lie there in the bed pretending to be asleep and wishing he'd let me help him.

One morning, I woke to the sound of rain drumming on the roof. I half sat up, nudged the curtains open an inch, peeked out...and stopped.

Cal was out there, standing in the rain. Naked.

He had his back to me and he was lathering himself with a bar of soap. The rain was washing the suds down his body and I followed them, transfixed. They slid over the huge, caramel bulges of his shoulders, then sped up as they slid around the islands formed by the muscles of his back. They followed the V-shaped form of him in towards his waist, then slowed as they crested his ass and trickled down over hard, perfect cheeks loaded with power.

I dragged my eyes away, flushing...and then stopped, my eyes locked on Cal's upper arm. There was a tattoo there, an eagle curled protectively around a globe with an anchor behind them. I was too far away to read the two words above the image, but I knew what they said. One of my flatmates had once had a boyfriend with that exact same tattoo. The words were *Semper Fidelis*.

Cal was a former Marine.

23

CAL

W E NEEDED to go to town. Normally, I could have gone another couple of weeks but we were getting through things faster, with her here: coffee, sugar, spices. Plus, she really needed some proper clothes and some boots that fitted. "We need to make a list," I told Bethany. "And it's got to be a really good list. Everything we need, and I mean *everything*."

She nodded, her eyes big. I could see it was sinking in: this wasn't like getting home from the grocery store and realizing you forgot the milk. If we forgot something, we'd just have to do without it for another three or four months.

She was assuming I made the trip so rarely because it was a long hike. But that wasn't the main reason. Going to town means *people*.

Together, we went through every damn thing in the cabin that could run out, everything that was broken and needed replacing, every job we needed to do that was waiting on a nail or a screw, wrote it all down and then checked it. Twice. Doing it on my own would have been a royal pain in the ass: I'd rather be swinging an axe or hunting or, hell, doing just about anything other than writing lists. But Bethany actually seemed to relish it and doing it with her was almost...*fun*. She thought of some things that I wouldn't have remembered and she added one or two things that we didn't strictly *need* but that sounded good. Like chocolate. I couldn't even remember the last time I'd had chocolate but now that she'd suggested it, I couldn't wait.

It was just one of the ways that things were changing, around the cabin. The previous morning, she'd walked in and told me that she was done with Betsy.

I blinked, thrown. "Betsy?" Then I looked at the bucket in her hand. "You gave the cow a name?"

She flushed, then lifted her chin and looked defiant. "Cows need love too."

I shook my head, bemused, but I was smiling. "Okay."

"And the same goes for Hank."

"Han—You gave the *goat* a name, too?" I thought for a second. "Please tell me you didn't name the chickens."

"Amy, Adele, Florence, Whitney, Madonna, and Beyonce."

"But not the—"

"Winklenose, Snortle and Rolypoly." And she looked me right in the eye, daring me to laugh at her. But I didn't. I just nodded and thought it was adorable.

There'd been lots of little changes like that. Like seeing her boots, stuffed with newspaper, lined up next to mine by the door. Like all the jars in the cupboard suddenly having labels, something I'd never gotten around to doing. Like, when I went out hunting with Rufus, how he'd bound the last hundred yards back to the cabin, excitedly barking, and then leap up at Bethany as she opened the door and not stop running around her until she tickled his tummy.

Ever since I'd built the cabin, there'd been something missing, something I'd never been able to put my finger on. I only knew that it didn't feel like the place I'd been raised in. It was warm and dry but it didn't feel like a home.

Until she arrived.

I didn't know what to do about that. Everything was getting too damn comfortable. Sometimes I'd be sitting with her on the steps, drinking coffee, throwing a stick for Rufus to fetch and I'd almost slip into thinking that this could work, that she could just stay here forever.

And then the past would hit me, a freezing wave that swamped me, drowned me, left me choking for breath. How could I forget, even for a second? How could I forget what I'd done? I didn't deserve Bethany, didn't deserve any sort of peace. Being out here, far from people, was my punishment and my escape. But it was no life for her. She might be enjoying things now but long term, this solitude would drive her crazy. She needed people around her, friends...and one day, a husband and kids. I couldn't give her that.

I had to keep the two of us apart but that was getting harder and harder.

The next day, we set off for town before dawn. It was a six-hour walk each way, so with a little time in town to buy supplies, it would be dark again before we were back.

It was a beautiful day. As the sun rose, we came out of the pines and into an area of aspens. Their leaves were changing from gold to deep orange and with the rising sun blasting warm light through every brightly-colored leaf, it was like walking through a palace of stained glass. We didn't speak, just watched in amazement, soaking it up. And it hit me that I'd never had anyone to share this stuff with, until now.

Mid-morning, we came to the top of a rise and stopped for a water break, looking out over an unbroken sea of yellow and scarlet treetops. Bethany sat on a log and Rufus immediately laid his head in her lap for ear scratches and head ruffles.

"You ever think about living somewhere a little less isolated?" she asked.

I stared out at the trees. "Tried the city, back when I was in school. Didn't like it, much."

"I thought you were homeschooled?"

"This was later. When I was a teenager."

I was going to leave it there. But I could feel her listening and she was so damn good at it, so patient and calming, that all the stuff that normally stayed locked up safe in the depths of my mind started slipping out. "I went to a school in the city for a little while. A big school, in a lousy area. Everything was concrete and it smelled bad." I looked down at my oversize body. "And the desks were too small, I always felt clumsy. I was this big dumb kid from the country. I knew how to hunt deer and how to find wild mushrooms, not...which bands were cool. The other guys thought I was weird. The girls, even more. Everybody called me Bigfoot."

She stood up and put a hand on my shoulder, cool and gentle. "You're not dumb," she said fiercely. "Or weird." She looked around at the forest. "You were just out of place, there."

The memories bubbled up, but where they'd normally catch and stick painfully in my chest, now they just seemed to escape, like her hand on my shoulder was making them as insubstantial as ghosts. I still didn't want to talk about this stuff, but getting it out actually felt good. "Everything was so busy, and there were no animals. I tried to find some parts of the city with some green, where there might be some birds, some squirrels, but when I went off on my own, just for a little walk, like...three or four hours, my aunt *freaked out.*"

I suddenly realized I'd said too much. I went quiet and hoped she wouldn't pick up on it, but this was Bethany: she was good with people. She left it a moment, and then gently asked, "Why were you living with your aunt?"

Dammit. I shook my head and stood up. "We should get going."

"Cal," she said softly. "Cal, I'm sorry...."

I nodded quickly to let her know that it was fine, then picked up the pace. I figured if we got busy walking, there wouldn't be time to talk. I could feel her watching me, concerned, as she trailed along behind me. I moved even faster.

I slipped under some overhanging branches and—

A big, dark shape, no more than ten feet ahead of me, its rump covered in thick, dark fur.

I had time to think *fuck.* And then it heard me and turned to face me. A grizzly bear the size of a small car. And *shit,* I could see a cub. I'd startled a mama bear. I'd done what even the dumbest hiker knows not to do in an area with bears: I'd moved too fast, too silently, so she'd had no warning. All because I'd been so determined not to talk.

"*Get back!*" I yelled, already trying to back up. But the branches I'd ducked under slapped the back of my head and I had to awkwardly shuffle under them—

And then the bear gave a long, bellowing roar that I felt in my chest...and charged towards me.

24

BETHANY

I HEARD CAL yell to *get back* and I backed up as quickly as I could, but then he was racing back towards me and—

Oh Jesus.

It was huge but it moved with terrifying speed. It came thundering out of the trees and I could feel the weight of it in the way the ground shook. Cal dodged to the side, waving his arms, and I realized he was making sure it followed him, not me. The bear turned to face him, lowered its head and roared. I had to slap my hands over my ears, it was so loud. *What the hell are we going to do?* This thing could kill us in the blink of an eye.

It lunged towards Cal and I caught a glimpse of long, curving teeth. Cal brought his arm up to protect his face and the jaws snapped closed—oh Jesus, it had hold of his shirt, and now it was shaking him like a doll with its jaws, trying to knock him off his feet so it could tear at him. Cal was grunting, trying to break free, but even he was no match for the bear's strength. He staggered...and went down. The bear's body blocked him from view but I could see it slashing with its claws—

He was dead unless I did something.

"*HEY!*" I yelled at the top of my voice. "*HEY!*" The bear didn't turn around. But then I circled to the left, towards where the bear had come from.....

That got its attention. It let go of Cal and turned to face me, then gave another of those ear-splitting roars. I froze. *Now what?!*

"Bethany!" Cal, from somewhere behind the bear. His voice was ragged: was he just scared for me, or was he hurt? "Don't run!" he yelled. "Play dead!"

I took an instinctive step back. Every nerve was telling me to bolt, to get away. *Play dead?!* Just lie down and let it bite and claw at me?!

The bear lunged forward, close enough for me to feel the heat of its breath.

"Play dead!" yelled Cal again. I could hear the raw terror in his voice.

The bear opened its jaws—

I threw myself to the ground and lay face-down in the dirt, eyes closed.

I heard the bear's heavy breaths and then the ground shook with each thump of its paws as it came closer. *Oh God—*

I felt fur brush my bare hand. It was right up against me.

Then a hot waft of air on the back of my neck. It must have its head down, jaws open, right over my head and neck, deciding whether to bite. Something warm and wet plopped onto my ear and I tried not to twitch.

A growl and a tug on my hip and I was rolled with terrifying ease. I tried to keep everything loose and floppy. One of my arms actually brushed warm fur as I was flipped onto my back. *Keep your eyes closed, keep your eyes closed—*

Warm breath against my chest. My neck. My face. A wet nose brushed my cheek. Then it nudged me, testing me. I tried to stay ragdoll-limp. Tried not to imagine those jaws snapping, my skull crumpling—

The wet nose found my ear and snuffled. I forced myself to keep still.

And then the ground shook again as it lumbered away.

I lay there not daring to move. I couldn't hear its footsteps anymore, but the wind was rustling the trees and I couldn't tell if it had wandered off into the forest or if it was just standing silently ten feet away. If it was safe, why hadn't Cal come? He must be playing dead, too, and it wasn't time to come out yet. I'd just have to wait until he gave the all-clear.

Then my stomach knotted. There was another possibility. What if he was hurt? I'd lost sight of him, when the bear attacked him. I'd heard his voice but it had been strained, ragged...what if he'd been clawed in the neck or the chest? What if he was bleeding out and I was lying there not helping him, scared of a bear that had long gone?

What do I do?!

I lay there motionless, the sun soaking through my closed lids, the breeze on my face. I strained my ears but I couldn't hear anything. I had to help him, even if it was risky.

I opened my eyes just as a huge form loomed into my vision. I flinched and cried out in panic—

Cal grabbed my shoulders. "It's okay! It's okay! It's gone."

I stared up at him, unable to speak. Then I grabbed hold of him and pulled myself to him, burying my face in his chest.

25

CAL

I'D BEEN SO SCARED. She'd been lying so still, as I approached. Had the bear shaken her, and snapped her neck? Then she opened her eyes and my heart just *lifted*. And then she threw her arms around me and lifted herself off the ground, crushing herself to me, and—

I melted. I wrapped my arms around her, wanting to never let her go. God, we'd come so close! My heart was still pounding. And I could feel the hot dampness of her tears soaking through my shirt. *I nearly lost her.* All because I hadn't wanted to talk.

I tightened my arms around her.

She suddenly drew her head back. "R—Rufus!" she spluttered through her tears. "Where's—"

"Rufus!" I called. A few seconds later, he appeared through the trees and bounded over to us. Bethany freed one arm and stroked Rufus, reassuring herself that he was okay. "I've trained him," I told her. "He knows to lie low, if he sees a bear."

"I thought—" She looked up at me, eyes still full of tears. "I thought you—" She reached up and touched my arm. One whole sleeve of my shirt, from the elbow to the wrist, was shredded where the bear had caught it with its teeth. "Oh God."

She'd started shaking and that scared me because I had no clue how to deal with it. I wasn't used to having anyone to comfort. "It's okay," I told her. "It's okay." And I clutched her close, closed my eyes, and just held her, and that seemed to work. Gradually, our breathing slowed. I was in an awkward position, knelt beside her with my upper body twisted, supporting her weight...and it felt so right, no force on earth could have moved me. We stayed there for a long time.

When we eventually unwound and got to our feet, she looked down at my chest and her eyes went big. "Cal!"

I looked down. The front of my t-shirt was stained red. I hadn't even felt it at the time, but the bear must have just caught me with her claws. I peeled the cotton away and looked down: yep, three red lines slashed across my left pec. "Not deep," I told her. "I'll be okay." I looked at her. "You could have been killed. You know it was crazy, what you did?" I tried to be gruff, because I needed to make sure she never did anything like that again. But one look in those big brown eyes and I just melted all over again. "And brave," I allowed. Then, "Thank you."

She looked away, embarrassed. But when she looked back at me, I was still gazing at her. *I mean it.*

She reluctantly nodded. And then we were caught, trapped in each other's eyes. The forest seemed to go quiet around us. I felt us start to move, so gradually it was almost imperceptible, both of us leaning closer—

I caught myself just in time and stopped, my heart thumping.

She stopped, too. "Those scratches need to be cleaned," she told me, all brisk and business. "Sit down."

I sat down on a log and took off my shirt and t-shirt, and she got the first aid kit from my backpack and went to work.

I sat there silently watching her for a few minutes. She was leaning close to my bare chest, her face only inches from my body, her long black hair thrown back over her shoulder so that it didn't get in her way. Those soft brown eyes were laser-focused on what she was doing and it was a rare opportunity to just gaze at her without getting caught doing it.

Her lashes were so long and those lips, the way she nibbled at the lower one when she was concentrating.... I felt like I had when I'd seen that deer in the forest, on our hike to the smallholding. Like I was lucky, like I was seeing something truly special. I felt that *pull* again. It would be so easy to just reach down and take her under the chin, tilt her head up to look at me and—

I looked away before I did something stupid. "You always want to be a doctor?" I muttered.

"My mom is a physiotherapist," she told me. "Her mom was a pediatrician. *Her* mom was a nurse, during the war. It's what we do. Instinct, or something."

Instinct. She just wanted to help people. She'd helped Rufus, she'd tried to help me. And I'd clammed up and pushed her away...and nearly lost her.

Before I knew what was happening, I was speaking.

"I used to dream about the city," I said. "Not any particular city, just *the city*. Someplace with skyscrapers and sports cars and everything made of concrete and glass. All I'd ever seen was the local town, and that was no bigger than Marten Valley. I used to lie in my room, when I'd done all my chores, and just think about city life: the parties and the technology and the cars and the w—" I cut myself off before I said *women*. "I begged my dad for a trip to the city," I told her. "Finally, for my fifteenth birthday, he says we're going to Seattle. We'll do all the tourist stuff, have a meal, and stop in to visit with my mom's sister, who's just moved there from Europe."

Bethany was looking up at me in shock. In the whole two weeks we'd been together, this was the most I'd said in one go. This was stuff I'd buried deep, long ago, and it hurt, coming out. But it was nothing, compared to the fear I'd felt when I'd seen her in danger.

"For weeks, I can't think of anything else," I said. "The day comes and I'm sitting there next to my dad in the pickup, craning forward in my seat, watching the city get bigger and bigger on the horizon. Then we're moving through it and it's *crazy*...so many buildings, so many cars. Pretty much the only cars I'd ever seen were pickups and station wagons and now suddenly there were stretch limos and sports cars: a

Porsche drives by *right next to us*, bright blue, and my dad was laughing because my jaw was on the floor. I'm hunkered down in my seat, trying to see the tops of the skyscrapers."

Bethany had started working on my wounds again but her hands moved slowly as she listened. There was something about her that was so calming...it eased the tightness in my chest, allowing the words to flow.

"We spend all day looking around. Everywhere I look, there are reflections and technology, big animated signs, beautiful people. My dad starts saying we should head home—it's a long drive back. But I keep asking to stay one more hour. Night falls and the whole city lights up. I'm standing there gaping at billboards and restaurants, theaters covered in millions of little lights. It's incredible." My voice caught. "I want to do everything. I want to get one of those coffees everybody's carrying, in the huge cups with the whipped cream on top. I want to ride an elevator up to the top of one of the skyscrapers. I want to go to one of the clubs with the music pumping out of it."

"And then..." I slowed. Stumbled. "We hear a...scream. A woman's scream. From an alley just a few steps from where we are. We look at each other and then look around. There were no cops on the street and the other people walking past....they don't stop. They just give this worried look and keep on walking. And suddenly, the city doesn't seem exciting." My voice went cold. "It just feels scary as hell."

Bethany had stopped dressing my wounds. She looked up at me, her eyes huge.

The memories were jagged, now, razor-sharp. They sliced at me as I dug up each one, and even shaping them into words was painful.

"My dad says to me, *stay here*. And then he's gone, running into the alley. Because that's just who he is. And I strain my ears but there's traffic going past. I can hear him talking to someone in that voice he does, the one he learned in the Marines, the *don't fucking mess with me* voice, but I can't hear the words. And then..." I stared at my boots. "Then I hear him just...*stop*. The words are cut off and he just gives this little grunt. And then *I'm* running into the alley and—"

"It's dark in the alley and my eyes haven't adjusted, yet, after all the bright city lights. I stumble in, feeling my way along the wall...I hear footsteps, someone running away. And then I see my dad, sitting with his back against the wall, and his white shirt has this big black stain on it. Then a car drives by on the street and its headlights light us up, and I see the black is really red."

I glanced at Bethany for a second. She was staring up at me, her mouth open in horror, her eyes shining. I looked back at my boots. It was the only way I could keep talking.

"He's trying to speak, but he can't. He's taught me first aid, I know I need to keep pressure on the wounds but he's been stabbed three, four times and he's bleeding *so fast* and I'm calling for help, again and again, and I'm—I'm crying. But it's a long time before someone comes and when they do, when a passer-by finally hears and flags down a cop...he's dead."

"*Cal...*" Hands brushed my face, cool and smooth against my beard and cheeks. She gently lifted my chin so that I was looking at her. "Oh God...."

I took a deep breath and looked right into her eyes. "The cops take me to the police station. I hear that they've caught the guy, and they found the woman he was mugging, when my dad ran in to help: she's going to be okay. And I'm sitting there thinking, *I'm going to have to go home on my own. I'm going to have to go all the way back to Idaho on my own. How will I get there?* But it's worse than that. One of the cops manages to track down my mom's sister and she races there. She has to tell me who she is because it's the first time I've seen her since I was a baby. And she tells me I'm going to come stay with her."

Bethany just knelt there staring at me. She opened her mouth to speak and then closed it again. I nodded. There was nothing to say.

What surprised me was...sure, it hurt, just as I'd known it would. Telling her had brought everything back. And the pain was vicious and bright but...*clean*. Like a wound that could now heal. And the best treatment for it was looking into those big brown eyes, letting that soothing presence wash over me. I took a deep breath and slowly let it out. I sure wasn't healed, but it felt better.

For a few minutes, I just watched her work. She was quick and neat with the stitches and she had a gentle touch: I barely felt a thing. "So what happened in med school?" I asked at last. I was trying to be gentle, like her, but I wasn't used to this stuff: I felt like an elephant trying to turn around in a room full of Ming vases.

She drew in a long breath and let it out. "It went well, for the first few years. I loved the work, I loved helping people. And then...I was on my ER rotation and one night, this woman comes in with her little girl. The kid's got asthma, and croup on top. You ever see a kid with asthma? It's terrifying for them. They can't breathe and they don't understand why. Her chest's heaving and she's not getting any air and she's *so scared.* And the mom's in pieces, she's begging me to help them. But just as I'm about to get them some Albuterol, it comes out that they don't have any insurance. And my boss says rules are rules, I have to send them to a different hospital. But that's right across town, it'll take hours, they'll have to wait in chairs all over again and the kid needs the medication *now.* So..."—she took a deep breath—"I snuck into the drug locker, when no one was looking, and got the kid an inhaler." She sighed. "I didn't know they had cameras in there. They kicked me out."

My whole body had gone taut with anger, listening to the story. "For handing out one inhaler?!"

"You know how much it cost?" she asked, her voice bitter. "Forty-three dollars. I could have paid for it myself, I literally offered them the money out of my purse, but the money wasn't the point." She shrugged. "I get it. I broke the rules. But—"

"They didn't have to kick you out!" I stared down into those big brown eyes. She suddenly looked so lost and I knew why. Medicine was what she was meant to do, she had the instinct for it. "Can you go back?"

"I could start over at another school, but there's no way I could afford it. Do you know how much debt you build up, as a med student? I still have it. There aren't that many jobs for people with half a medical degree. That's how I wound up at the call center. It barely paid enough to cover the interest on the loan." She blinked a few times and I could see her eyes getting wet. She taped some gauze over the scratches. "There. You're done." She jumped to her feet.

Without thinking, I grabbed hold of her wrist. As soon as I did, it was like I'd touched a live wire. Her skin was so soft, so smooth, and a heated, urgent energy throbbed through my fingers. She caught her breath and froze, gazing down at me.

I struggled for words. "You would have been a great doctor."

She nodded quickly and looked away.

I got to my feet and looked down at her. I just wanted to pull her into my arms and hug her. But the way I felt right now, the hug would turn into a kiss. And I couldn't let that happen.

"Come on," I forced myself to say. "We still have a long way to go."

26

BETHANY

AROUND MIDDAY, we jumped across a small creek, climbed a rise, and suddenly there it was below us: Marten Valley.

It was a tiny place with old-fashioned, wood-built stores, some of which looked like they'd been there a hundred years or more. Lovingly-painted gold lettering on the windows invited you to come and browse in McLeary's General Store, or wrap up warm with a jacket from Arlan Co. Outfitters. With the sea of red and amber forest around it and blue sky overhead, it was beautiful.

Cal had explained on the walk that north of here, the woods got more populated and that this was the nearest town for everyone within ten miles or so. You could tell. The sidewalks were packed: people were carrying sacks of groceries back to their pickups, taking dogs and cats to the veterinarian or bringing armfuls of mail to the post office. And everyone knew each other. They stopped to gossip, leaning against shop fronts, sitting on steps, or slowing their pickups (*everyone* seemed to drive a pickup) to say hello.

Except for Cal. As we walked down the street, no one greeted him. He'd been in the area for six years, surely by now they'd know him, even if he only visited town every three or four months?

Then I turned and looked at him. He was walking head down, jaw set, a scowl on his face, just as he'd been at Tucker's gas station. His whole posture screamed *leave me alone!* And with his huge, muscled body, no one dared to argue. When we got off the crowded street and into a store, the scowl faded but he was still unsettled: he kept glancing out of the windows, looking longingly at the forest. Rufus pushed up hard against his legs, aware that something was wrong.

He didn't want to be around people, around civilization. And if a place as small as Marten Valley bothered him this much, then going to Seattle must have been pure hell. Whatever he'd been doing there when he first met me, it must have been something that meant the world to him.

We stopped at the outfitters first, where I picked up jeans, t-shirts and a few thick plaid shirts in my size. Then a few tank tops, because sometimes when we were sitting around in the cabin in the evening with the stove on, it got pretty warm. I held one up against me for Cal to see. "You think this is okay?"

He looked at it, and for just a second, his tension seemed to dissolve. He looked away, his cheeks going pink. "Fine."

I looked down at the tank top, mystified. I guess the scoop neck came a little low, but I was holding it up on top of my clothes. Wait, was he imagining how my breasts would look in it? Now *my* cheeks colored and a rush of heat went snaking down my body.

We found me a pair of boots and several pairs of socks and the simple pleasure of having footwear that fit, after weeks of hobbling around in Cal's newspaper-stuffed boots, was amazing. I was very glad to get hold of some bras and panties, too.

Cal counted out some bills and put them in my hand, motioning me over to the register. That woke me up to the fact that I was carrying probably a few hundred dollars worth of clothes. I shook my head. "I can't let you pay for all this!" I thought about what we still had to buy: food and supplies, all of which we were using up faster because I was at the cabin. "This isn't right—"

He shook his head. "It's fine."

I looked up at him helplessly. I didn't like it but I didn't have much choice: my purse was still at the mansion. "You know that I'll pay you back when all this is over? Every cent."

He nodded. And as he looked down at my serious expression, he smiled just a little. "I know," he said softly.

I paid, and changed into some of the new clothes right there in the store's changing room: my new boots, a green plaid shirt, and a pair of black jeans. We moved on to the General Store and I noticed how Cal's tension increased as soon as we were back on the crowded sidewalk. The town was getting busier as the day went on: the bar served food and it seemed as if a lot of people were coming into town to eat lunch.

The General Store took a good hour, carefully picking out everything we needed, from spices for cooking to cotton thread for fixing clothes, coffee and matches, and a new potato peeler...everything that had been on the list.

I rejoined Cal and we double-checked we had everything. Then, in a quiet corner of the store, we carefully packed everything into our backpacks.

"Ready to head back?" Cal asked.

I thought for a second. I actually wanted to stay. After weeks of isolation, I was craving people: not even necessarily talking to them but just being around them, hearing voices. I wanted to see the rest of the town, maybe check out the bar and get lunch there. But I could tell something was wrong. I'd never seen Cal so unsettled and the longer we stayed here, the worse it was getting. I wasn't going to make him stay here a second longer than he had to. "Ready," I said.

I noticed he took a deep breath just before he stepped out of the store, like he was steeling himself. Then we were on the sidewalk, with Cal marching fast towards the end of the street and the path that led into the trees. I thought of an animal, speeding up as it gets closer to the safety of its burrow. Rufus, who'd had to wait outside the store, trotted happily alongside us. Another thirty seconds and we'd be into the trees.

And then Cal just...froze. He stopped dead in the middle of the

sidewalk, a rock in the river of people, staring at something ahead
of us.

I moved closer and followed his gaze. An SUV had pulled up
ahead of us and he was staring at the mother, as she lifted a toddler
out of her child seat. An older child was helping, a third one was
clinging onto her mother's skirt. Dad was hurrying around the car to
help.

I looked at Cal. His *keep away* scowl had fallen apart and what
had replaced it was heartbreaking. He was the biggest, strongest guy
I'd ever known but right then, he looked utterly destroyed. His face
was twisted into an expression of raw horror and his eyes were
distant: he was somewhere else. And whatever he was reliving, it was
tearing him apart.

27

CAL

ALL MEMORIES FADE. That amazing sunset, your first kiss...with time, the colors fade, the rough edges get smoothed by nostalgia, the pain dulls.

But some things never become memories. They're too ugly, too painful. They live on in your head, a piece of the past that stays crystal clear forever.

I was *there*. Cicadas chirping, a warm wind rustling the trees. The scent of burning petrol crinkled my nostrils, roiling black smoke blowing in my face and catching in the back of my throat.

I leaned left and right as I approached the SUV but the windows were tinted: all I could see was my own face: younger, my chin dark with stubble. I reached for the handle but stopped just before I burned my fingers: I could feel the heat coming off it. The flames had left the metal too hot to touch.

I used the toe of my boot to pull the handle and open the door a crack. Then I hooked the edge of it and swung it wide—

I felt the world open under me and I dropped into blackness, guilt that crushed my chest and tore at my soul. *What have I done?!* And the realization, the horrible certainty that what you've done is irreversible.

Not the day I became a monster. The day I realized I'd become one.

I kept falling, down and down into the blackness, the pressure building and building as I went deeper. I could feel myself imploding, and there was no one to hear my scream because down here, I was all alone.

Then I felt a hand in mine. *Bethany.*

A determined wet nose found my other hand, licked and then snuffled. *Rufus.*

I wasn't alone.

I blinked my way free of it and looked down at the two of them. Both had the same look of concern on their face. Shame bloomed across my face.

I marched off down the street towards the path that would lead home. I could hear Bethany hurrying to catch up. "Cal!"

My shoulders rose. I scowled at the ground and kept walking.

"Are you okay?" Bethany asked from beside me.

I nodded quickly, still walking. The shame was turning to hot, dark rage, turned inward.

"We can talk about it," she said. She was having to almost run to keep up with me.

I gave a quick shake of my head, still refusing to look at her.

"We *should* talk about it."

I finally stopped and rounded on her. "I don't need to talk about it!" I snapped. I was mad at myself, not her, but I was such a mess, it just boiled out of me, seeking any target that was there. "I was doing fine until—"

I managed to cut myself off, but it was too late.

Those big brown eyes stared up at me, as shocked as if I'd slapped her. She looked away, and when she looked back, her eyes were shining. "Until I came along?" she asked, her voice cracking.

Shit.

She set off along the street. Rufus looked up at me, worried, and then trotted after her. I raced after them. "Bethany!" I called. "Bethany!"

She slowed but didn't stop. I had to grab her arm and spin her around. "Stop!"

She looked up at me, guarded and hurt. I felt about an inch tall. And I had no clue how to handle this, I wasn't used to talking to people, least of all women, *least* of all tearful women I'd upset. "Sorry," I said at last. Then, "I wasn't."

"You weren't what?" she asked, her voice shaking.

I took a deep breath. "I wasn't doing fine before you came along."

She looked right into my eyes, checking to see if I was telling the truth. I stared right back, because I was, and eventually, she gave a quick little nod, a blink and a sniff. "You *do* need to talk about it," she said. "To someone, even if it's not me."

I gazed helplessly into her eyes. I've never felt so vulnerable. "There ain't no one but you."

And suddenly, she just lifted her arms and...I don't know how it happened, exactly, I don't know if I went to her or she went to me, but suddenly we had our arms around each other and it wasn't about sex, it wasn't even about love, it was something deeper. A promise that she'd be there for me, when I was ready, and that I'd always be there for her.

Aw hell. I tightened my arms around her back and crushed her close. This girl was special. *So* special. I inhaled the scent of her hair, felt the softness of her mold to me. I didn't just want her, anymore, I needed her. But nothing had changed. I couldn't have her. Didn't deserve the way she made my chest lift and my lungs fill. I didn't deserve one second of that peace, that happiness. And she deserved a hell of a lot better than me.

I knew all that. But I still couldn't let her go.

And then, over her shoulder, I saw something weird. We were next to a store window and in the glass, there was a reflection of Bethany's face. But it wasn't her face casting the reflection: this was a bright, black-and-white image, like from a TV. I frowned at it, then slowly released Bethany, trying to figure out where it was coming from. Was there a TV inside the store? No....

I turned the other way. A State Police car was sitting right next to us at the curb. It must have pulled up while we'd been busy hugging, and the cops must have gone into one of the stores because there was no one sitting in it. But the computer monitor between the seats was lit up, and on it was a full-screen picture of Bethany.

I let go of her and gently turned her around so she could see. Together, we moved closer to the car, peeking through the window. I could just make out the words *Alert,* and *Arrest and Detain.*

The men at the mansion weren't waiting for her to go to the police. They were using the police to find her. Her picture was probably all over the state. *Shit.* We'd completely underestimated them.

At that second, the bell on the store next to us rang and two cops strolled out, takeout coffees and donuts in hand. They noticed us immediately, shooting me a warning look for being so close to the car, then casting a much more appreciative look at Bethany's curves. *Fuck.* I backed away from the car, holding up my hands in apology, and hustled Bethany away. "Walk," I hissed in her ear. "Don't run."

She gulped and nodded, her face pale.

We started walking. I was visualizing the scene behind us. We had maybe five seconds before they reached the car. They'd have to stop to put their coffees on the roof while they opened the doors. Then they'd settle into their seats, see the message that had arrived while they were in the store. A second of shock: *that's the woman we just—* And then....

"*Hey!*" one of the cops yelled. I felt Bethany tense but I tugged at her hand, keeping her walking.

"*Stop!*" My shoulders tensed but still I kept walking: every second counted.

"*You! Black hair, green shirt! Stop and turn around!*"

"*Run!*" I yelled.

We ran.

28

BETHANY

J UST A FEW weeks ago, the woods had been the scariest place I
could imagine. Now, all I could think of was getting back to
them. We sprinted down the street, Rufus racing alongside us.

The cops dived back into their car, figuring they could chase us
down on the streets. So when we turned onto the path and raced
towards the woods, they were taken by surprise. They had to pull up
and jump out of their car again, but that only bought us a few
seconds.

We had to climb up out of the valley as we left the town. What
had seemed like a gentle slope on the way in was a punishing climb
on the way out, especially loaded down by our full backpacks. I was
panting by the time we neared the top and then I made the mistake of
looking back. The two cops were sprinting up the hill behind us,
already horribly close. The cops were unladen and fresh; we were
weighed down and tired from a whole morning's hike. They were
easily faster than us.

Cal heaved on my hand, hauling me up the last few feet, and then
we were running down the far side, sliding on loose pine needles, our
legs almost running away with us. We jumped the creek at the

bottom and ran for the forest. The cops were already cresting the hill behind us. I was frantic, now, lungs burning *They're going to catch us!*

But then we plunged into the trees and things changed. The cops weren't used to moving through the wilds: they were like me when I first arrived. I could hear them tripping on branches and cursing, crashing through the forest instead of slipping through it. My legs ached and I was fighting for air but, each minute we kept up the pace, I could hear them falling a few more seconds behind us.

Cal suddenly cut left, away from the course we'd been following, and the noises grew more distant as the cops carried on in a straight line. A moment later, Cal pushed me up against a tree, his finger to my lips. We went motionless, his arms protectively around me, his hard body pinning me to the trunk. Rufus flattened himself to the ground and lay still.

We waited, hearts thumping, straining our ears. Distant footsteps, rustling undergrowth, and a lot of cursing. The footsteps came closer...then retreated. A few moments later, Cal relaxed and stepped back, leaving a fading, warm imprint of his body on mine. "They're gone."

The rush of relief only lasted a second. "They have the *cops* looking for me?!"

He nodded, his face grim. Neither of us had predicted this. We knew the club would monitor the police, watching in case I went to the authorities, but we hadn't thought they'd be able to use the police to actually search for me. They were a lot more powerful than we'd thought. I wondered what crimes they'd framed me for. Maybe fraud —they could say that they gave me the relocation money and then I ran off. But it didn't matter. What mattered was, every cop in the state, maybe every cop in the country, was looking for me.

"They'll get me," I said in a small voice. "If I go to a city, even a town, they'll get me."

"Then don't go to a town," he growled. "Stay here with me."

He'd tried to sound firm, but something else crept into his voice. A need. I looked at him and he looked away. Then met my eyes, defiant. Possessive.

"I can't stay in the cabin forever," I said softly. "And they know the area we're in, now! They know you must live somewhere hiking distance from town. They can sweep the whole woods, find the cabin. Find you and Rufus."

Cal's jaw set firm. "Let 'em come."

I bit my lip. He meant it. He'd fight off the whole club and an entire army of police, if it came to it. He'd die to protect me.

And that was exactly why I had to leave.

29

CAL

THE NEXT MORNING, back at the cabin, she confronted me. The day before had been exhausting: all the way to town and back in one day, plus the stress of her nearly being caught. We'd pretty much eaten and then fallen into bed. But when she sat down at the table, I could see the dark circles under her eyes. She'd been awake all night thinking and worrying. I sat down opposite her on the new chair I'd made: still rough-hewn and in need of sanding.

She looked at the table for a moment, drew in her breath, and said, "I need to go to Canada."

Cold shock, then fiery rage, disturbingly strong, at the thought of being separated from her. "What?! No!"

She put her hand on mine. The touch of her was calming but I didn't *want* to be calmed, right then. "It's the only way," she said. "I can't go to the police or the FBI: they control them. I can't go to another city or another state: my picture's everywhere by now, they'd arrest me and then disappear me. And I can't stay here. They'll find this place eventually." She shook her head. "I don't know why they can't just let me go. I'm just one woman. I'm no threat to them!"

I nodded. It *was* weird. They knew that if she ever went to the authorities, they could make sure it came to nothing. So why go to all the trouble of hunting her down? It almost felt personal.

"Canada's the only safe place," she said. "They don't have any pull there...I hope. I can start fresh." She met my eyes. "I won't be a threat to you and Rufus."

Hearing his name, Rufus strolled over and looked from Bethany to me, his tail wagging. I stared stubbornly at Bethany and shook my head. *No. No way.* I wasn't going to let her run off on her own, just to protect us.

She squeezed my hand. "It's the only way," she said gently.

I sat there fuming. Wasn't this exactly what I'd wanted? For her to leave, so everything could get back to normal? Except I hadn't expected it to feel like this. I'd been secretly imagining some fairy tale ending where I beat the club, vanquished them like some heroic knight, in a way that let her get her old life back. I wanted to think of her happy and free, not hiding out in Canada.

But none of that changed the fact that she was right. If these bastards were prepared to use the entire state police to search for her, they'd do whatever it took...even searching the woods. "How do you even plan on getting there?"

"Walk," she said defiantly. "We're in Idaho, the border can't be that far."

"It's a *hundred miles!*"

"We could do that. If we did it together."

"You mean, I see you to the border?"

She bit her lip. "No.,," she said tentatively.

Go with her? Something inside me soared and for a glorious few seconds, the idea seemed golden and bright. A new life. A new start. The two of us together. It wasn't like I couldn't build a new cabin, buy a new cow. There was plenty of wilderness in Canada.

Then I woke up. Nothing had changed. What had happened in Marten Valley—something we still hadn't talked about—was a reminder. She was still a city girl and I was still a fucked up mess who couldn't be around people. I couldn't give her the life she needed.

And after what I'd done, I didn't deserve to be anywhere but out here on my own.

I shook my head and forced my voice to be hard. "How would you get across the border? You have your passport with you?"

She blinked, shocked and a little hurt, too. That made me feel like shit, but it was the only way. "No," she said, "But we could sneak across, there must be places—"

She still said *we*. She was still hoping. My guts twisted, but I pressed on as if I hadn't noticed. "Even if you could, how are you going to live? How are you going to get a job, without any ID?" I sighed. "If we're going to do this, we're going to do it right. You need a whole new identity: a Canadian passport, driver's license, everything, so you can start a new life. And we need to get you to a proper border crossing, and get you in officially."

She stared at me in miserable silence for a few seconds. And I realized that this whole idea: leaving her life in the US behind, starting a whole new one...that wasn't what scared her. What scared her was doing it on her own. I almost reconsidered.

But I couldn't doom her to a life with me, either. She deserved better.

That's what I told myself, but I knew it was more than that. That offer she'd made me in Marten Valley...she wanted to know me, know why I was out here on my own. If we stayed together, sooner or later she'd get me to open up.

I couldn't let that happen. She thought I was a hero. I couldn't take the look of disappointment and disgust on her face when she found out the truth.

This is better, I told myself.

Better for who?

"It's the only way," I said out loud.

She bit her lip, looked away and nodded. "But how do we do it? How do we get a new ID and everything?"

"We need to go see Jacques."

30

BETHANY

CAL STOOD UP and motioned for me to get up, too. He pushed both chairs and the table down to the other end of the room. Then he knelt down, took out a knife and started gently prying at one of the floorboards.

I stood there numbly watching him. He wasn't coming with me. I'd known he wouldn't but a little part of me had held out hope. The worst part was that I could see he wanted to: he'd tried to hide it but I'd seen the way he had to fight himself. He wanted to, but he wouldn't let himself be with me. He was still keeping me at a distance and soon, he was going to separate us forever.

I wasn't ready for how that felt. When you're sharing every waking moment with someone, two weeks can feel like two months. It wasn't just the sexual tension, that thick heaviness in the air that made every look loaded, that made us freeze each time we accidentally brushed fingertips as we passed a dish or folded a blanket.

I'd gotten closer to him than I had with anyone, despite the mysteries of his past. He'd taught me a new way of life and I'd gradually gotten him to talk, even if it wasn't about himself. We were changing each other.

And now I was going to leave. And I'd never see him or Rufus again.

The floorboard came loose and Cal put it aside. Instantly, Rufus trotted over and immediately decided that the hole was the most interesting thing ever, and stuck his head down into it. I had to put my arms around him and haul him back so that Cal could reach down and pull out what was hidden in the dark space: a dented metal lockbox.

When he opened it up, it was full of tight wads of bills. I stared at it, open-mouthed. "Where did you get *that?*"

"Selling animal hides. I only hunt what I need to eat, but the hide would just go to waste if I didn't sell it."

I picked up a wad of bills. Rufus sniffed them, then gave a snort, disappointed that the treasure was boring human things, and trotted off for a nap. I examined the bills, then did some rough math in my head. "But there must be twenty thousand here!"

"'Bout eighteen, I think. About three thousand a year, for six years."

I stared at him. "This is all the money you've earned, the whole time you've been here?! What about what you spend, in town?"

He shrugged. "Things like coffee, matches...that barely makes a dent. A few hundred dollars a year." He frowned regretfully "Had to get a new coffee pot, last year because I couldn't fix the leak. *That* cost me a bit."

While he counted the money, I eyed one of the patches on his shirt. He'd been brought up make-do-and-mend. He spent virtually nothing. In fact, that trip to town, buying me all those clothes...that had probably cost him more than he'd spend in a whole year, but he hadn't hesitated.

"Closer to nineteen," he announced, putting the money back in the lockbox. "Should be enough to buy you a new identity."

My jaw dropped. "Wha—*No!* No, you can't spend all that on me!"

"I don't need it." He put the floorboard back and gave it a thump with his fist to lock it into place. Then he stood and offered me his hand. "Let's go see Jacques."

"Cal, I can't. It's too much!"

"You said yourself," he said firmly. "It's the only way."

His jaw was set. He wasn't changing his mind. And Canada *was* my only hope, and his plan for getting there sounded a lot better than mine. But why did it have to involve clearing him out of his life savings...and worse, leaving him behind?

"When it's all over, when I'm settled, I *swear,* I'll pay you back," I told him.

He looked away as if the promise weakened him for a second. "I know," he said. Then he offered me his hand again.

If I did this, it set me on a path...one that ended with me saying goodbye forever. But I didn't have a choice. If I stayed here, Cal and Rufus were in danger.

I took his hand. He pulled me up so fast, so effortlessly, that I went light-headed. I tottered in front of him and he put his hands on my hips to steady me, the warmth of his palms soaking straight inward to my groin. I looked up into those cornflower blue eyes and tried to imagine never seeing them again.

"This is the right thing to do," he rumbled. It sounded like he was trying to convince himself, as much as me.

I swallowed and nodded.

And we went to see Jacques.

31

BETHANY

"So who is this guy?" I asked as we tramped through the undergrowth. We were heading in a direction we hadn't gone before, not towards Tucker's or town. It was a beautiful clear, crisp day and each gust of wind made a few more gold and scarlet leaves flutter down from the aspens, slowly building into an endless soft carpet that looked like frozen fire. I was luxuriating in my new boots and everything was perfect...except when I thought about the future.

"He's a smuggler," said Cal. "Lives on the river. Moves stuff back and forth over the border in trucks, then uses boats on the river to distribute it." He glanced across at me and must have read my expression. "You thought criminals only lived in the city?"

"No," I said defensively. *Yep.* "How do you know him?"

"He doesn't live that far away. Five hours' walk or so."

I shook my head in disbelief. I was still getting used to Cal distances, where a five-hour walk was nothing.

"Basically my closest neighbor," Cal continued, "So I made sure to check him out before I built the cabin. I see him a few times a year, but I stay out of his business and he stays out of mine."

It was mid-afternoon before I glimpsed the first sliver of gleaming blue through the trees. As the forest thinned out, the slivers joined together to form an endless blue expanse. It was a river hundreds of feet across, big enough to have a few small islands a little further downstream. "Tell me we don't have to wade across *that,*" I pleaded.

"Nope." And Cal pointed.

As I stepped out from behind him, I saw a tiny square of wood about half a mile upstream. A raft. People still used *rafts?!* And on the far side of the river, moored at the bank—

"Is that what it looks like?"

Cal nodded. "That's where he lives."

It was a steamboat, the sort of thing Huckleberry Finn would wave to, and it must have been well over a hundred years old. Its white paint was faded and it looked like it hadn't moved in a long time, but it still had a proud beauty about it, with its tall chimneys and high wheelhouse.

We hiked down the side of the river to the raft, a square of tied-together logs and barrels no more than eight feet per side. A rope stretched across the river, threaded through iron rings hammered into the deck, so that you could stand on the raft and haul yourself across. As soon as we got on, the whole thing started leaning and rocking drunkenly, but once we balanced our weight, it settled down. Then Rufus leapt aboard, woofing excitedly, and we had to tame the raft all over again.

Cal leaned down to the rope and began to pull us, the muscles in his back stretching out his shirt as he heaved. I bent down next to him and helped and gradually, the far bank crept closer. I realized after a while that the raft was a pretty good defense. Any visitors were slowed down to a crawl as they made their way across, and they were helpless, out here, hands too busy with the rope to reach for a gun and with nothing to take cover behind. I guessed it was deliberate.

Something else occurred to me. How did Cal know so much about buying new identities, and how much they cost?

The rope took us right to the steamboat. We stepped off onto the deck and were met by a woman in her late thirties in a silky black robe patterned with pink roses. From her bare feet and the way she held it tightly closed against the breeze, she wasn't wearing anything underneath. "This way," she told us in an accent that might have been Italian, and she led us below deck.

It was dark, down here, the only light coming from fairy lights strung along the ceiling. I couldn't see the floor underfoot and when I stepped on a plank and felt it move and sink a little, my stomach knotted. The entire boat creaked each time the wind moved it against its mooring. How close was this thing to going to the bottom?

We passed through a narrow passageway, Cal's wide shoulders almost brushing the walls. As my eyes adjusted to the gloom, I realized there were cabins on both sides of us, their doors open. Every one was stacked high with goods. I saw bottles of whiskey, cigarettes, and a tall pile of small white boxes. At the end of the hallway, the woman opened a door and led the way into a much bigger room, which must have been a grand stateroom when the boat was built. It still had its wood paneling and ornate holders for lanterns.

Jacques was at least fifty but could have been over sixty. The dark hair, still almost black in places, was stylishly cut and made him look younger, but his pointed beard was pure silver. His pale blue eyes still had that joyful, youthful sparkle but the smile lines must have taken decades to form. He was wearing a chocolate brown, pin-striped suit that would have cost hundreds at some Seattle vintage store, but might well have just been something he'd kept since his twenties.

He lounged in a scarlet, wingback armchair as if it was a throne. He had a tumbler of brandy in one hand, a lit cigar in the other and he gave off the air of a man for whom everything is right in the world. The woman who'd led us in perched herself on his knee, crossed her legs and regarded us with suspicion and just a little protective jealousy.

"Cal," said Jacques warmly. His accent was smooth as caramel and impossible to place, as if all the rough edges had been melted away by hard bargaining and hard liquor in a hundred different ports around the world. "Haven't seen you in a while." He turned to look at me and gave a roguish grin. "I see you finally found someone to warm your bed."

I swallowed and flushed.

"It's not like that," said Cal.

"Oh really?" asked Jacques. I felt his gaze sweep down my body. But it didn't feel cold and ugly, like when the men at the mansion did it. It felt flirty and flattering and there was something about Jacques, despite him being more than twice my age. I felt myself flush again. I saw Cal's whole body stiffen in response and the woman on Jacques' knee narrowed her eyes at me: if she was a cat, her ears would have gone back. I quickly looked at the floor.

"She needs help," said Cal. "She needs to get into Canada. And she needs a Canadian identity. I figure you can do that."

Jacques considered. "As it happens, I do know someone who's good with passports. She's retired, but she owes me a favor." He stroked his beard and looked at me. "I can get you to the border and make sure you get through. I even have an apartment you can use, while you get settled. Call it twenty thousand, all in."

Cal brought out the lockbox. "We have almost nineteen."

Jacques gave him a reproachful look. "Then you can *almost* have a passport."

"C'mon, Jacques, you know I'm good for the rest." He glanced at me. "She needs this." His voice was tight with emotion in a way I couldn't have imagined when I first met him.

Jacques' heard it, too. His salt and pepper brows came together in a frown and he sat back in his chair, suddenly serious. "You better tell me exactly what we're dealing with, here."

And so I told him. I told him about the club and the mansion, about Ralavich and the attorney general and the senators. His face grew darker and darker, his mouth going tight. When I'd finished, he downed the bourbon and slammed the glass down on a side table. "*Bastards,*" he spat. The woman on his knee had changed her expression too: she'd softened, watching me with almost motherly concern. I decided I liked these two.

"You can have your new identity," he told me. "And I'll drive you up to Vancouver myself. Be back here at noon in three days' time. Sweetpea, take the lady upstairs and get some photos, will you? I need to talk to Cal."

The woman nodded and rose. She slipped a protective arm around me and led me upstairs, Rufus following behind us.

32

CAL

JACQUES ROSE and poured himself another bourbon, then looked questioningly at a second glass. I shook my head.

He sipped. "Senators. The goddamn attorney general." He shook his head. "I'm too old for this crap." He spread his arms wide. "I should have handed this all off to my son, by now."

"Why don't you?"

"Well, *then* what would I do?" He sighed. "Cal, on account of you being one of the last few honest men in the world, I'm going to make you an offer. But you've got to promise not to tell anyone. I don't want people to think I'm going soft."

"What's the offer?" I asked, suspicious.

"Since I'm getting one person into Canada," said Jacques. "I think I might just be able to stretch to *two* sets of papers, for the same price."

I looked him right in the eye. "Told you, it's not like that. I'm just...looking after her."

"You're a hell of a marksman, Cal, but you're a terrible liar." He sat back in his chair. "Don't forget, I know you. I remember when you first showed up here, wanting me to haul that damn stove down the river. You weren't much of a talker *then,* but I've watched you get worse each year. Last time I saw you, you barely said two words. Then today, you show up with her and suddenly you're talking again. You got fire in your belly. You look at her and I see your face light up." He leaned forward. "A man's not meant to be alone, Cal. Go with her."

Dammit. I lowered my eyes to the floor. "She's better off without me," I said. I could feel his eyes on me, watchful and sad. "But I'll take that bourbon now."

He poured it silently and put it in my hand. I knocked it back and let the burn of it wash the pain away. For a while. *Three days. Three days and then I'll never see her again.*

"Thanks for the drink," I told him. Then I handed him the lockbox and headed upstairs.

Bethany was standing in front of a wall, where a sheet of gray fabric had been pinned as a background. The woman in the silk robe was just lowering a digital camera. "All done. See you in three days."

We climbed back onto the raft. Rufus decided he'd swim, this time, and doggy-paddled alongside. As we hauled the raft along, Bethany asked, "What did Jacques want?"

"Nothing," I told her. "Nothing at all."

33

BETHANY

I T WAS THE first day after meeting Jacques and I was deep in the
woods with Cal. That morning, he'd told me that he wanted to
teach me to hunt. It caught me off guard. I was only going to be there
a few more days and Cal brought home all the food we needed
without breaking a sweat, and even if I did learn, I wasn't going to be
anywhere near as good as him anytime soon. But he wouldn't take no
for an answer.

First, I watched how he did it. He'd sight a target, way off in the
distance, and circle a little so that he was in its path. Then he'd go
stock still, becoming one with the forest. He was like a rock,
unmoving, unblinking, barely breathing. And then a *crack* and the
target fell to the ground as if he'd reached out with an invisible hand,
and Rufus ran off to collect it. I shook my head in wonder. "You're
amazing," I muttered.

He shook his head and shrugged. "I started young."

Then it was my turn. He handed me the rifle and showed me the
basics. I handled it like a live snake, terrified I was going to drop it
and blow my head off. But he stood behind me, his warm body
pressed against my back and his big hands covering mine, and
helped me load and cock it, bring it to my shoulder and sight on a

paper target he'd pinned to a tree. And when it was time to pull the trigger and I just couldn't, too scared of the explosion, he whispered in my ear that it was okay, that I could do it. He was a good teacher, gentle and patient. *He should be out here doing this with a son or a daughter.*

I fired. The rifle kicked and boomed and I stumbled back, shell-shocked. I didn't think I'd hit anything but he showed me the ragged hole that had been punched in the corner of the paper target. I fingered the shredded edges and thought *I did that. I shot something.*

After ten shots into paper, he led me further into the woods. He took my hand in his and walked with me, teaching me step by step how he moved. I'd already learned to be quiet, but he wanted me to be silent.

When I could do that, he stood me in the middle of a clearing, brought out a neckerchief and tied it over my eyes. I swallowed. I'd read enough books that being blindfolded, with him standing so close, triggered a million filthy fantasies. My whole body seemed to throb, my skin suddenly alive and aching to be touched. *Down, girl!*

"You hunt with your ears as much as your eyes," he told me. "Now *listen.*"

And once I'd gotten myself under control, I listened. *Really* listened. And after a few minutes, I started to hear things I hadn't, before. There was the background sound of the woods: the wind rustling the leaves, the creak of branches. But layered on top of that was a second layer, one made up of movement. I could hear birds flapping as they haggled over the best perches, mice scampering through the grass, twigs being brushed aside by rabbits and deer. I looked around at the darkness, following my ears, entranced.

Gentle hands slipped the blindfold off and I looked up into blue eyes. He looked questioningly at me. *Understand?*

I nodded.

What I didn't understand was why he was doing all this. Was he trying to fill the time until I left, so we didn't have to think about it too much?

An hour later, as we crept silently through the undergrowth with

Rufus slinking along next to us, he held up his hand: *Stop.* He pointed and I caught my breath. A deer, grazing peacefully, completely unaware of us.

He nodded to me and my heart sank. I raised the rifle and took off the safety. Sighted on the center of the deer's body....

I lowered the rifle and looked at the ground. "I can't. I'm sorry, I can't." I felt stupid. We'd eaten venison plenty of times. Where had I thought it came from?

He put his hands on my shoulders and gently turned me to face him, then used one big hand to raise my chin to look at him. "It's okay." He didn't sound patronizing, or like he thought it was cute. He sounded sincere. But I still looked up at him doubtfully. *He must think I'm so weak.*

He jerked his head to the side. "Come look at something." He led me over to a tree and took a little bag from his pocket. Then he tipped some of the contents of the bag into his palm and held it out. *Acorns?!*

He went still, and I went still next to him. After a moment, there was movement in the tree as something scampered from branch to branch. Then a little furry head peeked around the trunk. Two quick jumps and a scurry, and it was hanging from a branch just above us, regarding us with shining, suspicious eyes. A squirrel.

Cal stayed completely still. The squirrel looked at him, looked at me, then suddenly leaped, so quickly it seemed to vanish and reappear on Cal's shoulder. It jumped down his arm and onto his wrist, grabbed an acorn and sat there eating it, the forest so quiet we could hear its little teeth nibbling. I watched, amazed, until it had finished. Then it grabbed a second acorn for later, sprang back to the tree, and was gone.

"People say they're vermin," said Cal. "They're what people learn to shoot when they start out. But I never could bring myself to shoot 'em." He turned to me. "You don't want to shoot animals, don't shoot animals. C'mon, let's try the paper target again."

I was still getting over the insane cuteness of this big, hulking guy feeding squirrels. I blinked and frowned. "What's the point, if I can't shoot animals?"

He looked at me, determined and powerfully protective. "Just because," he said.

And realization hit. This wasn't about hunting for food, or filling the time until I left. He wanted me to be able to look after myself once he wasn't there to do it. In case the men from the club caught up with me, on the journey or even when I got to Canada.

If it came to it, he wanted me to be able to shoot them.

34

CAL

THAT EVENING, I sat brooding. Bethany was outside, milking Betsy and Ha—

Milking the *cow* and the *goat*, dammit.

I had plenty of stuff to be doing: there was wood to be chopped, grain to be milled, and the hinge on the chicken coop door needing fixing. But I just couldn't seem to get going.

The day after tomorrow, she'd be gone.

I knew I was making the right decision. It was better for her, better for everyone. That's what I kept telling myself.

But I knew she was hurting, just like I was hurting. I wanted to do something nice for her. And there's only so much you can do, in a backwoods cabin. It wasn't like I could go buy her a box of cupcakes.

Maybe there was something I could do, though. While she was busy in the barn, I hauled it out from behind the cabin and wrestled it through the door. Then I got some big pots of water boiling on the stove and filled buckets from the well. By the time she came back in, it was ready.

"Figured you might want a bath," I mumbled, looking at the floor. "Sorry: I don't have any stuff to make bubbles."

She stared at the big, cowboy-style metal tub. A smile spread across her face and something inside me *lifted* and tugged so hard I had to look away. So I didn't get any warning when she ran over and threw her arms around me. *"Thank you!"* she said, her breath little hot gusts against my pecs. "Thank you!"

I swallowed and grunted. Her breasts were pillowed against my chest and when I breathed in, I could smell the sweet, feminine scent of her. I could feel my cock swelling in my pants and any second, she was going to feel it, too. I nodded and backed away. "I'll be outside."

I opened the door...and stopped. Heavy gray rain was just starting to fall. I shrugged. "I'll be okay."

"No. Don't be silly. Stay here," said Bethany.

I turned around and caught her eye. She looked at the tub, then down at her clothes. The tension in the room rose a little more.

"One second," said Bethany in a strangled voice. She pulled the sheet off the bed, then got a ball of string, climbed up on a chair and tied it to a rafter. In a few moments, she had the sheet dangling like a curtain from the rafters, forming a screen between me and the tub. "There."

I sat down by the stove to wait. It was quiet in the cabin and from behind the sheet, I could hear the sound of shirt buttons popping through holes. Then the soft *whump* as it fell to the floor. Next, her t-shirt. Then the heavier sound of her jeans. Her bra, her panties, they were so light that I had to strain to hear them. *One. Two.*

She was naked.

The soft padding of her feet across the floorboards and then—

What I hadn't counted on was, the lantern was behind her and my end of the cabin was dark. So as she stepped in front of the light, it threw her shadow onto the sheet. I could see every gorgeous curve of her body in silhouette: her lush hips, her rounded ass, the sway and bounce of her breasts.

"It's too quiet," Bethany said. "Talk about something."

I couldn't answer for a second. I was watching her lower herself into the tub, her back slightly arched, breasts upthrust, bracing herself for the shock of the hot water. "Ah—*Ahhh,*" she breathed. I felt myself redden like a damn teenager, but I couldn't look away. "Like what?" I muttered.

"Anything," said Bethany. I heard her scoop up water and slosh it over her upper body, and imagined her breasts, glossy and shining. "How'd you join the Marines?"

I sat bolt upright in my chair, the leg squeaking. *How did she—*

"I saw your tattoo," she said softly.

I rubbed at my upper arm through my shirt. She didn't miss a thing. "My dad was a Marine," I said at last. "I wanted to serve, just like he had. And I was living in the city, then, and I hated it. Figured that the Marines would suit me better than sitting in some office: at least it'd be outdoors. Signed up as soon as I was old enough."

"I'd like to hear about it," she said tentatively. "If you want to tell me."

I nearly said *no.* Better to keep everything before I came to the woods off-limits. Venturing into the past risked unleashing the memories and I wasn't sure I could deal with them, right now, not when the countdown to her leaving was tearing away at me.

But Bethany was easy to talk to. I *liked* talking to her. And this might be the last chance we really had to talk.

And the Marines...that was a good time in my life. Maybe it wouldn't hurt to visit it, just this once. I could stop before everything went wrong.

I leaned forward in my chair and began to speak.

35

BETHANY

"The first day of boot camp, I'm wondering if I've made a mistake," said Cal. "We're in these big, concrete buildings, and it's almost as bad as high school: all the other recruits are into video games and cars and I'm this big, shambling teenager from the country."

I wrapped my arms around my knees, wishing I was wrapping them around Cal: I could imagine the big, awkward, teenage him and I just wanted to give him a hug.

Cal's voice lightened. "But then training starts. And on day one, the drill instructor yells that we're going to do a ten-mile hike. And I thought: *this,* I can do."

I smiled, imagining Cal effortlessly pounding through the miles.

"Then they put us on the rifle range. The instructor lies me down on the ground, hands me a rifle, tells me to shoot at the target. So I line it up, squeeze off a shot. Right through the middle. The instructor says *beginner's luck* and tells me to try another. So I fire again, but this time no hole appears. I shoot again. No hole. Instructor says, *what the hell happened, you aren't even hitting the target anymore?* And I say, Sir! I think I am, Sir!"

"And the instructor gives me this *frown*...and then he takes a pair of binoculars and looks down at the end of the range and tells me to take one more shot, and I do. And he stands up...lowers the binoculars...and calls for the whole range to stop. Then he walks down to the end of the range, gets the target, and brings it back. And he pokes his pinky finger through the one hole that's there, the one that's gotten just a shade bigger each time I hit it, and he says *where the hell did you learn to shoot like that, son?* And I say *Sir! Shooting dinner, sir!"*

I could hear him smiling at the memory and I grinned, too.

"I finished my training. Got sent out to Iraq, Afghanistan. Seemed like I was suited to it: I could move quietly, I was a good shot." I heard his shirt rustle as he shrugged those big shoulders. "Got promoted. They gave me some medals."

He sounded almost embarrassed about it. I shook my head in wonder: he was so modest! I'd seen how silently he crept through the forest, how effortlessly he hunted his prey. He must have been an amazing soldier. "Did you enjoy it?"

His voice changed, taking on a tone I hadn't heard before. He sounded wistful. "I loved it. Loved...." He trailed off, searching for the right word.

"Serving?" I offered.

"Protecting people," he said at last.

I nodded to myself. I'd seen that fierce, protective instinct in action. It was who he was.

"It felt like I'd found my place," said Cal. "The guys you serve with, they get to be like family. I guess jarheads aren't much more imaginative than schoolkids because they called me *Bigfoot,* too. But...it was okay, coming from them."

I nodded silently. I understood.

"I did four years, then applied for the Marine Raiders. They taught me a whole bunch of stuff."

He said it like it was nothing, but my eyes were bugging out. He was *Special Forces?!*

"Got sent around the world, helping out here and there," he said. "I was in for eleven years, all told."

"You miss it?" I asked.

He didn't answer for a while and I realized he was thinking about it. Either he hadn't thought about it, all these years, or he hadn't let himself.

"Yeah," he said at last. "Yeah, I miss it."

And then he just went quiet.

I waited. Nothing.

"What happened then?" I asked, keeping my voice light.

Silence. I sat up in the bath, staring at the sheet, wishing I could see him. "Cal?"

I strained my ears. I could hear his breathing, ragged with pain. Just as I was about to say something, he spoke. "I'm going to go check on the animals before we turn in." His heavy footsteps, clumping across the wood floor, then the door opening and banging shut.

Something had happened after he left the Raiders, something that had led him to isolate himself out here. Something he couldn't talk about. I sat there in the cooling water, arms around my knees, my chest tight with worry. In two days, I'd be gone. And whatever demons Cal had in his head, he'd be left alone with them forever.

36

RALAVICH

I STOOD on the mansion's balcony, looking out at the view as the sun went down. To the left, lights were gradually coming on, pinpricks of white and orange that joined up to form towns, with crawling caterpillars of car lights inching between them. To the right, there was...nothing. Just the blackness of the woods.

Bethany was in there, somewhere.

It had been two days since some cops had seen her in Marten Valley. They'd questioned the locals and someone had recognized the man she was with: some big, bearded loser who lived out in the woods—no one was sure exactly where. And—I felt the anger start to boil inside me, thick and dark as bubbling tar—Bethany was presumably spreading her legs for him, in return for living in his hovel.

She'd regret it. They both would.

Cairns had pointed out that the woods covered hundreds of square miles: we could search forever and never find them. His plan was to wait them out, catch them when they next came to Marten Valley.

But I'd had enough. The mansion was a pleasant enough place to spend time: I could run my business from here easily enough, they'd brought in a case of vodka, the good stuff, and there were plenty of girls to fuck. But I wanted *her*. And I wasn't going to wait any longer. I'd kept my best attack dog on a chain for over two weeks. It was time to let him loose.

I summoned Alik. "We're taking matters into our own hands." I pointed to the woods. "Go out there and find her."

Alik gave a long sigh of relief and a big, honest grin spread across his face. There's something about soldiers, especially Special Forces soldiers. They can't be idle. They need a mission or they get restless, even depressed. "My pleasure," said Alik with feeling. As he turned to leave, he said, "Things may need to get...messy."

"Do whatever you need to," I told him. "Let's show these idiots how we deal with problems in Russia."

37

CAL

THE NEXT MORNING, I woke early and lay there on the floor looking at her in the bed. She was on her side, turned to face the wall, but even through the blankets, the glorious hourglass shape of her made me stare.

Today was her last full day at the cabin. Tomorrow morning, I'd take her to Jacques, and then she'd be gone. I wanted to spend every moment with her but at the same time, I couldn't be around her. The feelings I'd been crushing down inside me for weeks were just too strong, now. Every second I was in her presence, that *pull* drew me in until I couldn't speak, couldn't think, couldn't do anything except what it demanded. Tell her how I feel. Ask her to stay. Put my hands on her waist, pull her to me, and kiss her.

And then what? What would happen, if I gave in? I couldn't get close to her. Not without coming clean about what I'd done. And if I did that, and she looked at me in horror....

I rolled over, jumped to my feet, and grabbed some clothes. Within a minute, I had my rifle and my backpack. I'd spend the day hunting. That would keep me safely away from her.

Rufus lifted his head from his spot curled up next to Bethany. I told him to stay and he looked offended, but put his head back down.

Outside, I saw black storm clouds piling up on the horizon. *Dammit,* I'd have to make sure I was back before that hit. But it looked like it was a way off: I could still be out for most of the day.

Normally, hunting calms me. There's something about being in nature that gives me peace: that's why I came to the woods. But now, it didn't seem to be working. I kept going, moving further and further from the cabin but I still had this sense of unease, like something was missing.

Her. It was her. For years, I'd sought solitude. But I'd gotten used to having her around and now, it wasn't the same without her. Tomorrow, she'd be gone forever. The woods would never feel the same again.

I pushed on, determined to prove my heart wrong. If I went deep enough, found a spot lonely enough, maybe I could get that peace back. But all that happened was that I missed her more. *Goddammit!*

Then the first heavy drop of rain hit my cheek. I looked up to see clouds rolling overhead, dark mountains that flickered with lightning. They'd moved a lot faster than I'd thought and I was much further from home than I'd planned.

The wind started to rise, setting trees rocking and bending, whistling between the trunks. *Shit.* This was going to be a bad one. A dangerous one. Bethany hadn't been through anything like this, not out here in the wilds. And because I'd been selfishly trying to protect my own feelings, I'd left her all alone.

I started to run. And prayed I'd be in time.

38

BETHANY

"Ready?" I asked Rufus. He gave an ear-splitting *woof* and leaped around like an eighty-pound puppy. "*Go!*"

I hurled the ball. It bounced off the ground, bounced off a tree, flew over my head, and arced down towards the undergrowth. Rufus ran one way, skidded to a stop, and bolted back the other way, almost knocking me off my feet as he passed, then leaped and caught the ball just before it hit the ground. He trotted back to me and dropped it at my feet, then nudged it with his nose: *again, again!*

I'd picked up the ball while we were in Marten Valley and I was hoping it would last for a good while after I was gone, something for Rufus to remember me by. Just the thought of that made my chest ache. Tomorrow, I'd be off to Canada. A new start, no more looking over my shoulder for the club...but I'd be on my own. And I couldn't forget about the other women Ralavich had abducted. Maybe, once I was across the border, I could find someone in the Candian authorities who'd listen. But what if I couldn't? What if they said it was a US problem and that the FBI should handle it? Then the club would have plenty of warning and would just shut down for a few months until the investigation was over. They might even kill the women at the mansion, just to cover their tracks.

I had to go, or I was putting Cal and Rufus at risk. But it felt like I was running away.

Rufus suddenly sat bolt upright and barked at the sky. A breeze was ruffling his coat and a few big drops of rain plopped into the dirt. I looked up to see huge black clouds covering the sky. I hadn't noticed it getting darker but now, as the clouds covered the sun completely, it was like night had come early.

I wasn't too worried. I was in a forest, so I'd be sheltered, right? How bad could it be?

But then there was an eerie, rising howl from the trees. I knew the sound, that wail you get when the wind whistles around a tree, like a reed vibrating in a flute. But I'd never heard the wind filtered through ten thousand trees, before, or felt the way it broke apart into a million separate currents, only to recombine and blast you from every direction at once. The hairs on the back of my neck stood up, and Rufus nudged me with his head. "Okay," I said. "Let's get inside."

We were halfway to the door when I remembered Betsy and Hank. Both were outside grazing. *Crap!* I hurried to where I'd left them and tried to get Betsy moving towards the barn, but she was unsettled by the wind and wasn't feeling cooperative, edging to the side instead of going forward. Then the rain started, not so much drops as a constant, hissing stream that plastered my hair to my face and turned the ground to sticky mud. And the whole time, I was looking around me frantically, thinking *where's Hank?* The goat was nowhere to be seen.

It took me a good ten minutes of battling and pleading with Betsy before I got her safely into her stall in the barn. By then, my shirt and jeans were soaked and I was shivering from the brutal gusts of wind that seemed to cut straight through my wet clothes. The wind had risen to an ear-splitting screech and lightning flashed overhead. Rufus, who'd stayed loyally pressed to my side the whole time, was shivering, his coat sopping wet and heavy.

I'd seen plenty of big storms in Seattle, but I'd always been safely sheltered inside, watching the lightning while cradling a mug of coffee. Being out here in the wilderness was very different. The temperature had dropped and the wind was so cold, that my head throbbed. One second, a gust was trying to punch its way down my throat, the next, it changed direction and I could barely breathe. It was terrifying, and getting worse.

I raced back to where I'd last seen Hank, but as I rounded the corner of the cabin, a gust took me right off my feet and I went full-length in the mud. I lay there stunned for a moment, the cold ground sapping my body's heat.

Rufus licked my cheek, worried. I hauled myself to my feet, one whole side of my body coated in glutinous, gray-brown mud, and started searching through the trees for Hank. But it was almost completely dark, now, and he could be in any one of the patches of thick shadow. Worse, the wind was picking up anything that wasn't bolted down and sending it scuttering along the ground. A watering can bounced past me and hit a tree. Then a branch as thick as my arm was bounced along the ground, spinning and twisting, and I had to dodge out of its way. If something like that hit Hank, he could be killed. Or he could run off into the woods, terrified, and we might never find him. I ran back and forth, venturing further and further from the cabin, Rufus nervously trotting at my side. "*Hank!*" I hollered. Nothing.

There was a *crack* that could have been the world snapping in two, and I was thrown to the ground. The air smelled like the photocopier at the call center and all I could see was red: throbbing, violent scarlet with a purple-white blob searing through the middle. It took a while for me to realize that I'd screwed my eyes shut and I tentatively inched them open, but the after-image the flash had left was so bright, it took me a few moments of blinking before I could see again.

Lightning had struck a tall pine right in front of me, splitting it halfway down and turning the top into a raging orange plume too fierce for the rain to put out. Burning branches started to creak and thump to the ground. Rufus gave a whine of fear. *I have to get him out of here.* But I couldn't leave Hank...

And then, in the flickering light of the fire, I saw two big, scared eyes peeking out from the middle of a bush.

I raced over there, stumbling on legs that had gone numb and shaky. I didn't have any time for niceties: the tree was cracking and leaning, the wind finishing what the lighting had started, and we were close enough that I could feel the fire's heat on my face. I reached in, scooped Hank into my arms and staggered away with him, Rufus running alongside me. Embers were falling all around me and the icy rain hadn't let up: I could feel myself being singed and soaked simultaneously, water pouring down my face and making it difficult to see. But I kept my eyes on the silhouette of the barn up ahead and kept putting one foot in front of the other. Just as we arrived, there was a groan and then the sound of snapping wood, and the pine that had been struck toppled to the ground.

I got Hank into his stall and shut the barn doors tight, then ran for the cabin, staggering as the gusts caught me. I was almost there when a branch came sailing through the air and punched end-on into one of the windows, shattering the glass and leaving the branch wedged in the hole. *The shutters! I have to close the shutters!* I ran around heaving them closed but they were made of thick, heavy wood, and the wind was trying to tear them out of my hands. Twice, I nearly had my fingers broken when I lost my grip and a shutter slammed back against the wall. Rufus barked and butted up against me, trying to nudge me towards the door and safety. "I know!" I told him. "One more!"

I heard the whistle of something rushing towards me a split second before it hit. I started to turn away, which may have saved my life. A branch slammed into my arm just above the elbow, making the whole limb light up with pain. I fell sideways, the pain bad enough to make me nauseous. I tried to get to my feet but every movement of my arm made me freeze and grind my teeth as a new wave of agony flashed through me. The wind was howling, now, blasting past my face so fast I couldn't breathe. I tried again to get up but slipped in the mud and fell back on my ass, jolting my arm again. I cursed, hot tears filling my eyes.

And then suddenly, an arm was slipping under my legs and another under my back and I was being lifted into the air and tipped to rest against a broad, plaid-shirted chest. The final shutter was slammed closed and then we were running, with Rufus a dripping missile next to us. We barreled through the door and then we were in the luxuriously warm, dry air of the cabin.

He set me gently down on the edge of the bed. I blinked through my tears and then I was looking up into cornflower-blue eyes, frightened and angry and gorgeous.

39

CAL

I STARED DOWN AT HER, my heart pounding against my ribs. I'd run all the way home, dodging loose branches and a few times nearly being blown off my feet by gusts coming across a clearing. But when I'd seen her, outside in all the chaos, when she should have been safe in some apartment in the city, that's when I'd gotten really frightened. Then I'd seen her arm, hanging limply by her side, and my chest ached with guilt. I'd failed to protect her.

"What happened to your arm?" I didn't mean for it to sound so angry, but I was mad at her for being outside, mad at the men in the club who'd put her in this situation, mad at myself for not being here.

"Branch hit it," she said through chattering teeth. The cold was starting to hit her, now. The cabin was warm but her thick plaid shirt and jeans were soaked through with rain and mud and they were leeching all the heat from her body. "B—Betsy and Hank are in the barn. A w—window broke."

She'd run around out there in the middle of a storm saving the damn animals. Did she know how brave she was? I looked over my shoulder at the branch that was sticking through a window. "I'll nail a tarp over it. We need to get your clothes off." I grabbed a blanket from the bed and hung it over the stove to warm. Then I started popping buttons on her shirt without really thinking about what I was doing. It was only when I was halfway down and looking at her soaked, translucent t-shirt and her bra-clad breasts beneath that it sunk in that I was undressing her. I felt my face heat, but we didn't have a choice: she couldn't do it herself with one good arm.

I kept popping buttons. Her breasts pushed forward through the open shirt, almost brushing my chest. I helped her gently pull the shirt over her shoulders and off her arms, wincing along with her as we worked it past the place that hurt. I reached down and popped the button on her jeans, and now it was impossible not to feel like I was undressing her, scrambling to get her out of her clothes so that I could—

I pushed that thought down and crouched, dragging the mud-soaked jeans off her legs, trying not to look at the long, pale curves of her thighs or the dark shadow visible through her soaked panties. I stood up. "T-shirt," I ordered. I tried to sound all businesslike and neutral, like a doctor, but it didn't come out like that.

She tried to struggle out of the t-shirt but she was shaking too much and it turned into a wet tangle around her shoulders. I helped her pull it free. God, her skin was icy, the smooth paleness going goosebumped. Every nerve in my body was screaming at me to warm her up the way I wanted to: pull her to my chest and run my hands all over her—

She looked up at me, her eyes huge.

I forced the urge back...*just*. For her own sake, I had to keep her away from me and I was so nearly there: she'd be gone, tomorrow. I grabbed the warm blanket from the stove and wrapped it around her like a poncho. "Your bra and panties, too," I told her.

She fumbled beneath the blanket for a few moments. She didn't always have a hand free to hold the two sides of the blanket together and I kept getting glimpses: a pale breast swinging, a pink nipple, crinkled with cold, a curl of soft hair—I forced my eyes to her feet until I saw her bra and panties hit the floor. "Now give me a look at that arm," I ordered. I figured if I was terse and gruff, maybe I could cover up how I was aching for her.

But to show me the arm, she had to twist the blanket around until the gap was at her side and then stick her arm through. And even with the blanket clamped together at the waist, I still couldn't help but see her whole side-boob. And then *below* her waist, her entire leg was exposed, like some Hollywood starlet on the red carpet, and my eyes just kept climbing upward, right up to that bare patch of hip that reminded me she wasn't wearing panties—

It scared me, how much I wanted her. And the lust was just the surface layer, white water on a wave so deep, so powerful, it was close to sweeping me away. I could hear the blood rushing in my ears, feel my eyes flicking over her too fast: her eyes, her hair—

Her *lips....*

I tore my gaze away and took her hand in my hand. When I felt how cold she was, I came dangerously close to melting. And when I ran my fingers up her arm, probing and testing, a big swell of protective need rose up in me and I had to stare hard at the goosepimpled flesh because I didn't dare look into her eyes. "Nothing broken," I muttered. "But you're going to have a hell of a bruise." I tried to let go of her arm but I couldn't seem to. "You could have been killed! If it had hit you in the head—"

"I just—I wanted to make sure everything was okay!" she said. "I didn't want you to get back and find the cabin wrecked."

That very nearly did it. My heart went caramel soft and it took a superhuman effort to growl at her. "I don't care about the damn cabin —" Her wet hair was falling over her face and I brushed it angrily out of the way—

And suddenly, I was looking right into her eyes.

The rest of the world ceased to exist. *I don't care about the damn cabin*...something in my eyes must have completed the sentence because I saw *her* eyes widen, her pupils grow.

Her lips parted.

And I just growled, grabbed her waist with both hands, plucked her up off the floor, and brought my lips down on hers.

40

BETHANY

H E KISSED ME and nothing else mattered. I didn't feel cold or wet or even in pain. My eyes closed and in the warm blackness, all that existed were his lips. They owned me, made me his, then spread me open and damn well plundered me, and I flowered open beneath him, inviting him in as urgently as he invaded. I could feel his panting breaths and that *I* was panting, just as hard. Everything that had been building up for weeks was finally being released.

His hard upper lip demanded every part of me, wouldn't stop until he knew me completely. And just behind it, that wonderfully soft lower lip, brushing over my sensitive flesh, making me tremble. Other sensations started to trickle in, now, one by one. The brush of his beard against my neck, that reminder of how wild he was, the hair so gorgeously soft. The heat of him through the blanket, his body like warm rock. His hands—oh God, his hands, big and powerful, gripping my waist under the blanket and holding me in the air like I weighed nothing.

That silver wire inside me, the one that was drawn so achingly tight whenever I was around him, was vibrating and dancing, singing in harmony with every hard press of his lips. And all those vibrations were bouncing and echoing, low in my belly, triggering a deep, scarlet, bass drum rhythm that made me squirm and crush my thighs together, and that got more powerful with every kiss.

He growled low in his throat and pulled me to him, my upper body pressed tight against his chest. My legs kicked either side of his waist and hooked around him as if it was the most natural thing in the world, as if I belonged there. My groin settled against his abs and a flutter went right up my body, leaving me light-headed. In some ways, it was just like when he'd carried me over the gorse bushes, that first day. But then I hadn't been naked and wrapped only in a blanket, my legs entirely nude as they encircled him, one bare breast spilling through the opening in the fabric to press against his shirt.

I was breathless and desperate: the feel of him against me was amazing. My hands dived through the opening in the blanket and slid over the swells of his biceps and the wide curves of his chest, and with every brush of my palms over soft cotton and warm muscle, I felt myself melt. There was something about the effortless strength of him, the way he could hold me so easily. It made me feel small and weak in an entirely good way. My legs tightened around him and I ground myself against him, flushing but unrepentant, and he cursed under his breath.

With my legs around him, he could free one hand from my waist. He slid his fingers through my hair, burying them deep in the cool wetness, using his thumb to wipe beads of water from my forehead as he kissed me. His palm was deliciously warm against my cheek and he used it to guide me, turning me how he wanted me for his kisses. They were becoming deeper, the tip of his tongue playing with my lips and then darting between them, seeking out mine and dancing with it.

He started moving around the cabin. Each one of his heavy footsteps bounced me against him, rubbing the washboard of his abs against my groin. At first, he was just turning around and around, too fired up to stay still. But then his steps grew purposeful and he marched us over to one particular spot and stopped. I still had my eyes closed but after a few seconds, I figured out where we were. I could feel heat bathing my back through the blanket and warming my soaking hair. He'd moved us next to the stove.

Realization hit. *He's moved us next to the stove so that I won't freeze when he takes the blanket off me.* My groin tightened and that scarlet drumbeat inside me boomed louder, faster.

His hand started exploring me under the blanket, running up from the naked curve of my waist, his thumb brushing the side of my breast and making me heady. Then down, sliding around the crease of my hip to cup my ass cheek and tug me harder against him. Both of us panted harder and he broke the kiss, lifting my head so that he could shower kisses down my chin and down the length of my throat. Between his warmth against my front and the stove warming me from behind, the last of the chill was chased from my body. I fumbled with the blanket, but it was trapped between us. I wanted to be naked against him, *needed* to be, but I wasn't sure how to go about—

The hand that was exploring me slid around my back until he was holding me under the arms. Then he lifted me up and away from him. He used his other arm to gather the blanket and pull. Soft wool caressed my nipples for a second as it was whipped away and then it was fluttering to the floor and I was hanging there nude, dangling in his grip, my toes kicking just clear of the floor. I opened my eyes and found that he was looking right at me, his gaze raking up and down my body. I stared back at him, lips parted in shock. I'd never been so utterly naked before, not just bare but *displayed,* hanging there helplessly just a few feet from his eyes. I'd never been confident about my body but the way he looked at me, the way his gaze just ate me up, made me light up with pride.

He brought me closer to him and used both hands to lift me higher, so that my breasts swayed towards his face. I realized what he was about to do a split second before he did it and felt my lips open in an O...then his mouth enveloped my nipple. I arched my back, pressing against him as his tongue worked at the hardened bud, hotly bathing it and then circling around the edge in a way that made me grind my hips in mid-air.

He licked my breasts for long minutes, until I was a writhing, groaning mess. I could feel the heat of the stove baking my naked back and ass, blasting away the last of the water. But now my front was glowing, too, the heat of his mouth making me throb and pant.

He slid one arm around my waist and pulled me against him, and I threw my arms around his neck. That freed one of his hands and he slid it slowly down between us...and between my legs. When he cupped me, I went weak...and then a thick finger was sliding up into me, finding me wet and ready.

He carried me across the room and my heart sped up as I realized we were heading for the bed. When we reached it, he bent low and then dropped me the last few feet, so that I landed with a gasp and a bounce. His finger only left me at the last second and I lay there staring up at him, feeling the emptiness, the ache where it had been. And he gazed right back at me, eyes locked on that exact place, and then lifted his head and looked me straight in the eye as he pulled off his clothes.

His shirt first, tossed on the floor to reveal the caramel boulders of his shoulders and biceps, the chest so wide and strong that it made my pussy twitch and my skin tingle, my whole body anticipating the hard press of him against it.

Then his jeans, his shorts, his boots, all kicked down his legs and off in one urgent tangle. His thighs, thick with muscle, and, between them—

I gulped and my ass tensed and shifted on the bed, my body reacting on primal instinct: first inching away, a little scared, then lured closer, hypnotized. *Big.* Not just long but thick, the head silky smooth and the shaft weighty and hard as rock.

He put one knee on the bed, between my ankles. He glanced at my legs and took a breath, but no words came out. He met my eyes and I saw how his eyes were hooded with lust: he was too turned on to speak.

I opened my legs and felt his eyes shoot up my thighs to the soft lips of my pussy. My breath was coming in fevered pants, now, the drumbeat inside me thundering and crashing.

He climbed fully onto the bed and the way it sank under his

weight, the way the muscled bulk of him nudged my thighs further apart, made my stomach flip-flop. *This is real. We're really doing this.* His hands thumped down either side of my head, trapping me, his arms solid as tree trunks, and the drumbeat inside me became a continuous roar. I grabbed hold of his wrists, running my fingers over their hardness, hanging onto them to ground me as I went spacey and light, my ass making slow circles on the bed in anticipation.

He dipped his head and kissed down my body: between my breasts, over my stomach and all the way to my pussy. Then he moved forward, looked down into my eyes—

God. I felt the silken touch of him against my wet lips. For a second, we stayed there, those cornflower-blue eyes staring right into my soul. Then the arrow-shaped head of him was parting me, opening me...*stretching* me, my hands climbed his wrists, clinging on—

I rolled my head against the pillow, arching my back as he pushed deep. The heat of him...God, the solid girth of him, plunging into me. Every new millimeter he touched set off new streamers of pink and silver pleasure, making my eyes flutter closed and my lips open wide. He drew back and the pleasure became a needful ache. He thrust deep again and it compressed, glowing hotter and brighter.

His hips sunk between my thighs, opening me wider, and that hard, muscled ass came into play, driving him into me. Three hard thrusts and he was in me to the hilt, my hands clutching at his shoulders and my lips forming his name. Then he lowered himself to his forearms and began to fuck me, the weight of him pinning me to the bed, his pelvis grinding against my clit on each thrust. God, the feel of him, the hard solidness of him after weeks of imagining it. His body was like a drug: the more I ground my softness against him, the more I needed to.

For long minutes, the bed creaked in rhythm, the hard swells of his pecs grazing my nipples and the pleasure flaring hotter and hotter, compressing with each stroke until it was as dense as the core of a star. I felt my mouth moving but I didn't know what I was saying. At first, he kept his control, coaxing me closer and closer to the edge with a steady pace. But the more I writhed and gasped under him, the more turned on he got and the more his control began to shred, until he was hammering into me full speed, pounding my softness into the bed with his body. My hands clawed at his back, my legs came up and cinched tight around him. The pleasure was filling my whole body, taking me over. Somewhere in the distance, I could hear myself begging for release.

He suddenly stopped, grabbed hold of my waist and *twisted,* and with a yelp I was rolled over so that *I* was on top, my knees spread wide to straddle him. He guided my movements for a few strokes, lifting and dropping me, and then as soon as I started to move myself, his hands went to my breasts. Now I knew why he'd wanted me this way. There was something in the way he touched them—delighted, lusty but almost reverent—that told me he'd been dreaming of doing this for weeks. He *gloried* in them, filling his hands and squeezing, using his thumbs to stroke my nipples to aching peaks, and I'd never felt so proud of my body, so...*worshipped.*

I could run my hands over him, now, use that hard chest to press against as I rode him. My ass bounced atop his thighs, my back arched and I moaned, moving faster and faster, the pleasure swelling and tightening, urging me on. I could hear the wind howling outside, branches slamming against the walls, but nothing could touch us, in here. We were safe and warm and all that mattered was the perfect, hard slide of him inside me, the trembling streamers of pleasure it threw out, the feel of his fingers as they crushed my breasts just right—

"*God, Bethany...*" he said it in a low growl and what I heard in his voice, that mix of disbelief and victory and sheer joy, made that silver wire inside me draw tight, vibrating and singing right down into my soul. I panted for breath, almost slipping over the edge—

And then he grabbed my ass with both hands, drawing me down hard as he thrust *up* hard, his thumbs stroking along the crease of my hips, and that *did* send me over the edge, the orgasm corkscrewing up through my body, rippling along my spine and making me lift my face to the ceiling and cry out. My hips twisted and bucked against him as I felt him shudder and shoot jet after hot jet deep inside me.

Then I was slowing, wilting, collapsing forward onto his chest to lie panting atop him. And he brushed the hair back from my face and kissed me long and deep and tender.

When we eventually disentangled and stretched out, I found that, lying on his back, Cal's big body took up most of the bed. But I discovered a perfect, Bethany-sized space between him and the wall where I could lie on my side and cuddle up against him, his arm around me and my cheek on his chest. Outside, the storm still howled but with the wall behind me and Cal between me and any danger, I felt utterly protected.

There was a *whump* as Rufus jumped up onto the bed. He padded all around and over our legs in excitement: he'd never had *two* warm humans to cuddle up to at once before. He found a spot where he could wedge himself, turned around three times and then cuddled in, sighing contentedly.

For a while, I just basked in the afterglow, tired and happy. And then, with his pec as my pillow, I dozed off to sleep.

41

CAL

I LAY STARING UP at the ceiling as Bethany slept, her long dark hair spilling down my torso. As my body cooled and my breathing slowed, reality was setting in.

What have I done?

I'd known from the start that I couldn't have her. I'd told myself I had to keep my distance. Then I'd broken every rule. And now....

Now all I wanted to do was take Rufus and go to Canada with her.

For six years, I'd been existing, not living. Serving my sentence in my self-imposed exile. These last few weeks, she'd given me a taste of another life.

But I couldn't have it.

Bethany thought she knew me, but she didn't. I couldn't let it go on like that. I couldn't be close to her and not tell her what I'd done. And if I *did* tell her....

I looked down at her, peacefully asleep with her head on my chest. I imagined those big brown eyes going wide: shock, then disbelief. Then finally horror.

I couldn't take that. Not when I felt like this about her. Anything was better than that.

Even saying goodbye to her forever.

42

RALAVICH

I SNATCHED UP the satellite phone on the third ring. "Alik?"

Alik is not an emotional creature but for once, he sounded happy. "Got something," he told me. "I'm with a local smuggler. I thought she might try and get out of the country and I was right, she was here, arranging for passage to Canada."

A scream. A woman's scream can be a beautiful thing, a sound that gets me hard. But this was a man's scream, raw and agonized. I winced and held the phone away from my ear. "What are you doing to him?"

"I make little slit in his balls," said Alik. "And then with fork, pull out—"

"I understand," I said quickly. "Ask him when she'll be there."

Another scream. It went on and on. Then a man's voice, cultured and refined but ragged with pain. *"Tomorrow! They'll be here tomorrow!"*

43

BETHANY

NEXT MORNING, we had to leave early to be at Jacques' boat for noon. The wind had stripped every last leaf from the trees and blown them like snow into huge drifts. The ground was littered with branches and some trees had been felled completely, ripped out of the ground to lie on their sides with their roots dripping dirt, or snapped completely in two, exposing creamy, pale wood. It was awe-inspiring and scary, a reminder of how powerful nature was. Any other time, I would have been fascinated. But today, I crunched through the leaves head down, miserably brooding.

I'd hoped. I'd thought that after last night, he might have changed his mind. But when I woke, he was sitting next to the bed, already dressed. Next to him was my backpack, already packed for me with all my clothes and supplies for the journey. But there was no bag for him. I'd looked into his eyes, my own eyes filling with tears, and when I saw the sadness there, I knew I wouldn't be able to change his mind.

We reached the raft. I could see Jacques' steamboat on the far side and Jacques was standing by the door that led downstairs, waiting for us. But between us and him was the river and it was nothing like the calm, sunlit scene it had been last time. The storm had swollen it and it was raging and foaming as it rushed downstream, the water a dirty grey-brown with white caps to the waves. I saw branches being tossed and tumbled by the current. Sometimes they'd disappear, sucked beneath the surface and I waited for them to pop up again...and they didn't. It had gotten colder, too, and the water would be colder still. I shuddered.

One at a time, we gingerly boarded the raft. Then Rufus jumped excitedly aboard, setting it rocking, and I had to grab hold of the rope and tell him sternly to *sit!* If any of us wound up in the water, I wasn't sure we'd make it to shore.

Rufus grudgingly sat. I ruffled his fur and Cal began to haul us across. I tried not to think about how hard it was going to be to say goodbye.

Last time, it had seemed to take hours to get across the river. This time, it felt like seconds. As the steamboat came closer and closer, I felt the emotion welling up inside, unstoppable. *This can't be the end!*

The raft bumped up against the steamboat and I turned to Cal, feeling tears hot in my eyes. "I don't—" My voice caught.

Cal put his hand on my shoulder. "You've got to," he said. "It's the only way."

"Then come with me," I blurted. "Come to Canada with me, I'm sure Jacques could fix it. We can bring Rufus—"

He shook his head.

"Cal *please!* I'll help you build a cabin—"

He looked off into the distance. His mouth twitched but then he pressed his lips together as if he didn't trust himself to speak. He shook his head.

I could feel tears escaping and trickling down my face, and I had to look away too or I would have started full-on sobbing. I squatted down on the raft and wrapped my arms around Rufus. "You are a *good boy,*" I told him, my voice shaking. "The best. You take care of each other, okay?"

Rufus licked my cheek and woofed, looking worried for the first time. He looked at Cal, then at me. *What's going on?*

I swallowed and breathed deep, trying to hold myself together long enough to say what I needed to say. I stood up and put my arms around Cal, nestling my face into his chest for the very last time. "Thank you," I said. I took a shuddering breath. "Back in Seattle, I felt like my life was ticking away, one day at a time. I've lived more in these few weeks than I have in a year."

And I lifted up on tiptoes and pressed my lips to his. His whole body *tensed*...I felt him growl, deep in his chest, and his arms twitched, *trembled,* about to grab me and pull me close—

He broke the kiss. "Goodbye." He looked quickly away, but I saw his eyes were shining.

I nodded. Blinked. Turned around and stepped off the raft and onto the steamboat. Jacques was waiting for me, looking pale and drawn. He held out a Canadian passport and I took it, my chest beginning to quake—

Jacques staggered to the side. The man who'd pushed him stepped out of the doorway and grabbed my wrist. I blinked uncomprehendingly at him, my eyes still full of tears.

Alik. Ralavich's bodyguard. In his other hand, he had a gun and he lifted it to point at the raft.

"*No!*" I screamed, lurching forwards.

There was a *boom* that made my head ring.

I saw Cal jerk as the bullet hit him...and then he fell from the raft and was swept away by the river.

44

CAL

PAIN EXPLODED like white fire, searing down my arm and across my chest. I was spun around, a puppet with its strings tugged, and then I was falling, falling....

I hit the water and the shock of the icy cold made me gasp and inhale water. Choking, I tried to kick for the surface but the current had me now, tumbling me over and over, and my cheek scraped the bottom. I tried to stabilize myself but as soon as I used my left arm, my whole upper body lit up with agonizing pain.

I was moving too fast and spinning too much to figure out which way was up. And now I *really* needed to breathe. I kicked at the water but that just tumbled me more. My back scraped along the river bed, drawing blood, and my mouth opened in a scream, choking down more water. My boots dragged against the mud, kicking up brown clouds until I couldn't see anything. The cold was soaking into my bones with each passing second, draining my energy and turning my muscles to concrete. The aching pressure in my lungs grew and grew and the world went black around the edges.

Teeth closed on my arm and I was dragged determinedly upwards. Once I knew which direction to move in, I started weakly kicking, helping a little. And then I saw sunlight and—

My face broke the water and I sucked in half the air in Idaho. My vision cleared. I was downstream from the steamboat, half a mile or more, and Rufus was towing me to shore by the arm. I let him.

Clambering up onto the bank took everything I had. I fell to my knees, coughing, each cough sending fresh waves of pain through me. I looked down to see a ragged slash in my shirt. The bullet had grazed my shoulder, leaving a long, shallow gash that wouldn't kill me but hurt like hell. I wasn't in good shape. Pain throbbed from the wound, radiating through my whole body, and it got worse when I moved. Plus, I was soaked to the skin, shivering with cold and still coughing up river water.

But they had Bethany.

I gritted my teeth and with sheer stubbornness, I heaved myself up to one knee. Even that small act made the world go gray around the edges. A dripping Rufus inserted himself under my arm and helped and together, we got me up to my feet. I coughed, shivered, and waited a second until my vision cleared again. "Good boy," I rasped to Rufus. He gave a short bark and shook himself.

I lumbered into a run. Each step sent a shockwave up my leg, through my spine and into my shoulder. The pain was so bad I staggered and nearly fell.

But the pain had another effect, too. It made me mad.

Mad at them for taking her. Mad at me, for letting her go alone to Canada, just because I didn't want to tell her the truth. Thanks to me, she was on her way back to the mansion, so that bastard Ralavich could—

The image of it scalded my mind, igniting the rage. It drove me forward and every fresh wave of pain fed back into the rage, the red clouds filling me, powering me on.

He will not have her. I was going to get her back. And when I did, I wouldn't let anything come between us.

I kept my gaze fixed on the steamboat, forcing myself forward in long strides with Rufus running along beside me. By the time I reached it, I was panting and grunting with pain, and my shirt was soaked with blood. But I was ready to tear someone apart.

I found Jacques slumped against a wall, with his girlfriend tending to him, tears in her eyes. He lifted his head to look at me. "I'm sorry, Cal. He got it out of me."

I squatted down. Now I was close, I could see how pale he was, and his face was soaked with sweat from the pain. He was cradling his groin protectively: God knows what that bastard had done to him. "Not your fault." I turned to his girlfriend. "Will he be okay?"

She nodded. "I'll get him to a hospital."

Jacques knew what I was going to ask before I asked it. "Four men. The Russian and—and three other guys. Black SUV, heading west, they're taking the old logging road."

I nodded and ran. They had a big head start but the logging road was unpaved: you couldn't drive fast on it. And it took a winding path through the forest, where I could go in a straight line. If I was fast, I might still be able to head them off before it joined the main road.

I pounded up the side of the valley and then started to descend. There was no path to follow. I was going purely on instinct and the mental map I'd formed in my head over the years, racing through thick trees and praying I came out in the right spot. The hill got steeper and steeper and soon I was sliding as much as I was running, doing my best to stay on my feet because if I fell, I wouldn't stop rolling and bouncing until I hit the bottom. But I didn't dare slow down. I was imagining Bethany, terrified and alone in the back of that SUV. I had no idea where the mansion was. If they reached the main road, she was lost forever.

My shoulder was sending out zig-zagging bolts of pain right through my body, now, every movement agony. The trees got thicker. Soon, I could only see six feet in front of me and I was moving so fast, I covered that distance in a half-second. If I saw a cliff in front of me, there wasn't going to be time to stop.

I plunged on, branches scratching at my face, loose rocks tumbling beside me. I was going too fast, now, out of control, but I still wouldn't slow down.

And then I burst through a line of trees and saw the logging road below me. The slope leveled out a little and I veered to the side and managed to slow myself down. Even so, I didn't manage to stop until I hit one of the huge piles of logs, and that damn near finished me off. My shoulder slammed into a log full force and the only reason I didn't unleash every curse I'd picked up in the Corps was that every scrap of air was knocked out of my lungs. I slumped to the ground, panting. Rufus skidded to a halt beside me and nudged me with his nose, worried.

Then, in the distance, the roar of an engine.

I heaved myself to my feet. I was in time: just. Now I needed a plan. I was outnumbered and they had guns. If I ran down to the road and tried to stop them on foot, they could just drive past me or straight over me. I had to force them to stop, somehow.

I looked at the log pile. There were maybe twenty logs, each as thick around as my waist and twelve feet long, stacked on their sides in a triangular pile, ready to be loaded onto a logging truck. The road was maybe sixty yards below, down the slope.

The engine noise grew louder. Through the trees, I saw a flash of black paint. It was them.

The log pile was held in place with wooden chocks to prevent exactly what I was planning. I heaved the first one free, then the second. But the logs didn't move. Combined, they weighed thousands of pounds. They were going to need some help.

Just raising my arm to push made me want to throw up with pain, and when I actually leaned against the pile and heaved, I got spots in front of my eyes. But the roar of the car was getting closer. I pushed.

Nothing happened. It was like pushing against a mountain. *They're going to drive right past. They're going to drive right past and I'm never going to see her again.*

I growled and turned around, putting my back against the logs and digging my boots into the mud. *Push. Push!* The noise of the car filled the valley. I let my fear flood through me, let it fill my veins and surge into my heart, and I growled. *Push, you fucker, push, or she's on her back under that Russian bastard and—*

The logs creaked and rocked. My shoulder lit up in agony and I let it out as a guttural yell, pushing even harder, giving it everything I had—

There was a rumble like thunder as the first log started rolling. Then the second log, freed by the first, rolled after it and the noise grew and grew. The logs higher in the pile crashed to the ground, bouncing off each other and arcing through the air. All of them were on the move, now, rolling downhill and picking up speed.

I didn't time it exactly right, but with twenty of them, I didn't have to. The SUV braked hard when the driver saw the first logs cross the road, but it was too late to stop and a log slammed right into its side, knocking it across the road. More logs spun it around and it came to a stop facing the wrong way, dented and battered.

I raced down the slope to the road, my heart thumping. It had been the only plan I could think of, but what if she was hurt? What if she was dead?! I ran over to the car but the windows had shattered and I couldn't see through the frosted safety glass. I wrenched open the door—

Bethany was in the middle of the back seat, wedged between two of those guards from the mansion in the black combat gear. The big guy who'd shot me was in the passenger seat and another guard had been driving. Everyone looked stunned from the crash and the driver was bleeding from a cut on his head. But Bethany, thank God, seemed to be okay, probably because she'd been in the middle of the car. She was awake and blinking up at me in disbelief.

I grabbed the nearest guard and hauled him out of the car, dumping him on the road. Then I reached in and pulled out my girl. My shoulder screamed in protest but I ignored it, refusing to stop pulling until she was pressed up against me. Then I grabbed her cheeks in both hands and kissed her again and again, my fingers sliding deep into her hair. I've never needed anything in my whole life as much as those soft lips. I had to know she was okay, that we were back together. I filled my soul with the sweet, warm softness of her, my chest rising and falling as I breathed her in. Then I hugged her to my chest, my voice ragged with emotion. "From now on," I told the top of her head, "you're staying with me."

She nodded and clutched me tight. At that moment, Rufus arrived. He raced around and around our legs and then leaped up and wouldn't take his wet paws off Bethany's shoulders until she ruffled his fur.

The guard I'd hauled out of the car tried to get up. Rufus immediately growled and bared his teeth and the guy changed his mind. But the others were starting to come to their senses, too: the big guy who'd shot me, especially. There were four of them, and they had guns. "Come on," I told Bethany. "We've gotta go." And I took her hand and ran with her into the trees.

I got my bearings and headed straight for the smallholding. But as the adrenaline wore off, the exhaustion started to kick in. The wound in my shoulder didn't help. After a mile, I was panting and wincing and I had to slow to a walk.

"Cal!" Bethany dragged me to a stop. "You've been *shot!* Let me—"

I shook my head. "Later. We need to keep moving."

At that second, there was a rustle of foliage behind us. I spun around. Was someone there?

Seconds passed and no one emerged. But I kept waiting, just in case. I waited long enough for any pursuer to get restless and make a noise....

Nothing. It must have been a bird or the wind in the trees. I let out a long breath and turned to Bethany. As soon as I looked at her, I felt that *pull,* the one I'd been trying to crush down inside me all along, the one I'd finally realized I couldn't.

I reached out and took her hand, then pulled her close. She looked up at me, surprised, but squeezed my hand, and my heart just goddamn melted.

As soon as we were safe home, I was going to tell her what I'd done, why I was out here in the woods. Maybe she'd hate me, maybe that would be the end of us, but at least there'd be a chance.

"C'mon," I said. "We got a long way to go." And we started walking, hand in hand.

45
_____

RALAVICH

"You let her *go?*" I roared. "Three of you, with guns, against one man, and you just *handed her over?*"

The guard shrank back. Cairns, the head of the club, looked like he was about to say something, but I glared at him and he lowered his eyes. The bruises on his neck were still visible. He knew who was in charge, now.

"And where's my man?" I demanded. "Where's Alik? He was with you in the car!"

At that second, the satellite phone rang. I mashed the answer button. "Alik?!"

Alik spoke in a hushed voice. "I have them," he said with great satisfaction. "Tracked them all the way back to their house. The bastard's good, he nearly spotted me a few times. But I got them."

"You're there now?" I asked, incredulous. "You know where they live?"

"I'm looking right at it," said Alik. "A cabin in the woods."

"Send your coordinates," I said breathlessly. "I'm coming." I suddenly knew exactly what to do. How to make Bethany suffer, how to break her forever, and get my revenge on the man who'd kept her from me. I turned to Cairns. "You said you have a helicopter?"

He swallowed. "Y—Yes...."

"Get it ready. And get the other members. Tell them I've got something special for them."

46

CAL

W E WERE BACK at the cabin and I was sitting on a chair with my shirt off. My eyes were locked on Bethany as she laid out first aid supplies on the table. I hadn't let go of her hand the entire way home.

She cleaned the wound, then picked up a needle and thread, ready to suture. "Sorry," she said with a grimace.

I nodded for her to go ahead and she began. It hurt...but she had the gentlest damn hands I'd ever known and watching her was the perfect way to take my mind off the pain. Those soft lips were pursed in concentration and I was transfixed by them, and soothed by the brush of her cool fingertips as she worked. She'd tied her hair back to keep it out of the way and she was wearing a plaid shirt with the sleeves rolled up. She'd changed so much since I first met her. And she'd never looked more beautiful.

"Cal?" she asked quietly as she worked. "What now?"

I'd already made up my mind. Had decided as soon as I climbed out of that river. "Still got that passport Jacques gave you?"

She nodded.

"That offer still open?"

She drew in her breath. "You'll come with me?!"

I nodded somberly. "If you'll have me."

She threw her arms around my neck and hugged me close. There was something inside me that felt like it had been locked up and buried, right down in the depths, for six long years, and I felt it tentatively lift and pull against its chains. I was just beginning to let myself hope.

But something had to happen first, if this was to have even a chance of working.

I drew gently back from the hug and let her finish the last few stitches. I pulled on a fresh shirt and then took her hands in mine. "Need to tell you some stuff," I said. "Why I'm out here."

She nodded and squeezed my hands. I took a deep breath. I'd been planning this the whole walk back but it didn't make it any easier. My heart was suddenly racing. If I did this, I might lose her. But if I didn't, I couldn't be with her. I just had to do it and hope we came out the other side.

"After the Raiders," I began, "I got—" My stomach knotted. Dammit, this was harder than I'd thought. "Some guy approached me and—"

Rufus suddenly unwound himself, scrambled to his feet and alerted, ears high.

"What is it?" Bethany asked, worried.

Rufus was staring out of the window, his eyes fixed on the sky. He let out a sharp, short bark, then another. I stood up and walked slowly to the window, Bethany right beside me. But it took another few seconds before my ears made out the sound. A low thrumming, getting louder.

A helicopter. I looked at Bethany in panic, all my protective instincts taking hold.

They'd found us.

47

BETHANY

C AL GRABBED HIS RIFLE and we raced outside. But by then, the helicopter was already descending, creating a downdraft that nearly knocked us off our feet. It was a huge, black thing as long as a bus. It rammed air into our lungs, making us choke and gasp, and our eyes were tearing. The noise was like someone hammering nails into our eardrums and it was even worse for the animals, who charged around in fear. Rufus pressed hard against my legs, his worried barks almost lost in the roar.

The helicopter touched down in the clearing in front of the cabin and almost before it had stopped moving, four guards had jumped out and pointed their guns at Cal, ordering him to drop his rifle. Cal stubbornly stood there, his rifle trained on them and his lips drawn back from his teeth in a snarl, until I grabbed his arm. "They'll kill you!" I told him. Reluctantly, he lowered the muzzle and then dropped the rifle to the ground.

Only then did Ralavich climb from the helicopter. He looked around at the forest, then shook his head and spat on the ground. "Why the *fuck* would anyone want to live all the way out here?" He looked at me and I saw his face light up with that horrible, cruel lust.

Cal stepped protectively in front of me and the two men eyed each other. "That's him?" muttered Cal.

I nodded, so scared I couldn't speak.

Cal gave a low growl and took three steps forward. His whole body had gone tense and you could feel the primal rage rolling off him in waves. Each footstep seemed to shake the whole forest. The guards looked at each other uncertainly and the barrels of their guns wavered.

But Ralavich walked forward as well, and the two men didn't stop until they were just a few feet apart. "*You!*" snapped Ralavich. "You're the one who's been hiding her!" Ralavich's eyes flicked to me and then back to Cal and his face twisted in—

Oh God. *Jealousy.* My guts twisted. Ralavich thought I was *his.* The idea made me shudder.

And Cal recognized the look, too. His hands curled into fists. Rufus shot past me and ran to stand beside him, baring his teeth at Ralavich and making that chainsaw growl.

"I'm gonna give you one chance," said Cal. His voice was low, but it carried. "You get back in that thing and fly off, right now, and I won't come after you."

For a second, Ralavich just blinked, incredulous. Then he gave a short, sharp laugh with no humor in it. "*That's* your offer?"

"You should take it," said Cal. His voice was shaking with rage. "Because if you try to take her from me, I'll kill you."

"Oh, don't worry," said Ralavich. "I'm not going to just take her. You've pissed me off enough that I'm going to do something much more entertaining."

He turned and waved at the helicopter. More men climbed out, but they weren't guards. They were the men from the mansion, eight of them. They were carrying rifles and they were dressed in camouflage gear. Some of them seemed to be half-drunk and they were grinning and excited, messing with their guns and fiddling with the unfamiliar camouflage clothes, like men on a—

Oh God. Oh no.

Ralavich grinned as he saw realization dawn. "That's right, we're going to have a hunt. And guess what we're going to be hunting?"

I felt my knees weaken.

Ralavich's grin grew wider at my terror. "And guess what we're going to do to you when we catch you?"

I drew in a choked gasp. *No.* This couldn't be happening. My brain was still struggling to process *them, here,* in our safe little haven in the center of the forest. And what he was describing: no, he couldn't be serious.... I imagined them tracking me. Chasing me. Cornering me and pinning me down—

Ralavich looked at Cal. "Don't worry, we'll make sure you're there to watch."

Cal roared and started forward, but suddenly every guard had his gun up and pointing at him. I ran to him and grappled him around the waist, pulling him back. "No! Cal, no!" But he wouldn't move. His eyes were locked on Ralavich and he looked ready to tear his throat out.

"We'll give you a ten-minute head start," said Ralavich. He made a big show of checking the time on a gaudy gold wristwatch.

A head start. It suddenly all became real and I was so frightened I wanted to throw up. They were going to *hunt us.* They were going to hunt us like animals and rape me. I looked at Ralavich, aghast. *Why?* He had me. Why not just take me back to the mansion?

Then I saw what was in his eyes and I understood. This was how he'd break me. He was going to toy with me like a cat with a mouse, let me run just so he could catch me, so he could show me just how powerless I really was.

"You're wasting time," drawled Ralavich lazily. "Closer to nine minutes, now."

Cal lunged forward again, seething, but I grabbed his arm. "We have to go," I told him. "Cal, we have to go!"

He was so angry, it took several seconds before I got him to look at me. Then he nodded, scowled at Ralavich one last time, and grabbed my hand, pulling me towards the cabin.

Inside, he started grabbing things from shelves and throwing them into two backpacks: food, water, a first aid kit, a tarpaulin. He pulled something small and slender from the back of a shelf: his passport. The guards watched over us to make sure we didn't try to take any weapons.

Cal threw me one of the backpacks and we hurried outside. Rufus came with us, but Cal crouched down and ruffled the fur on his head. "You have to stay here," he told Rufus. "It's too dangerous for you." Rufus whined but reluctantly sat down just outside the door, doing it as slowly as possible in the hope we'd change our minds.

"Eight minutes," said Ralavich from the doorway.

Cal took my hand.

And we ran.

48

RALAVICH

I WANDERED around the smallholding, snorting in disbelief at the pathetic life the man lived. No power, no phone, scratching a living from the earth like a peasant, living within a dozen feet of animals. *What does she see in him?*

There was a *boom* of gunfire and everyone jumped. One of the men from the mansion, a senator from Chicago, raised his hands apologetically and looked sheepish. He was carrying both a rifle *and* a shotgun and the shotgun had gone off accidentally while he'd been showing it to a friend. About half the men were like him, city dwellers who'd barely ever held a gun. But they didn't have to be experts to run down a couple of unarmed civilians. And the other men were hunters, rich guys from places like Montana and Wyoming, who spent the hunting season bagging game. They'd soon find them. And when they did....

I raised my voice so they could all hear. "Shoot him if you have to, but don't hurt her. And if he's still alive, make him watch while you have your fun with her."

A ripple of excitement went through the men. This was even better than what they got at the mansion. Maybe, if this went well,

Cairns could turn this into a regular event and pay me a royalty for thinking of it.

I checked my watch, counting off the seconds. I could feel my own pulse racing, too. There was something primal about it, the thrill of the hunt. And the knowledge that soon, that curvy beauty would be broken and submissive to my will.

"Time's up," I announced. "Let's go."

49

BETHANY

W E RAN. It was a beautiful day and the forest was still and quiet. It must have looked to someone watching like we were running from invisible demons, sprinting headlong through the trees with nothing behind us. But we knew we had to put as much distance between us and them as we could. How long had it been? Three minutes, four? How long until they came after us?

We were heading uphill, the slope gradually getting steeper. "What's the plan?" I asked breathlessly.

"Stay ahead of them," said Cal. "Keep heading north. Get to the border."

It seemed impossible. The border was at least a hundred miles away.

He must have seen the doubt in my eyes because he grabbed my hand and squeezed. "I'm getting you to Canada," he told me, his voice iron-hard. "And I'm coming with you."

I squeezed back.

A joyous whoop went up behind us, echoing through the trees. They were coming. *Already?!* I looked back down the slope and my heart started to pound. It felt like we'd barely moved!

We ran harder but the slope was still getting steeper and soon we were scrambling, hanging onto trunks and branches to haul ourselves up the hill. Each time we glanced behind us, we could see the trees moving as the men advanced through the forest. The ones who were out of shape were a fair way behind but the younger, fitter ones were right on our tails.

Cal knew the forest and could lead us on the fastest, easiest route. And I was used to long hikes, now, and could keep up with him. But as the forest thinned out, we hit a problem. We had to keep to cover, sticking to the trees so that they didn't catch sight of us and open fire, whereas they could just move in straight lines across open ground. And where we had to move stealthily, in case they saw a bush move and took a shot at it, they could make as much noise as they liked.

Second by second, the hunters crept closer.

A sick fear spread through me, chilling me from the inside out, and it got worse with each excited yell and drunken cheer from behind us. It was the power imbalance, the feeling of them being all-powerful and us being...*nothing.* Just prey. However fast we ran, they'd catch us. However well we hid, they'd find us.

The panic set in and I started to make mistakes, stepping on twigs I knew to avoid, dislodging loose rocks that went rolling down the hillside, giving away our position. I tried to move faster and that just made it worse. *They're going to catch us. They're going to catch us and then—* I knew Cal would die before he let them touch me. *I'm going to get him killed. He's going to get shot and it's my fault—*

Cal stopped and turned to me, his big hands stroking down my upper arms. "Stop," he said softly.

I stared at him, gulping in air in huge panic breaths. *Stop? But they're coming!*

"You can do this," he told me. He wasn't even out of breath.

I shook my head.

"Yes," he told me, "you can." And his voice took on that tone that left no room for argument. "You're braver than you think. Tougher than you think. You got away from these bastards once. You're going to do it again." Those cornflower blue eyes looked right into mine and—

He believed in me.

I swallowed and nodded. The panic didn't disappear but my breathing eased a little.

He took my hand and pulled me into a run.

We pushed hard and a half-hour later, we finally made it to the top of the hill. Then the blessed relief for my aching legs of going *downhill,* not *uphill,* and at last, it felt like we were putting some distance between us and them. The sun was getting low in the sky and the trees threw out long shadows to help us. I started to think that maybe, *maybe,* we could make it.

But then the hunters started to crest the hill. They came down the other side with horrible speed: they were fresh, they'd spent the day lounging around at the mansion whereas we'd hiked all the way to Jacques's and back. Our pace started to slow. That sick fear started to grow in my stomach again. They were going to catch us.

We reached a clearing and Cal stopped and turned to me. By now, even he was panting. "We have to stop," he told me.

"*What?!*"

"It's our only chance. Hide and let them go past. Once we're behind them, we'll have the advantage."

I stared at him, then turned to look behind us. I could hear them crashing through the undergrowth, only a minute or two behind us. Every instinct was telling me to run. But I trusted him. I nodded.

He looked around the clearing. There was a gentle, bowl-shaped depression off to one side and he led me over to it. He quickly scooped out the dead leaves that had drifted into the depression, covered it with a tarpaulin from his backpack, and then pushed the leaves back over it. I quickly got the idea and helped, camouflaging the tarp until it was invisible. Then we got down on our bellies and slithered under it.

It was pitch black. Twigs were poking into me in about a hundred places but before I could fidget and get comfortable, I heard footsteps approaching. Next to me, Cal went utterly still and I tried to do the same.

The scrunch of boots on dried leaves. More than one man. A

group of them, moving together. Our little hollow was off to the side of the clearing. Their instinct would be to walk right through the middle...right? I pressed my cheek against the ground and tried to be calm, to think of nothing, to become stone.

The footsteps got louder and louder. I was pressed so tight to the ground, I could feel the vibrations right through my body. Closer and closer. God, they were heading straight for us! I could feel myself tensing, my shoulder blades hunching together. What if they noticed something? Was a boot showing? Had I pulled all my hair under the tarp? I held my breath, waiting for the rush of air and light as the tarp was pulled off us—

In the darkness, Cal found my hand with his and squeezed—

Two sets of footsteps...no, three. One of them passing so close I could have reached out and touched him. He was right by my feet, then my legs. He was almost past....

Then his boot came down right on my hand.

50

BETHANY

THE PAIN rocketed up my arm: agonizing, nerve-shredding. I wanted to scream, to curse, to twist and buck...but I couldn't. Because if I so much as twitched, it was all over. So I lay there silently howling, waiting for him to take his next step. *Come on! Come on!* His foot lifted—

And then settled back down, even heavier than before. I felt bones grind and fresh pain washed over me, so strong I wanted to be sick. He'd stopped. He'd stopped, and he was standing on my hand.

I still had hold of Cal's hand and I squeezed it so hard it must have been painful. It was the only outlet I had. He took it without flinching and squeezed back. *You can do this.*

But I wasn't sure I could. The hunter had started to chat with his friends, who must have stopped too. And he was moving. I'd never realized until then just how much we move, even when we're standing still. Every tiny little motion he made caused him to shift his weight around, his foot lifting and pressing and rocking from side to side. *Stand still,* I silently begged. *Please stand still!*

I heard a lighter flick open and then shut. He was smoking, and chatting with his buddies, twisting this way and that to look at them. The pain was throbbing through me in great waves of purple and black, now. I could feel the sweat rolling down my face and I was sucking in quick, shuddering breaths through my nose.

"I figure we're almost on 'em," said the man. "And when we get 'em...shit, did you see the tits on that girl?" He let out a long, low whistle and the other men laughed. And then, as they smoked, they talked about what they wanted to do to me, and which of them would be first. I screwed my eyes tight and tried to shut it out. Next to me, I could feel Cal's body go hard with anger, ready to throw off the tarp and launch himself at them, and I squeezed his hand in panic: *don't*. He stayed tense but didn't move, holding himself back...just.

The man finished his cigarette and moved off. His foot lifted from my hand and there was a brief instant of relief followed by burning, searing pain as all the blood rushed back into the bruised flesh. They were still too close to risk a sound. I let the pain come out as hot, silent tears.

At last, their footsteps receded. Then Cal was moving, flowing effortlessly up from under the tarp and creeping silently forward, following the hunters into the lengthening shadows. Now *he* was behind *them*.

And hunting was what Cal did.

51

CAL

TRACKING HIM was easy. He was an amateur, the sort of guy who sits in his Washington office all year, then goes to the woods and sprays a thousand rounds in a day in the hope that he'll get lucky and hit something and can pose with the body of a deer for a photo. I could smell the stink of his cologne and the cigarette he'd just smoked, and he was making enough noise that I could have followed him with my eyes closed.

The problem was me. This wasn't like stalking an animal or even like stalking an enemy, in combat. This was personal. My body was shaking with rage and I had to force myself to be calm, to go slow, because what I wanted to do was to run at him and tear him apart. Lying there, hearing what he wanted to do to Bethany, was the hardest thing I'd ever done.

Well, now he'd pay. They all would.

I waited until he lagged behind his buddies by a few steps. Then I clapped a hand over his mouth and with my other arm choked him around the throat until he went limp. I lowered him to the ground without a sound and his friends never even noticed. I picked up his rifle and let out a long, slow sigh of satisfaction. *Let's see you try and take her from me now, you bastards.*

I crept back to Bethany and hugged her tight. Then I gently examined her injured hand. There was a lot of bruising and it looked like one of the fingers was broken, but she'd heal with treatment. I got out the first aid kit and strapped the broken finger to the one next to it. Then I took her face in my hands and just looked at her.

The sun was just sinking below the horizon and the last rays painted her black hair with amber and gold. Those big brown eyes looked up at me, still wet with tears but lit up with such steely determination. I couldn't imagine how much pain she must have been in. She was the bravest person I'd ever met. I bent down and kissed her. It was only supposed to be a quick kiss: we didn't have time for anything else. But as soon as my lips met hers, I was lost and I had to force myself to stop.

As the sun disappeared and the moon rose, I led her forward. The bastard who'd trodden on her hand had been in a group of three and the other two were still ahead of us.

We crept closer, Bethany moving as silently as I did. The other two had realized they'd lost their buddy and were calling for him. I raised my rifle and shot the first in the leg, the second in the arm. Given what they were involved in, I wouldn't have had much problem with shooting them right through the heart. But wounding them would tie up more men to help them limp back to the helicopter. I grabbed their rifles, threw one far off into the bushes, and gave the other one to Bethany.

Now there was no one in front of us. But watching through the trees, I saw another group of three behind us. *Dammit.* Beyond that, there was nothing: everyone else was either way behind or had spread off to the sides. There was an opening to escape, but we had to deal with these three first.

The moon went behind a cloud and I heard the hunters cursing as they peered into the blackness. *Maybe they'll go a different way.* I flattened myself against a tree and pulled Bethany hard against me, and we waited.

A river lay to the east of us. I heard the hunters wander that way and my hopes rose, but then they turned and headed back towards us. The sound of the river muffled their footsteps and I wasn't sure it was all of them, at first. Then they heard something move in the bushes and let off a flurry of shots, and I counted a rifle, a shotgun, and then the roar of an assault rifle. Three weapons. Three hunters. They were all moving straight towards us. My guts twisted. I'd have to ambush them, but this wasn't the same as the first three, when I'd been creeping up from behind. We'd be face to face. I wasn't sure I could take all three without them getting a shot off and in their panic, they might hit Bethany...

I thought desperately. What I had to do was get her somewhere I knew she'd be safe. The sound of the river made me look that way and an idea started to form. I knew this part of the forest and what I needed was just a few minutes away.

I led her to the river, keeping the hunters behind us. The river was only about ten feet across, but it ran along the bottom of a canyon, far too deep to climb down. And just a few hundred yards downstream, exactly where I remembered it, was a moss-covered log that formed a bridge across. It was the only way across the canyon for a few miles either way. And I knew all three hunters were behind us, on this side.

"What's the plan?" Bethany whispered.

I hesitated. The last thing I wanted to do was lie to her. But I knew she'd never agree to it and I had to protect her.

"We're going across there," I said, nodding at the log. "You go first."

She nodded and carefully sat down on the log, then inched her way across. When she was halfway, she looked back at me uncertainly.

"Go on," I told her. "I'm right behind you."

She nervously inched the rest of the way, then climbed off onto the opposite bank. She looked back at me in confusion. Then, when she saw me bend and pick up my end of the log, she went pale. "No!" she hissed. "What are you—"

I heaved the log around and let it fall into the river. There was an almighty splash and I heard shouts of surprise from the hunters. Bethany stared at me, horrified and scared.

"It's okay," I told her. "They're all on my side and they can't get across, now. You're safe."

"*Cal!*" she begged.

"I'll come back for you, when I've dealt with them," I told her. And then I ran, drawing them away from her. The last thing I saw was her agonized face, mouth open and pleading in a silent *no.*

I prayed I was doing the right thing.

52

CAL

I DREW THEM UPSTREAM, then found a fallen tree and lay flat on my belly, my rifle resting on the trunk. I went utterly still and waited for the first one to appear.

I knew Bethany would be upset and probably angry. Well, that was fine. There'd be all the time in the world to deal with that, once we were in Canada. Hell, I'd buy her roses and chocolates. Or shoes, that's what city girls went nuts for, right? She could be as pissed at me as she wanted, as long as she was safe.

The first one showed himself a few seconds later, an easy target. But I waited until the second one was in view, too, so he wouldn't have time to run. Then I fired two quick shots, hitting one in the shoulder and one in the hip. They fell to the ground screaming in pain and I waited for number three.

And waited.

And waited.

I lay there, adrenaline pumping through my veins, finger on the trigger. *Where the hell is the third one?*

I slowly rose and advanced, rifle up. I went over to the first hunter, who was rolling and cursing in pain, and kicked his rifle away. Then I approached the second.

Shit. He was carrying a rifle *and* a shotgun. He must have been taking potshots with both of them. What I thought were three hunters behind us had only been two. But I'd seen three in the group. Where was the third?

A rifle shot echoed through the trees and I spun to face where it came from. A fist clenched tight around my heart. I wanted to be wrong, but I knew I wasn't.

The shot had come from the far side of the river. One of the hunters must have crossed over before I sent Bethany over there. She was all alone with him. And, now that I'd pushed the log into the river, I couldn't get to her. *Oh Jesus, please no....*

I raced to the river and stood there panting, looking up and down its length, praying I'd see something, but it was just as I remembered it: there was no other bridge in sight.

For three beats of my heart, I stood there frozen, staring into the darkness, going sick with fear. She needed me and I couldn't get to her.

Then I turned and started to run. But the nearest crossing was at least a few miles away.

I wasn't going to get to her in time.

53

BETHANY

I WATCHED CAL turn and sprint away into the trees and it was like having part of me torn away, leaving me raw and exposed. As his footsteps faded, it went eerily quiet. The woods seemed to expand around me and the feeling I'd had when I first arrived, of being tiny and lost in their vastness, came rushing back.

Then I felt guilty for being scared. I was safe, thanks to him. He was the one who'd have to fight the hunters...alone. Icy fear sluiced through me and I stared at the last place I'd seen him, wishing him back. It was three against one. I knew how good Cal was, but what if one of the hunters got off a lucky shot? What if he got shot and I wasn't there to help him? I wanted to scream at him, pummel him in the chest. *Why? Why did you do this?*

But I knew why. He'd done it to protect me, just like he'd been doing right from the start. I'd be okay: I just had to do my part by not panicking and we'd be back together soon.

I moved just far enough from the river that a hunter on the far bank wouldn't see me. Then I found a fallen tree and sat down. After a moment, I thought to look in the backpack Cal had given me: everything had happened so fast at the cabin, I wasn't sure what he'd put in there.

I found a bottle of water, a flint and steel for starting fires, some energy bars, and a first aid kit. I pressed my lips together tight, my chest dissolving into warmth and then imploding into an aching, tight center. He'd made sure I could survive on my own. Not just the supplies, but what he'd taught me. He'd known there might come a time when we had to separate, when he sacrificed himself and I went on alone—

Don't think like that. He'd be back. Everything would be fine.

To try to take my mind off it, I ate an energy bar and drank some of the water. I wished Rufus was there. I was glad he was safe, back at the cabin, but being out here without him felt wrong. Right now, ruffling his fur and feeling him push himself up against me would be very, very welcome—

A noise, off in the distance. I froze, listening. A rustle, as if someone had pushed through some undergrowth. What scared me, was, it had sounded like it came from off to the left, as if there was someone else on this side of the river. *That's impossible.*

I sat there stock-still, listening. But there were no more sounds. I slowly relaxed. It must have been the wind, or a rabbit or a squirrel or—

The snap of a twig, definitely from the left, this time. I scrambled to my feet, stuffing everything back in the backpack and swinging it onto my back. Then I ducked behind a tree, putting it between me and the source of the sounds, and pressed myself to the trunk so hard I could feel my heart slamming. I stared into the darkness, willing the forest to remain still. Nothing happened for five seconds, ten. Maybe I was wrong....

A figure, moving slowly between the trees. A man, a rifle gripped in his hands. He was staying low, head swiveling to check in every direction...and he was creeping directly towards me.

I ducked back behind the tree. *How? How is that possible?!* Cal had said all three of them were on his side! I tried not to panic. I just had to stay ahead of him, cross back over the river and find Cal—

My stomach dropped as I remembered. The log over the river was gone. I was trapped over here...with him.

I peeked around the tree again. At first, I couldn't see him. Then he appeared and my throat closed up in panic: he was so much closer! And this time, as the moonlight lit up his face, I recognized him. It was the attorney general.

I had to move. I had to move *now*. If I ran, he'd hear me. I had to move like Cal taught me, quick and silent.

I started moving, but it was much more difficult, in the dark. I couldn't see where I was putting my feet. If I didn't want to make a noise, I had to test the ground each time I put a foot down. And that slowed me.

I went as fast as I dared. But I could hear him gaining.

54

CAL

I WAS RUNNING flat-out, crashing through the undergrowth and ramming branches out of the way with my forearms. I didn't care about making noise. In fact, I *wanted* to make noise, I wanted to draw the attention of the bastard on the other side of the river, make him focus on me instead of on Bethany. I was running close to the bank, hoping that he'd see me and start taking shots at me across the river. But there was no sign of him and that meant he must be deep in the trees. Hunting her.

I pushed myself even faster, my arms pumping and my thighs screaming. But the nearest crossing point was still a mile away and once I crossed, I'd have to run all the way back. I was going to be too late.

I made a decision and skidded to a stop. Then I stared at the river in breathless panic and tried to think.

It was way too wide to jump across. The canyon walls were too steep to climb. But some of the trees had branches that extended out over the water. Maybe...

I hunted around until I found what I was looking for: a cluster of trees where the branches from my side almost touched the branches from the other. The problem was, the trees around here were bigtooth maples and river birches. The trunks were sturdy enough but the branches were spindly. Fine for a kid, but I weigh almost three hundred pounds. I'm built for strength, not acrobatics.

But I didn't have a choice. I swarmed up the trunk and started out along the thickest branch I could find. At first, it was fine. By the time I was over the edge of the canyon, though, it was starting to creak. I went full-length and hauled myself forward, trying to spread my weight. What I needed to do now was go slow, plan each move. But I couldn't afford to go slow. Not when she was trapped over there with a hunter.

I climbed higher, and further out. I was making progress but the branches went from the thickness of my upper arm to the thickness of my wrist. They were bending under my weight and the creaks were constant, now. When I looked down, the canyon was a pitch-black void, right below me. If I fell now....

Ahead of me, the branches became twigs and brushed the twigs of the branches of the trees on the other side, like two lovers leaning out from balconies and touching fingertips. The twigs wouldn't support me. I'd climbed as far as I could. There was only one thing left to do.

I grabbed a branch above me for balance and rose up to a crouch. The branch was slender enough that I had to put one foot in front of the other and even then, only the middle of my boots were in contact with the wood. The branch didn't like the shift in weight. It creaked and the creak didn't stop, building and rising. I hesitated for a second. I had to choose: fall to my stomach and shimmy back to safety or—

I glanced down. The canyon was like an open mouth, ready to swallow me.

But she needed me.

I grunted, pushed off hard, and leaped. I flew through the air like the world's heaviest, least agile monkey. The branch I was aiming for rushed up to meet me—

And then passed me, rushing upwards as I fell. I'd missed it by six inches. I plummeted, crashing through leaves and twigs, frantically reaching for—

My hands found a branch but it was too thin. It bent and then snapped and I tumbled again, swinging off to the side. My hands clawed at the air—

My hip hit something solid and I bounced and then slithered past it, the bark lifting my shirt and drawing blood from my skin. Just as I passed it, I managed to hook an arm around it and—

With a jolt and a creak, I stopped. I was dangling from one arm on the very lowest branch of the tree on the far side. I hauled myself up, got my legs onto the branch, and panted in relief. Then I crawled along it all the way to the trunk and finally I climbed down onto the far bank. As soon as my feet hit the ground, I was running, heading back along the river to where I'd left her. *Hold on*, I willed her. *Hold on, Bethany, I'm coming.*

55

BETHANY

H E WAS ALMOST ON ME. The problem was that I had to go slow to avoid making noise, but he could just push forward as fast as he liked. He might come from the city but he'd obviously done some hunting before because he was methodical, sweeping his rifle around to check a wide fan in front of him. I was pretty sure that he didn't know I was there: he was just following a plan, or a hunch, checking this side of the river. But any second, I'd slip up and make a sound, and then he'd have me. Either he'd shoot into the trees and wound or kill me, or he'd hold me at gunpoint and call for the others. And then....

The panic drained my strength and made my muscles weak and shaky. I was prey again, a mouse running for cover, feeling the chill of the hawk's shadow. *It can't end like this.* I was trying to breathe quietly but when I thought about him catching me, about them holding me down while they— My breathing went ragged and I blundered on with tears filling my eyes. *This can't be it.* I was meant to have the same rights as them, they shouldn't be able to do this—

And then the rifle slung on my back bumped against me, reminding me it was there.

I stopped and stood there, frozen. Then I slowly turned around and looked towards the rustling foliage behind me.

No. No, Jesus, I couldn't.

But if I didn't, he was going to— And this is why Cal had trained me. He'd known this might happen.

It's murder. I hadn't even been able to shoot a deer.

I unslung the rifle and held it in numb fingers. What he was going to do to me, he'd already done to other women. He'd do it again and again. Him and men like him, the club...they'd been doing this for hundreds of years. They'd keep doing it...unless someone stopped them.

I crept over to a tree and got behind it, leaning out just enough to see. I went through the steps Cal had taught me, checking the rifle was loaded, taking the safety off. As if I was shooting at a paper target. It didn't feel real.

I pushed the stock against my shoulder and squinted down the sights. Found the place where the branches were rustling, glimpsed a shadow beyond them. Another breath and the shadow became a figure. Another breath and the figure was a man, creeping towards me, and suddenly it *was* real, I was aiming at a living, breathing person and oh God, I couldn't. The sights wavered as my hands shook, tracing a path between his collarbone and his navel. Drops of sweat were running down my forehead and into my eyes, making them sting. *No. No, I can't do this.* I imagined the bullet punching into him, ripping into flesh and bone. My finger flinched away from the trigger. *I can't.*

Then I thought of the other women at the mansion. The nine others going to Russia with Ralavich plus however many were there for the other men to "enjoy." All the other women in call centers and warehouses who'd get into a black Mercedes on the promise of a better job and awaken to marble floors and chandeliers and a pack of hungry men who were too powerful to stop. If I got to Canada, I might be able to help them. But only if I escaped.

The sights steadied. He was so close, now, I could see the thread pattern on his camouflage coveralls. My finger found the trigger. I took a deep breath—

The attorney flew sideways through the air as if he'd been hit by a truck. Except it wasn't a truck that had hit him. Cal had charged in from the side and slammed into him, taking him right off his feet. They crashed to the ground together, the attorney general's rifle clattering to the ground. My whole body wilted in relief.

That's when the attorney general pulled out the knife.

He was much smaller than Cal and nowhere near as strong, but they'd rolled so that the attorney general was on top and Cal had to use both hands to force the blade away. And Cal's rifle was still on his back, trapped awkwardly beneath him. I brought my rifle up again. But they were rolling and twisting around. What if I shot the wrong one? I cursed, lowered the rifle, and ran towards them.

Any other time, the attorney general wouldn't have stood a chance. But Cal was panting and heaving for breath: he must have run here, giving it everything he had. And the wound in his shoulder had weakened that arm. Meanwhile, the attorney general had the extra strength of a man fighting for his life. He was trying to force the knife down to Cal's face and the blade was twitching and shaking as Cal's strength failed—

I swung my rifle around and hit the attorney general in the side of the head with the stock. He slumped sideways, unconscious.

Cal and I looked at each other. I let the rifle fall from my hands. And then I was throwing myself full-length on top of him, my arms wrapped around him and my face buried in his chest. He put his arms around me and it was the best feeling in the world, like cuddling up to the world's biggest, warmest teddy bear, one who could hug you back.

"I thought I lost you," he told me, the words rumbling through me from his chest.

I couldn't speak. I just nodded.

"Thought I was keeping you safe," he said, crushing me to him. "I'm sorry."

I nodded again. "Is it over?" I said into his chest.

He gently pushed me back so that he could look into my eyes. "Yeah," he said firmly. "I got the other two. That's everybody who was close to us. The others are way back. We can slip away, if we go now."

He helped me to my feet and passed me my rifle. Then he took my hand and as soon as his fingers wrapped around mine, I knew everything was going to be alright. He looked around, getting his bearings, and then we were moving, leaving the river behind and disappearing into the vastness of the landscape. Now we were together, the woods didn't feel scary. They felt like our territory, somewhere we could lose the outsiders.

We went at a fast walk for over three hours. The hunters knew the rough direction we'd taken but they'd still have to search a wide triangle either side of it and with every step we took, those triangles expanded. In a clearing surrounded by massive pines, Cal finally called a halt. "No way they've tracked us all this way," he told me. "Not those guys. We should rest."

I nodded gratefully and slumped down on my ass on the ground, and he sat down beside me. We were sitting on a carpet of soft pine needles and the pine trees formed a wall around us: we couldn't see more than ten feet in any direction. They deadened sound like a theater curtains: it was so quiet, we could hear our breathing and the slow creak of the trees as the wind played with them. All around us, it was dark and still, and high above, a circle of starry sky was framed by the treetops. Despite being outside, it felt private.

I took a breath of cool night air and realized it was the first time I'd really stopped since that morning, when we'd gotten up early to go to Jacques. We'd hiked to the river, then the raft and the ambush and being taken off by Alik and Cal rescuing me and then racing *back* to the cabin, and then I'd barely had time to patch up Cal's wounds before Ralavich had arrived and we'd had to run for our lives. I took another breath, slower this time, and felt my stomach growl. Breakfast was a long, long time ago and I'd only had an energy bar since. I thought about digging in my backpack and finding another one and splitting it with Cal, but that required effort, and suddenly...I sighed and let myself slump sideways into the comforting solidness of his shoulder. As the adrenaline wore off, the exhaustion was hitting me, turning my limbs to lead. I wasn't sleepy, but I didn't want to move for a while.

Cal slipped his arm around me and drew me close. The top of his shoulder made the perfect pillow and I sighed in satisfaction. But I could feel him brooding and when I turned to look, he was staring off into the trees. "What is it?"

"There's some stuff you need to know," he said, not meeting my eyes. "What I was going to tell you back at the cabin. Why I'm out here."

I smoothed my hand over his back. "There's no rush," I told him. "I know it's hard. We could wait till we're in Canada, when things aren't crazy."

He finally looked across at me. "You're the finest woman I ever met," he told me. "And I need to know if—" He broke off and glared at the ground.

Need to know what?

He looked at me. "I need to know."

In that second, he was more open, more vulnerable, than I'd ever seen him. I saw the pain I'd glimpsed before but something else, too. Guilt. Aching, soul-deep guilt that had been eating at him this whole time. My stomach knotted. He'd done something, and he needed to tell me so that he could find out if I still loved him. What if it was something I couldn't get past?

What if this was the end?

Part of me didn't want to know. *Can't we just carry on like this?* But I'd sworn that I'd help him. I could see how hard it was for him to tell me. I had to do my part and listen.

I reached out, took his hand, and nodded.

And he told me.

56

BETHANY

"It started in Afghanistan," he said. He shuffled around so that he was sitting facing me. The only light was from the circle of moonlit sky high above and deep shadows covered most of his face. Only those beautiful blue eyes gleamed in the darkness. He'd turned, I realized, because he wanted to look me in the eye when he told me.

"The Marine Raiders had done a whole slew of missions with these...well, they called them *intelligence personnel,* or *specialists.* But we all knew they were CIA. Sometimes, we'd have to escort them somewhere dangerous or keep watch while they met a contact. Sometimes, we'd have to help them capture a suspect, and it would get messy. Anyway, one time, I'm with a couple of these spooks and a couple of guys from my unit, and the CIA guys are meant to be meeting with some contact, up in the mountains, to get information. Only it turns into an ambush, and our vehicle gets shot up. We have to run on foot into the mountains and hide. No radio coverage, satellite phone is still in the car, so we got no backup. We have to get to the nearest friendly village on foot, while the bad guys try to find us."

"So I take charge. It takes us three days but I get everyone home safe, just—" He looked around at the dark woods and shrugged. "Y'know."

I did know. Just *doing what he did.* Navigating so easily in the wilderness. Knowing how to move silently and hunt for food. Avoiding and outwitting the people hunting them, just as he'd done tonight. Those people couldn't have asked for a better guide.

"Anyway, we get home, they give me a damn medal and I figure that's the end of it. But a few weeks later, a new CIA guy turns up at the base and asks for me. Asks me if I want to serve my country. And...." He stopped for a second and sat there brooding, searching for the right words.

I still had hold of his hand. I squeezed to let him know I understood. This big, gentle giant had *always* wanted to serve, just like his dad. I felt Cal relax a little.

"I ask the guy why me, and what they want me to do. And he says they need someone who can operate on their own, who can be dropped off a long way from the mission area and make their own way there on foot, undetected, and who's a marksman. And...well, I'm kinda unsure, because I feel like..."—he sighed—"The guys in my unit...they're like family, y'know?" He looked at the ground, embarrassed. "Not sure I *want* to be on my own."

I nodded. Cal was used to surviving on his own, going on long hunting trips on his own. He could be on his own for hours or days, when that would make more social animals like me go crazy. People who didn't know him—like this CIA guy—assumed that meant he didn't need people at all, but they were dead wrong. We all need people around us, sometimes. The difference between someone like me and someone like Cal is that I'd seek out company before I got too lonely. But a stoic, fiercely loyal soldier like Cal...put him on his own and tell him it's necessary and he'd accept it stoically...and slip slowly into isolation. What was heartbreaking was that after losing his dad and being on his own in the city, Cal had finally found exactly what he needed in the Raiders: a close-knit group of guys he really cared about. And this CIA guy had ripped him away from all that.

"So I say no," said Cal, still staring at the ground. "I want to help, but it feels like I'm right where I should be."

"But something changed your mind?" I asked quietly.

"The CIA guy, he leans in close, and he says, *Caleb*—no one ever calls me Caleb—*we need your help.*" And he tells me they're tracking people, around the world, people who are planning to do really bad shit. He says there are hundreds of thousands of Americans who don't realize how much danger they're in. Who are *dead*, if these guys get their hands on a nuke or a dirty bomb." He let out a shuddering sigh and looked right at me. "He says *they need someone to protect them.*"

My chest ached. I knew Cal. I knew that deep, protective urge that lived inside him. That had been all the CIA guy had needed to say...and maybe he'd known that.

"So I become a specialist, working for the Central Intelligence Agency," said Cal. "Three weeks later, they send me on my first mission, in Pakistan. Set me down ten miles from where I need to be, with a map and a rifle and some rations. Twenty-four hours later, I'm looking at a guy through the scope of my rifle as he goes outside for a smoke. He's the head of a cluster of terrorist cells, he's already organized an attack on an airport, an embassy bombing, he's planning more. So I line him up and I pull the trigger."

He looked right into my eyes. "No capture. No arrest or trial. I just kill him, like I've been ordered to."

I slowly nodded.

"There are more. In Yemen, Afghanistan, Iraq, Iran. All people plotting attacks. Twelve men, over about six months. And then they send me to Panama." His voice slowed. "The target's a private airfield, out in the middle of nowhere. I'm in the trees, watching this plane arrive, and...something doesn't feel right. Terrorists don't fly around in private jets." His eyes were distant, remembering. "The jet taxis to a stop and the door opens. A guy appears at the top of the stairs and...he's in a *suit,* carrying a briefcase. I check the photo they've given me. Definitely the right guy. And I realize that they haven't told me much about this guy, other than this might be the only chance to get him. But there's no one I can ask, I'm out there on my own, out of contact. So I line up the shot and I take it."

"He drops his briefcase as he dies and it goes bouncing down the steps and as it hits the runway, it springs open. It's full of money. Must be hundreds of thousands of dollars. The engines are still spinning and all the banknotes get blown around, the air turns *green.*" He inhaled, long and slow. "When I get back, I ask the CIA guy, who was that guy? And they say, he was a banker, he was moving money for the terrorists." Cal shook his head. "And I stew over it, for days, because it doesn't feel right. But eventually, I tell myself, these people need money to recruit, to buy weapons, to buy bombs and fake passports. If the guy had been supplying them with plutonium, would I have had a problem with it?" He sat there silently for a moment, his thick forearms resting on his knees, brooding. "So...I carry on."

I listened, a sick fear building. I squeezed his hand and I wasn't sure which of us I was reassuring.

"There are more, around the world," said Cal. "Libya. Turkey. Albania. They don't tell me who they are, they just give me a time, a location and a photo. Sometimes, I see a crate of guns, and I'm like...okay, these are bad people. But sometimes, it's drugs. And I ask questions and the CIA say, *you gotta look at the big picture,* because some of these people sell drugs to raise money for terror operations. But I'm thinking...isn't this stuff criminal, not terrorism? Shouldn't the FBI or Interpol or someone be doing this, shouldn't these people be being arrested, not—" His throat closed up. "*Murdered,*" he spat out at last. "But I wanted to help. I wanted to protect the people back home. I figured my bosses knew what they were doing. So I stopped asking questions."

"The months go by, and now, sometimes, I finish the job and I haven't seen anything at all: no guns, no drugs, not even cash. I walk away and I have no idea who I've just killed, or why. But I don't ask." He said it wretchedly. "I've *stopped asking.*"

"Because you were loyal," I said gently. "Because you trusted them."

He looked right at me, those blue eyes hiding nothing. He wanted me to know the truth. Needed me to. "Because I was afraid of what I might find out."

I nodded. I could imagine him, stumbling down the path they'd led him on, afraid to look over his shoulder and see how far he'd come.

"I didn't...." he began. "I couldn't...." He closed his eyes for a second and gave a low growl of frustration. His whole body seemed to throb with tension. "I didn't have anyone to—I was on my own, in this little apartment in the city, waiting for the next call. I knew that things were wrong, but I didn't know what to do."

I leaned closer, squeezing his hand, and put my other hand on his shoulder.

"Then...one time," he said, "I'm in Colombia. Creep through the jungle to the target and it's this big white mansion, in the middle of nowhere, with guards and a high wall around it. It's obvious that this guy must be part of a drug cartel. I don't like it, but I pull the trigger. Kill him while he's on his balcony, silenced shot, his guards won't even find him 'till morning. I'm just packing up to leave when I get a call on the radio. There's an SUV heading for the mansion and it's the brother of the guy I just killed, some bigshot who they've been trying to get for years. No matter what, I have to intercept the SUV and kill him."

"So I race through the jungle, find a bend in the road and lie in wait. The SUV shows up: big black thing, probably with bulletproof windows, too, but I know they won't stop a sniper round. As it comes up to the bend, I put one right through the windshield, right into the chest of whoever's driving. It swerves, goes full speed into a tree. I figure the guy's going to have bodyguards so I put more rounds through the windows: *one, two, three, four, five.* Six shots in all. Then I wait. Nothing moves. The car's burning."

"I walk closer, to check he's dead. Even ten feet away, I can't see because the windows are tinted. I go to the driver's door, pull it open. And the guy who was driving, this bigshot, he's dead. But in the passenger seat, there's—" He swallowed. "A woman. His wife. She's still alive but she's taken one in the chest and she's coughing up blood, and I've seen enough to know she's only got seconds. But she's not trying to save herself. She's trying to turn around."

Oh God. Oh God, no.

"I run to the back of the car and pull open the door. And there are —" He swallowed again. "Bethany, there are three children. All under ten."

Oh Jesus. My hands were over my mouth. *Please no.*

"I check them all, praying that one of them will be okay. I look up and the wife, she's craning round in her seat, and she doesn't even look angry with me, she's just begging, *begging* with her eyes, for me to tell her that one of her kids is still alive. But I shake my head. I see tears start to run down her cheeks and then she dies, too."

"I stumble back from the car. I get on the radio and I tell them there's been a mistake, the guy's family was in the car and—" He broke off and squeezed his eyes shut, his teeth clenched in rage. It was several seconds before he could speak. "*They just went quiet.* It wasn't a mistake. They knew damn well there were kids in the car. They just saw it as collateral damage and they thought I'd see it the same."

I wanted to throw up. "Oh God...."

"It was like I was waking up. Realizing what I'd become." He opened his eyes and looked right at me. "A monster."

I shook my head in horror, but I didn't know what to say. They'd taken this gentle giant, with all his hunting skills and bravery, and exploited him, used him as a weapon for their own needs, without any thought for what it would do to him. "You didn't know," I whispered. "You couldn't have known. It's not your—"

"I should have said no," he spat. "I should have got out. I should have asked questions, long before." He glared at me, but all the anger was turned inward.

I stared at him helplessly. All he'd ever wanted to do was serve his country. Those bastards had seen that patriotism when they recruited him and used it. Hell, that was probably part of *why* they recruited him. "Cal," I began. But I didn't know what to say.

"I'm standing there by the SUV," he said. "Just...numb. Wondering what I'm going to do because I can't believe *what I've done*. My radio's buzzing, the CIA want me the hell out of there before anyone comes along and finds me there, but I can't move."

"And then...I hear something. A little whine, from the backseat. And I know that all the kids are dead, but I lean inside the SUV again and down by their legs, there's something wriggling, wrapped in a blanket, too low to the floor for the bullets to have hit. I pull it out and unwrap it and I'm holding a little fluffy German Shepherd puppy."

"Rufus," I breathed.

"The parents must have taken the kids to buy him, just before they took them to visit their uncle. I stare at this little guy and I know that he'll die if I just leave him there to wander off into the jungle. And I'm not letting anyone else die. I need my hands for my rifle so I open up the top of my shirt and sit him in there, against my chest, with his head poking out, and I haul ass out of there. When I get to the extraction point, the CIA pilot tells me to leave it behind, and I just—I *glare* at him until he backs down. I guess that's the first time I did it. I keep the little guy with me all through two choppers and two flights, all the way back to the US."

"We get home and the dog looks around at this new home in a new country and he just looks... lost. I know how it feels. I give it one of my old shirts to play with and he loves it: he's small enough to go down the sleeves like a kid in a play tunnel and he does that over and over until he finally falls asleep. But I don't sleep. I'm seeing the faces of those kids, over and over."

"The next morning, it's raining. I take the dog out with me, and we go to the store to buy dog food and a lead and stuff..." He swallowed. "Everyone's...*normal*. And they think I'm normal, I have 'em fooled, but inside I'm—" He closed his eyes. "The girl on the checkout smiles at me and I want to yell at her, *don't you know what I did?!* And every time I see children, I'm—I can see their faces, I can feel their necks, under my fingers, as I check for pulses that aren't there...."

Silent tears were rolling down my cheeks. I leaned forward and put my hands on Cal's shoulders. I didn't know what to say to make it better but I needed him to know I was there.

"I get outside, start walking home...and everywhere, there's just people, normal people, and they don't realize there's a monster right there, walking next to them. I've killed a family. I've killed *children*. And the other ones...the people I assassinated. How many of them were innocent, just people the CIA decided were *inconvenient*? I'm crossing a bridge over a highway and the next thing I know, I've stepped up onto the parapet."

I stared at him in horror, unable to speak.

"I'm standing there, with the traffic roaring past below, and I'm thinking, *do it,* because I don't deserve to be in this world, anymore. And then I hear this little bark. I've dropped the puppy's lead, but it hasn't run away. It's just sitting there looking up at me and I think...who's going to take care of him if I do this?"

"And so I climb down, and I pick up the lead, and I figure out a different way. I go back to my apartment, pack a bag, empty my bank account. The dog picks up the shirt I gave him in his teeth: I guess it's his, now. And then we just walk out...and keep walking."

"You just...*left?*" I asked.

"I just left," he said. "Slept rough. Hunted for food. Kept going and going, getting further and further from the cities, from people, until I reached the woods. Found the spot where the cabin is, used all my savings to buy the land." He looked around him. "Monsters belong in the woods."

It was the most heartbreaking thing I'd ever heard. I flew at him and flung my arms around his neck. "*No!*" I told him. "Jesus, Cal, no! You're not a monster. It wasn't you. You were just trying to protect people."

He was stiff and unyielding under me. "Doesn't bring that family back, though, does it?"

I rested my head against his. "No," I admitted.

"You know why I was in Seattle, that day I met you?" he asked. He pushed me back just a little so that he could look at me. "I had a friend,

in the CIA...or as close to a friend as you can get, in that place. Shawn
Lox. Good guy. Military, same as me, except he was Airborne. They had
him doing what I did. He woke up and got out about the same time I
did." He looked away, off into the trees. "Except...he didn't go into the
woods, he crawled into a bottle. Wound up driving to a military base at
three in the morning, drunk out of his mind, screaming outside the
gate about the things he'd done. They were about to arrest him when
he pulled a gun and shot himself. It made the papers, even in Marten
Valley. I was in Seattle for the funeral, to say goodbye." He shook his
head and looked at me. "I don't know if there's any coming back, for
people like Shawn and me. I want you. I want to come with you to
Canada," he said. "I want...*this. Us.* But after what I did..."

"Isn't that for me to decide?" I demanded. I got to my feet. "Isn't
that why you're telling me all this? So there aren't any secrets, so I can
decide for myself?"

He sat there looking up at me, shocked. Then slowly nodded.

I've never been more sure of anything in my life. "Then, Cal, I've
decided! I want you. I need you. You—You put your arms around me
and I feel *safe.*"

He looked away. "But I'm a—"

"No! No, you're not. Maybe you *were.* Maybe, for those few years,
when they were using you, you *were* a monster. But not anymore." I
crouched down. "Look, I can't say it's okay. I can't undo what you did.
But you can't change who you were, who they made you. You *can*
change who you are."

He shook his head. "After what I did—"

"You can still make it right. I don't think anyone's beyond
redemption."

He looked up at me. For all his strength and size, at that moment,
he looked like a scared kid.

"Really," I confirmed. "But you can't do it out here." And I reached
down and offered him my hand.

He sat there staring at me for a moment and I saw a change come
over him. He seemed to lift. It wasn't that the pain was gone: he'd

carry that with him forever, and maybe he had to. But he had something else, now. He had hope.

He gripped my hand and I pulled him to his feet, nearly overbalancing. After sitting for so long, he looked even taller than normal, towering over me. Or maybe he was standing taller, now. He looked around at the forest, glanced up at the sky, took a deep lungful of air as if experiencing it all for the first time. Then he looked at me.

And for the first time, he was free. Those cornflower-blue eyes sparkled in the moonlight, eating me up, and instead of hiding it, or turning away, or scowling, it just went on and on, making my heart lift and bob and that silver string inside me draw tight and sing.

He closed the gap between us with two quick steps that shook the ground, then he scooped his hands under my ass and I yelped as I was suddenly lifted skywards. He stood with me clinging to him, my legs around his waist, and in the quiet stillness of the night, we just stared at each other. Both of us slowly realizing that there was nothing holding us back, anymore.

When he spoke, that iron certainty was back. "I'm gonna get you to Canada," he told me. "We'll get Jacques to bring Rufus. I'll build us a place to live. And no one's going to take you away from me, ever. Sound good?"

I couldn't speak. So I just nodded, very, very firmly.

And then I couldn't speak anyway because he was kissing me.

57

BETHANY

STRAIGHTAWAY, it was different. The storm clouds that had always gathered around him whenever he came close were gone and he was on me full force. I gave a little mewl of shock and delight as that hard upper lip spread me wide and left me helpless and his tongue plunged deep.

My hands came up and traced the muscles of his back through his soft cotton shirt. The kiss grew and built, the world spinning around me as his lips owned me, each hard press sending earthquakes down through my body, crumbling me, making me dissolve in his arms. His strength and size had always made me go weak but this was something else: he was finally unleashed to do exactly what he wanted and what he wanted was to make me his. His hands on my ass were squeezing and rubbing, teasing me with what was to come, and every time my breasts stroked across his chest through our clothes, he'd let out a low growl.

I felt like I was flying. Part of me had just surrendered. Something in him, in that raw, hard lust, had triggered something in me, making me go melty and soft with shocking speed. But at the same time, something else was happening. His hands, his lips, the feel of him against me...they were setting off explosions of pink, hot pleasure,

making me tremble and sigh. But the explosions had a silver edge to
them, and each kiss, each rub of his pecs against my nipples, made
that silver crackle down my body, the sensations twisting together
and becoming an aching need as they hit my groin. With each hard
press of his lips, my hands moved faster on his back, desperate to
know him, to touch every hard inch of him.

He broke the kiss and I felt us start to move. He walked with me
in his arms and each big, earth-shaking stride he took bounced me,
making my groin stroke along the washboard of his abs and my
nipples drag along the hard curves of his chest. My breathing
tightened and I clung to him, burying my face in his neck and
planting kisses there. I didn't know where he was going but I didn't
open my eyes. I trusted him.

He crouched and laid me down on my back on something soft. I
finally opened my eyes to see him kneeling over me, gazing down
into my eyes. Beyond him, the silhouettes of treetops rocking in the
breeze, inky black against a deep blue sky that was speckled with a
billion silver pinpricks.

He gazed down at me. "You're the most beautiful damn thing I've
ever seen."

I drew in my breath but before I could respond to that, he was
kissing me. Slower, this time, but no less possessive, and as his tongue
found mine and danced with it, I moaned. I felt my shirt lift away
from my breasts and the buttons being popped through their holes
until he could spread the sides like wings. Then I felt his hands on
my jeans and I swallowed, my breathing speeding up. One button
popped. Two. Three. I opened my eyes and saw him kneeling there,
eyes locked on my groin and the panties that were slowly being
revealed. The store in Marten Valley had been stocked with basics so
they were plain white cotton briefs, not some weapon of mass
seduction made of lace and air. But Cal was gazing down at them as if
they were the sexiest things they'd ever seen, his eyes blazing in a way
that made me crush my thighs together and squirm.

He undid my boots and pulled them off. Then he hooked his
hands in the sides of my jeans and lifted me effortlessly up off the

ground so he could slide them down my legs, taking my socks with them. I dropped back to the ground, panting, my pale legs gleaming silver in the moonlight. I saw now that I was lying on a patch of moss, lushly green and springy. It was late and I should have been cold but when he hunkered down over me, straddling my half-naked body, all I could feel was a deep, violent heat thundering through my body, leaving me panting.

He moved in close, slid a hand under my shoulders, and brought me up to sitting, handling my body as if I weighed nothing. The open shirt fell from my shoulders. He leaned forward and kissed me full-on and savage, nibbling at my upper lip with his teeth, then kissing just my lower, an open-mouthed, breathless kiss that went on and on. I felt his other hand lift my tank top inch by inch until it was gathered under my arms. Then he broke the kiss just long enough to whip it over my head and off. He looked down and the way he drank in the sight of me, his chest rising and falling with heavy pants of lust, made the heat inside me tighten and throb.

He slid his hands up my naked back and unhooked the clasp of my bra, and I lifted my arms as if in a stupor so that he could get it off. *Am I really doing this?!* I'd never been naked outside, before and—

The bra came off and I gasped. I could feel the breeze playing over my sensitive flesh, caressing it, my nipples rising and tightening. I inhaled, smelling the trees, the earth, the endless sky above. It felt so freeing....

Then Cal hooked his thumbs in the waistband of my panties and slid them down my legs and off. As my legs rose to help him, I fell back...and then I was lying there on the ground, completely naked, feeling the outdoor air waft over every inch of my skin. I swallowed. It was heady, exciting, but I was more exposed than I'd ever been. I looked down at my curves uncertainly....

Then I looked up and saw how he was looking at me, and any last-minute insecurities melted away. He was gazing down at me almost reverently as if I was some goddess of the forest he'd stumbled upon while hunting. Then, as his eyes swept down my body, his breathing changed and those blue eyes gleamed as if he couldn't decide whether to worship me or ravish me.

He sunk his fingers deep into my hair, fingering the strands, then cupped my cheek in his palm. His thumb brushed my lips and I panted against it. Then the hand was moving down: over my throat, over my collarbone...he cupped my breast. I gasped and my toes pressed against the moss as he rolled it in his palm and then began to stroke and knead, sending silver streamers of pleasure arcing down to my groin and making my hips rise and circle in time with what he was doing.

He dipped his head and I cried out as my hard nipple was enveloped in heat and wetness, his tongue lashing over it and circling around and around. My heels braced against the ground and my back arched, my hands going up to grab his shoulders and then tangle in his hair. The feel of those rough, powerful fingers squeezing and rubbing was already driving me crazy and now each swipe of his tongue sent an extra pulse of hot pleasure straight to my core. I began to pant, grinding my hips together, needing him.

He kept licking me, sucking more of my breast into his mouth, now, devouring me with lips and tongue as he growled low in his throat, a vibration that buzzed against my nipple. I could feel the tension in his hand as he fought to hold himself back, his touch becoming urgent and just the right kind of rough. Then suddenly, he couldn't wait any longer to explore more of me. His hand slid down my body, over my stomach, and then outwards, over my hip and down my thigh. Then it twisted inward and I groaned as it slid edge-on between my knees and upward. The edge of his hand kissed up against the softness of my lips and rocked there, knobbly and perfect, sending a ripple of heat slamming through me. My thighs closed tight for a second in response, trapping his hand. Then, as they relaxed, he twisted his wrist and easily pushed my thighs apart.

He cupped me there, fingers rubbing over lips that were already sticky and moist, and my breath caught. Without taking his mouth from my nipple, he looked up at me, watching my response as he plunged a thick finger up into me.

I bucked and trembled, rolling my hips up to meet him and arching my back off the ground. The firm, hot lashing of his tongue across my nipple, the hard, knobbly slide of his finger inside me...the sensations raced through my body and met, becoming one continuous throb of pleasure. I let out a high little cry and twisted around the finger, drawing a low groan from him as my satiny walls caressed him. With my legs open, he'd had to switch to straddling one of them, and that meant that I could feel the outline of his cock, hot and hard and straining against his jeans.

He finally lifted his mouth from my breast and the feel of the breeze on my spit-wet skin made me gasp. Then he was kissing me, hungry and quick, his tongue moving in the same rhythm as the finger in my pussy, and my body danced in response, my hands diving under his shirt to roam across his back and chest and my legs wrapping around his arm. The pleasure was twisting in on itself and building: tighter and tighter, hotter and hotter. I could feel myself slickly wet around his thrusting finger and I clawed at him, writhing, wanting him. When I couldn't take it anymore, I broke the kiss, barely escaping his chasing lips. "C—*Cal!*" I managed, panting.

He looked down at me, those cornflower-blue eyes hooded with lust. His finger slowed but still moved lazily inside me, throwing out pink blooms of pleasure edged in trembling silver each time it glided along my walls, its progress audible in the shudders of my breath. He knelt there, hulking over me, the hunter who'd captured his prey. The thought made me gulp and sent a dark spike of heat straight down to my core, boosting that needy ache even more. I stared up at him, pleading with my eyes. And he kissed my panting, desperate lips one last time and nodded.

He got to his feet and stripped off his shirt and then the white t-shirt beneath. He kicked off his boots and shed his jeans and shorts in one go. And then he stood towering over me, naked. His body was bathed in moonlight, each hard edge gleaming silver, each massive, solid curve shining as if he was carved from iron. Free of his clothes, he looked even wilder, even more part of nature. The beard, the

massive size of him, the huge pecs, and the brutal power contained in
that chiseled six-pack, he was a wild man, a barbarian of the finest.
He walked towards me and each heavy footstep vibrated through
the ground, making me bite my lip. He was big, but viewed from
down here, he was a giant. And lying at his feet, naked on the ground,
I felt like some village maiden laid out for him as an offering. My
groin twitched at the thought and my eyes went to his cock, the
shining head of it slapping against his abs with each step.

He knelt down, nudging my legs further apart, and I went weak.
There was something about the size of him, the way the width of his
hips forced me to open wider. He was gentle, kind...but physically, he
was a beast. And now, with nothing holding him back, I was about to
experience him unleashed.

He lowered himself atop me until his chest just brushed my
aching nipples. I felt the head of his cock nestle up against my
slickened pussy lips. His forearms pressed into the ground on either
side of my head and I swallowed, took a deep breath—

He drove into me in one long thrust, his muscled ass flexing and
pushing him deep, pressing me down into the earth. I cried out at
how good it felt: that long silken push, the hot girth of him stretching
me, and he let out a throaty groan at the feeling of filling me. His hips
drew back and then he was lunging forward again, plunging even
deeper into me, making me gasp and tremble. He pulled back again
and this time he pressed his elbows against the tops of my shoulders,
holding me in place. Then he plunged into me again and I rolled my
head back against the moss as he filled me completely.

We lay there panting for a few seconds. Then his hips started to
move again, a slow pumping that made me gasp and grab at the grass
with both hands. Each inward stroke squeezed the glowing pleasure
tighter, making it hotter and more needful. Each slow pull as he left
me was a sweet ache that made my toes dance and my hips roll,
urging him back.

He was taking his weight on his forearms and knees, taking care
not to crush me, but there was still something deliciously about
feeling his weight on me, being pressed down into the ground by it.

And the brute size of him as he rode me, his hips spreading my thighs wide apart, the huge hard curves of his pecs stroking against my breasts...the feeling of it as he slowly pumped me made me grind my ass in circles against the ground. And that in turn made him groan, and his slow pumping began to break down as he fought for control.

He frowned down at me and that stern mouth twisted into a lopsided grin. *Devilwoman! What are you doing to me?* And I flushed and smiled, embarrassed but delighted that I could do that to him. And did it some more.

Cal growled like, *well, fine, if that's what you want.* And he gave up on his slow rhythm and just fucked me. His cock pistoned into me, unstoppable, and I cried out and grabbed at his ass, running my hands over it. I could feel the hard smoothness of it, the dimples as it flexed, powering him into me. Thrust after thrust, compressing the pleasure inside me faster than I could release it, pushing me towards the brink.

He was slamming into me, now, his body slapping against mine, my pale body writhing and trembling under his much bigger, tanned one. I had my eyes closed and I'd forget, sometimes, that we were outdoors. Then the breeze would blow across us, heavenly cool against our heated flesh, and I'd remember and it would send a crackling burst of energy right down my spine and the pleasure would double, treble. It felt risky, dangerous, even though we were as private, out here, as it was possible to be. The heat compressed tighter and tighter, becoming a weighty, incandescent ball that begged for release.

He was getting close, too. His thrusts were rough, his breathing almost animal. I ran my hands over his hips and ass, up over his muscled back, loving the feel of him. He went faster, building to a peak, and I rocked my hips up to meet him—

Suddenly, he wrapped his arms around me, grabbed my ass, and started to get to his feet, taking me with him. I quickly slipped my arms around his neck and clung on. My eyes went wide as he came up to standing and I slid down him, bouncing against the root of him with each step he took. He carried me to a nearby tree and pressed my back against it to pin me there.

"Been wanting to do this," he growled, "since the first time I met you."

And he began to fuck me like that, holding me against the tree. I wrapped my legs around his waist and hung on to his shoulders and it was incredible. I was powerless, wedged between his muscled body and the unyielding trunk of the tree, so every thrust was deep and full, with no room to escape. And the feel of the rough bark against my back, the smell of the trees around us...it reinforced that we were in Cal's world. And *up against a tree* is exactly how he *should* fuck his woman.

His hands were free now, and he filled them with my breasts, squeezing the soft flesh and rubbing his thumbs across my nipples. That tight, hot ball of pleasure rocketed upward, heating my chest, my face, I was on the edge....

His thrusts built to a peak, his hips hammering between mine, and he kissed me, one hand squeezing a breast and the other sliding along my cheek and through my hair. He pushed deep and I cried out against his lips as the pleasure went *tight*...and then exploded. I shuddered and bucked as the orgasm ripped through me, and as I spasmed around him, he groaned and I felt him shoot jet after hot jet deep inside me.

I went limp in his arms, panting against his neck. He chuckled: a low, warm sound I hadn't heard before. He seemed lighter. Freer. "You're something else," he told me.

He let me gently down to the ground and then lifted my chin and we kissed again, long and tender.

"Well," said Ralavich from behind him. "Isn't this cozy?"

58

BETHANY

W E SPUN TO SEE Ralavich strolling out of the trees. By his side, his bodyguard Alik, an assault rifle pulled in tight to his shoulder and aimed right at us.

Cal shoved me protectively behind him. I huddled there, my brain going a million miles an hour, trying to catch up. *How? How did he find us?*

Ralavich grinned, enjoying our surprise. "Alik says that you're good. You almost lost him, a few times. He thinks that you are former military, perhaps. But Alik, you see, was *Spetsnaz*. Special Forces. And they know how to track someone."

Now it all made sense. I hadn't had time to think about it before, but now I wondered if that was how they'd found the smallholding. Had Alik tracked us all the way there?

Cal and Alik eyed each other. There was anger there but just a hint of respect, too. An acknowledgment that they were the same, in some way. Worthy opponents.

"Come out, Bethany," said Ralavich. "Let me see you."

When Cal said my name in his low, sexy rumble, it sent a warm ripple of heat through me. Hearing Ralavich say it was the exact opposite, a chilling violation. But I was worried that he might shoot Cal, just to make me comply.

I stepped sideways, into view. one arm protectively over my breasts, the other hand down over my groin. I crouched and reached for my shirt.

"Oh no," said Ralavich. "Don't bother putting your clothes on." He looked at Cal. "I only caught the end of your session, but I'll let you watch all of mine. Thank you for warming her up for me. I hope you didn't wear her out completely."

Cal gave a bellow of rage and ran at him. I saw Alik tense, the assault rifle aimed right at Cal's head. But Cal didn't stop until I got in front of him, both hands pressed against his chest. *"No!"* I begged him. "No, that's what he wants!"

Cal stood there panting, his eyes locked on Ralavich. I've never seen such an expression of raw hate.

Ralavich grabbed my shoulder and pulled me away from Cal, then pushed me towards the middle of the clearing, making me stumble. I turned to see him stalking towards me. *Oh Jesus.* This was really going to happen. And it was a thousand times worse than if it had happened at the mansion, because I knew what it would do to Cal.

Ralavich was only three steps away, now. "Lie down, you little bitch," he told me.

I stood there frozen, trying to cover myself again.

He was two steps away. *"Lie. Down,"* he ordered.

This can't be happening. This can't be the way it ends. Not after all this!

One step away. He was grinning. He *liked* the fact I hadn't complied, because it meant he got to hit me, instead.

Ralavich stepped right up to me and raised his hand.

And I felt that chip of diamond at the core of my soul. It was bigger, now, as if everything that had happened in the last few weeks had built it up, atom by atom.

I grabbed Ralavich's waist with both hands and brought my knee up between his legs as hard as I possibly could. There was a horribly intimate feeling of softness crushed against bone and then Ralavich was crumpling to the ground, his legs folding under him. He fell forward to his hands and knees and I had to jump back to avoid being crushed. Alik pointed his rifle at me, stepping back so that he could cover Cal as well. I raised my hands and froze.

On the ground, Ralavich was incapable of speech. I could hear him sucking in huge lungfuls of air but his breathing was ragged, as if even *that* hurt. When he finally managed to lift his head and look at me, it was as if all the blood in his body had gone to his ruined face. It was almost purple with rage and pain. "*You....bitch!*" he hissed. It took him nearly a minute to struggle to his feet. Then he staggered towards me and his arm whipped out, a move perfected by years of practice. I heard the sound first, the crack of his palm slamming into my cheek, hard enough to send me sprawling on the ground. Then the pain lit up the whole side of my face, stinging and throbbing and bringing tears to my eyes. I tasted blood, warm, and coppery.

I heard Cal slowly exhale. His eyes were locked on Ralavich and he was fighting for control, angrier than I'd ever seen him. His hands balled into fists and he leaned infinitesimally forward, ready to spring. But Alik had his rifle pointed at both of us. "Don't," I pleaded, my voice tight with pain. And Cal held back. Just.

"What do you want to do, boss?" asked Alik.

Ralavich's eyes bored into me. "Take them both back to the cabin," he rasped at last.

They let us dress, then they tied both of our hands and walked us all the way back to the smallholding, with Alik keeping a careful ten feet behind us the whole way, ready to shoot us if we tried to run. Ralavich brought up the rear, walking with difficulty and cursing.

By the time we reached the smallholding, the sky was growing lighter. The other members of the club were sprawled on the grass beside the helicopter, several of them nursing wounds. Even the attorney-general was there and he glared when he saw us, his hand going to the ugly bruise on the side of his head.

Ralavich had three of the guards from the mansion surround Cal. Then he jerked his head at the helicopter. "Everybody else in. We're going back to the mansion."

The other members of the club gratefully complied, the injured wincing and grumbling as they limped aboard.

Ralavich looked at the cabin. "Burn it," he told Alik.

"No!" I turned to Ralavich in panic. "Please!"

But he ignored me. Alik went into the cabin and we heard things being tossed around as he searched for flammables. Then the sound of trickling liquid: the kerosene we used in the lamps, being emptied over everything. Alik emerged, lit a match and held it ready—

"Please!" I begged. I looked at Cal, who was staring at Ralavich in brooding silence. "Please don't!"

Ralavich gave Alik the nod and he threw the match. There was a *wumf* and through the windows we could see the flames rush across the floor. I saw the bedding catch light. The curtains. Flames licked up the legs of the chairs and table Cal had made by hand. "No," I breathed.

In minutes, the fire had spread to the log walls and the whole building was ablaze. Cal lowered his head in defeat and a hand crushed my heart. *This is my fault!* Everything he'd built was being destroyed.

But Ralavich wasn't done.

"Make the man watch," he told Alik. "When there's nothing left, kill him."

Sheer panic erupted upward, icy and all-powerful, stealing my strength. "*No!*" I screamed. I ran right up to Ralavich, stumbling on legs that had suddenly gone weak, my hands still tied behind my back. "No, please! Please, I'll go with you! Please, I'll do whatever you want!" I hated the pleading tone in my voice. I knew that I was giving him what he wanted. But it didn't matter. I'd do anything to save Cal.

Ralavich looked at Cal, who had lifted his head and was glaring back at him defiantly. Then he looked down at me, as if considering. For a second, I dared to think that maybe, *maybe,* if I pleaded hard enough, I'd get through to him, that maybe there was some shred of humanity in him. I got down on my knees. "*Please!*" I begged. "Please."

"There was a dog," said Ralavich. "Where's the dog?"

I looked at him in horror, then looked around. Rufus was

nowhere to be seen. We'd left him sitting outside the cabin but he was nowhere in sight.

"Make sure you find it, before you leave," Ralavich told Alik. "And kill it too."

"*NO! No please!*" Tears were running down my cheeks, now. I saw Cal's body tense, his hands closing into fists. He stared at Ralavich, murder in his eyes, but bound and with three guns pointed at him, there was nothing he could do. The panic was filling me, rising up like arctic water, threatening to drown me. This was my fault. Because I'd dared to stand up to him, because I'd kneed him in the balls. If I'd just submitted, maybe he'd have left Cal alive, or spared Rufus.

Ralavich ignored me. "When it's done, call me and I'll send the chopper for you." Then he grabbed me around the waist and hauled me towards the helicopter. I was going back to the mansion. He'd use me, and then I'd be taken to Russia. It would be as if none of this had ever happened, as if I'd just submitted to him in the mansion instead of running. The only difference was, Cal and Rufus would be gone. Even the cabin would be destroyed. I'd ruined everything. The icy panic rose up over my chest, drowning me: I couldn't speak. "N—N—"

Ralavich looked down at me and grinned and that pushed me over the edge. I felt the fight drain out of me.

He'd won. He'd broken me.

"Give her something to make her sleep," he told one of the guards from the mansion. "She's been up all night. I want her rested and ready for me."

I glimpsed a hypodermic needle and then my head was being pulled to the side and held there, and I felt the needle jab into my neck. My muscles went floppy and I hung from Ralavich's arms like a ragdoll.

He lifted me aboard the helicopter. The three guards backed away from Cal, then they boarded too and the door slid closed. The rotors started to turn, kicking up loose grass and whipping the flames from the cabin sideways. My stomach lurched as we rose into the sky. The last thing I saw was Alik pushing Cal to his knees and moving to stand behind him, ready to execute him as soon as the cabin was just a ruin. Cal looked at me, agony in his eyes. *I'm sorry.*

No! I thought desperately, *no, it isn't your fault!* That was the worst part: I knew Cal and I knew his dying thought would be that he'd failed to protect me.

Then blackness descended and there was nothing.

59

CAL

THE SUN WAS RISING behind me, pushing back the darkness inch by inch. As it crept past me, it mixed with the false dawn in front of me, a roaring orange glow that had consumed the cabin and was slowly dying down, becoming a crackling scarlet fire among the blackened timbers. As I watched, the last of the roof beams collapsed inwards, taking some of the south wall with it.

I knew I should be feeling something. It had taken me a full year to build the place and outfit it. Months of chopping down trees, sanding wood and sealing cracks. More back-breaking trips to Marten Valley for supplies than I could count. Now, it was a ruin.

But I didn't care. Because the second she'd left, it had stopped being a home and had gone back to being a house, and now I knew how empty that was. She was gone. I'd failed her.

"It is done," said Alik. I heard him step back from me. Imagined him raising the gun.

"Don't shoot my dog," I said.

He hesitated. Then, "Have to."

"Ralavich isn't here," I told him. "He'll never know."

Alik gave a bitter laugh. "You don't know Ralavich. When I come back, he will ask helicopter pilot if he saw dog's body."

"*Please,*" I pressed. I wasn't ashamed to beg. Not when it came to Rufus.

Another pause. "I make it quick," Alik promised.

I closed my eyes. I'd lost both of them. The one companion I'd had for the last six years and the one woman who'd given me hope again. I felt like my heart had been ripped right out of me.

There was a sound, off to my left, barely perceptible. I only picked up on it because I'd spent so many years in these woods, waiting and listening. I knew the background creak of branches and rustle of leaves, I knew the birdsong and the chatter of the squirrels and chipmunks. And this sound didn't belong. It was the sound of threads ripping.

I let my head hang a little lower, as if I was sagging in defeat, opened my eyes, and looked to my left. Through the trees, I saw tan and black fur. *Rufus!*

He must have fled to the trees when all the hunters came back to the smallholding. But he hadn't left without his blanket, which he was dragging determinedly through the undergrowth in his teeth. Except it had gotten caught on some brambles and it was tearing as he pulled at it.

Rufus glanced to the side and saw me. The shirt dropped from his mouth.

Behind me, Alik racked the bolt on his assault rifle, putting one in the chamber.

Rufus shot forward, four powerful legs clawing at the ground.

The barrel of the gun pressed against the back of my head. "You want that I tell her anything?" asked Alik.

Rufus hurtled towards us. His paws barely seemed to touch the ground, now.

"Yeah," I said. "Tell her to remind me to buy dog treats."

At the last second, Alik heard Rufus approaching and spun to face him. But by that point, Rufus had leaped and Alik got eighty pounds of dog straight to the chest. He went down with Rufus on top of him, which both made him lose the assault rifle and knocked any remaining wind out of him.

My hands were still tied so getting to my feet wasn't the easiest, but I struggled upright and kicked the assault rifle out of range of Alik's hands. Then I squatted down, reached behind me and pulled the military-style knife from Alik's belt, and used it to saw through the rope binding my hands.

Alik coughed, wheezed, and tried to struggle free. Rufus lowered his head and growled, his teeth an inch from Alik's throat, and Alik reluctantly went limp.

"Good boy," I said, ruffling Rufus's fur. "*Very good boy.*"

There was a crash as part of the cabin's wall collapsed. I glanced over at the ruins. Ralavich thought he'd destroyed my life but I hadn't *had* a life here. I'd been surviving. Surviving isn't living.

I felt the rage starting to build inside me. I'd had a shot at a real life, with someone so loving, so caring, she'd accepted me as I was. And Ralavich had taken her away.

But I hadn't lost her *yet*.

I hadn't failed her *yet*.

I retrieved Alik's assault rifle and then walked back to him. With every step, I felt the anger spreading, charging my muscles and heating my blood. By the time I reached Alik, I was so mad I could barely speak.

"I'm only going to ask you this once," I growled. "Where's this fucking mansion?"

60

RALAVICH

CAIRNS WAS WAITING for us at the door when we got back to the mansion. His face colored with rage when he saw his millionaire members nursing gunshot wounds but I just shrugged. None of the injuries were life-threatening and I knew he kept a discreet doctor on call to treat the girls, when one of the members got rough with them. If need be, they could be taken to a local hospital, and their injuries explained as hunting accidents.

Cairns looked at Bethany, asleep in my arms. "I take it you're finally satisfied, Mr. Ralavich?" His voice was strained.

I nodded, laid Bethany down on a couch, and pulled out my phone. Within a few minutes, the money for all ten girls was transferred and Cairns was a lamb again, eager to plan future deals and asking if there was anything I needed.

I shook my head and hoisted the sleeping Bethany into my arms. "Just to be left alone," I told him as I headed for the stairs. I'd get her on the bed, then give her a shot of something to wake her up. I wanted her looking into my eyes as I took her.

Just as we reached my bedroom, my phone rang. I tossed Bethany on the bed and stabbed the button to answer. "*What?!*"

It was Vladimir, who was handling transport. "There's a storm

blowing in," he said apologetically. "If you want to leave today, you
need to get off now."

I cursed and let my eyes rove over Bethany's sleeping body. Her
shirt had ridden up to reveal a slice of pale stomach and those
gorgeous breasts were rising and falling under the tight plaid. *I could
stay one more day and enjoy her now....*

But I'd only ever intended to come to the US for one day and
thanks to this little bitch, it has already been over two weeks. If the
FBI realized I was in their country, they'd cage me like a dog and even
with all my connections back home, I might not be able to get out. It
didn't do to push your luck. "Fine. Get ready to go," I told Vladimir.

I summoned Cairns and told him to put Bethany with the others.
I watched as she was carried downstairs, her long black hair trailing,
a sleeping princess. It was a pity...but there'd be plenty of time to use
her on the way back to Russia.

61

CAL

W E WERE RUNNING. Running like we'd never run before. My feet pounded the ground, my legs eating up the distance in long strides. Rufus streaked along beside me, leaping over fallen trees and skidding around bushes.

We'd kept up the punishing pace for hours and somewhere, on some level, we were tired. I could feel my heart hammering in my chest like it was trying to break free and the sweat soaking through my shirt. Most of all, I could feel the muscles in my legs screaming for relief, begging me to stagger to a stop, just for a minute, just for a *second*.

But none of it mattered. The only thing that mattered was getting there.

Alik had told us the location of the mansion and as soon as I'd freed the animals and shooed them well away from the fire, we'd set off, following a dead-straight line through the forest. We'd left Alik alive, tied to a tree.

We came to a gully and both of us jumped across without breaking our stride. We raced through a thicket, down into a valley, and then up the other side. It got steeper and steeper until it was close to vertical. My feet began to slip and even Rufus, with four leg drive, had to scramble and claw. By the time we reached the crest, I was gasping for air and my legs were shaking and begging for mercy.

But they had Bethany.

We ran on.

62

BETHANY

I FOUGHT MY WAY upwards through layers of sleep, like tearing through black cobwebs. When I finally forced my eyelids open, I was lying on my stomach on a soft, squishy surface topped with red vinyl. My head throbbed and I cradled it in one hand as I looked around. I was in a long, thin room that reminded me of an indoor children's play area: every surface, even the ceiling, was coated in thick, squishy red vinyl padding. Light came from a battery-powered LED lantern hanging from a hook on the ceiling.

I wasn't alone. Nine other women, all about my age, were sitting slumped against the walls. All of them wore dresses or sexy, strappy tops and skirts. *The other nine.* The other nine women who Ralavich was taking back to Russia. And I was in here with them. I was going there too....

And then the drugged haze receded just enough and I remembered. *Cal!* Cal was dead. And Rufus, too. I'd pushed myself up to hands and knees but now I slumped back to the floor and wept. The kindest, gentlest guy I'd ever met in my life and he was *gone*, executed. And Rufus.... Who could shoot *Rufus?!*

I'd gotten them both killed. If I'd just accepted my fate, that night in Ralavich's bedroom, they'd still be alive.

I cried and cried until it turned into heaving, snotty wails. A few of the other women came and put their hands gently on my back but no one said *it'll be okay,* because we all knew it wasn't going to be.

I nearly gave up, right there. But then I thought of Cal and the way he'd looked at me when he'd given me that pep talk as we ran for our lives. He'd said I was brave. I sure didn't feel it, but he'd said I was. He'd believed in me.

Giving up isn't what he would have wanted.

And it wasn't just about me: there were nine other women here and I couldn't let them wind up in some Russian brothel. I had to do something.

I pushed myself up to standing, my legs shaking, and wiped the tears from my eyes. And then I started examining the walls, looking for a way out.

63

CAL

I JUMPED OVER A BUSH, crashed through some branches and—
An air horn blasted my ears.

I registered that the forest had stopped, but I was moving so fast that I was already halfway across the asphalt before I stumbled to a stop.

The air horn shredded my eardrums again. I looked that way and saw the eighteen-wheeler bearing down on me, the fender only twenty feet away. I dodged back out of the way and it blasted past, the slipstream stealing what remained of my breath. I checked around for Rufus, terrified, but then saw him safe at the edge of the trees. He was blinking at me, like, *what are you doing?*

The freeway. We'd reached the freeway. We were nearly there!

The mansion was on the other side so we had to wait for a gap in the traffic. I spent the time bent over, sucking in lungfuls of much-needed air. Now that I'd stopped, my muscles got in touch with my brain and started telling it about every mile they'd run. First, they burned like they were filled with lava. Then they started to tighten up and it was like the lava was cooling and setting into rock, shot through with jagged lightning bolts of pain.

A gap opened up in the traffic. We hurried across and ran on.

Just over the next rise, I saw a huge white mansion at the end of a long, winding driveway. We took cover in the scrubby undergrowth while I checked it out. There were high hedges and razor-wire-topped fences, guys on guard duty, and electric gates. This was the place.

I turned to Rufus. "You stay here. This is going to be dangerous." I ruffled his fur, then started across the open ground. Halfway to the hedge, I realized he was beside me. "No! Rufus, no!" I hurried back to the undergrowth with him and pushed him down into a sit. *"Stay! Dangerous!"*

I set out again. Before I'd gone three steps, he'd caught up and was running alongside me. *"Rufus—"* I began, exasperated.

He tilted his head to the side and gave me a look that very clearly said *you are* not *leaving me behind again!*

I sighed. I'd missed having him with me when we were being hunted. And we'd been in this together since the start. Plus, it wasn't like he was giving me a choice. "Okay, fine," I said and ruffled his fur. "Let's do this."

The hedge was designed to look pretty, not keep people out, and we just rammed our way through it. The real barrier was the wire fence just beyond it, but with Rufus keeping watch, I cut a hole with the knife I'd taken from Alik's belt and we belly-crawled through. Then we were up and running for the house.

A guard turned, saw us and brought his radio up to his mouth. I swung the assault rifle and clubbed him to the ground without stopping. Another one raised his gun. Rufus leaped and sank his teeth deep into the man's gun arm. He screamed and I punched him in the face.

We raced up the steps and I staggered to a stop outside the huge double doors. This was it. I could feel the rage thundering through my veins. This was the nest those rich bastards had slithered out of. This was where they'd taken her, and all the others like her. Where they planned to—

I growled and reached for the door handle. But before my hand could close on it, the door opened on its own. A tall, thin, bald guy in an expensive suit stood there, as surprised to see me as I was him. He took in my plaid shirt, torn and leaf-covered from racing through the forest; my mud-stained jeans and dirty boots, the panting dog beside me. His lip curled in disgust and he opened his mouth to banish us. Behind him, I glimpsed marble tiles and a huge chandelier. This was *his* world, and we didn't belong.

Then he saw the assault rifle slung on my back and all the blood drained from his face. He stepped back, turned to shout a warning—

I kicked the doors open with my boot, sending him staggering back to fall on his ass. Then I unslung the assault rifle and stepped into the enormous hallway. A few of the members who'd been at the hunt were standing around, drinking to numb the pain of their wounds, and they bolted as soon as they saw me. The other members just stood there staring. Two guards rushed towards me, drawing their weapons. I fired two quick shots at each of them and they fell. They were wearing body armor, so they'd survive, but getting shot is still like being kicked by a mule: they weren't going to be getting up in a hurry.

I turned to Rufus. "Find her. Find Bethany."

He lifted his nose and sniffed the air...then bolted up the main staircase. I ran after him, shoving aside anyone who got in my way. He ran straight up to the top floor, then down the hallway to a door at the end. I kicked it open—

A bedroom. Empty. But on the floor were those sneakers she'd worn when I first met her, the rubber soles still pure white. This is where that bastard had taken her, that first night. And maybe she'd been here since. But... "Where is she now?" I asked Rufus, ruffling his coat encouragingly. "Where is she now, boy?"

Rufus sniffed her sneakers. Turned a circle, sniffing the air again. Then he bolted back down the stairs. At the bottom, two more guards were waiting for us. Rufus shot straight between them, too quick to catch. Then I smashed through them like a quarterback, sending them sprawling.

I followed Rufus to a big, book-lined library. He turned a circle there, then looked confused and ran to the next room. I charged along behind him, grabbing members and hurling them out of the way, using the butt of the rifle or a few quick shots to take out the guards. A few of them got shots off, shattering a huge fish tank and sending a tidal wave of water thundering across the carpet. One of the members grabbed a shotgun and fired a couple of blasts at us, but only managed to destroy a bust and shred an oil painting before I clubbed him in the side of the head. We raced from room to room, until we'd been around the entire first floor and were back in the library. Rufus looked at me, confused.

Where is she?

64

BETHANY

I'D BEEN OVER every wall and even tried the floor and the ceiling but I'd gotten nowhere. Every surface was covered in the thick red vinyl padding and in the few places where I could force my fingers into a crack where two pads joined, all I felt was hard cold metal. There had to be a door somewhere—they'd got us in here—but I couldn't find it.

Panic started to rise in me, the cold nausea of feeling your time slipping away and not being able to do a freakin' thing about it. *We have to get out before they come for us and take us off to Russia!* But I'd searched every wall, felt in every crack....

Then I remembered what Cal had taught me. "Everyone be quiet for a minute," I told the others. "*Shh!*"

They quietened down and I closed my eyes and listened. I listened for the hum of air conditioning, the gurgle of water in pipes, the sound of footsteps. But there was absolutely nothing. Why couldn't I hear the rest of the mansion?

The room was soundproof. That's what all the soft padding was for. A soundproof, windowless box. A secret room, a place to keep women until they were needed, or to put them if the cops were about to search the house, a place where we wouldn't be heard even if we screamed for help. Where would you put a place like that?

Underground. We were down in the basement, in a locked box, where no one could ever find us.

65

CAL

RUFUS AND I ran back up to the third floor and worked our way down again, searching room by room. When guards got in our way, I clubbed them out of the way with the rifle or picked them up and threw them across the room, smashing furniture and knocking paintings off the walls as they landed.

Some of the bedroom doors were locked and when I kicked them down, I found guys in suits, along with the half-naked women they'd bought. That only fueled my rage. I hauled the guys out and punched them into submission, then told the women they were safe, now. But none of them knew where Bethany or the other women bound for Russia were. We cleared the whole of the third floor and then the whole of the second. *Nothing.* I stood there panting with anger and fear. Where the hell was she?

Rufus led me back to the library for the third time, then woofed, looking confused. Two guards ran in and I knocked one out with my rifle butt and punched the other in the face. The mansion fell silent. The guards and members were all lying injured or unconscious and the house itself was in ruins. The walls were peppered with bullet holes, antique tables and chairs lay in pieces, smashed apart in the fighting and the Persian rugs were soaked with fish tank water. The floor was covered with a carpet of crunching fragments: what used to be hourglass decanters and priceless Ming vases. I'd torn the damn place apart. But I hadn't found her.

I hunkered down and scratched Rufus's ears. "Talk to me, boy. Where is she? Where's Bethany?"

He sniffed the floor, turned a circle and woofed, as frustrated as I was.

"C'mon, boy." There was pleading in my voice. "C'mon, Rufus, she needs us. Where is she?"

Rufus lowered his nose to the floor and sniffed. For a few seconds, he seemed to follow a trail, but it ended with his nose against one of the book-lined walls.

I sighed. *Goddammit!* "It's okay," I told him. "C'mon, let's check outside."

But Rufus didn't move. In fact, he sat down. And let out another *woof,* right at the bookcase.

"Rufus, c'mon!" I even patted my thigh.

But he just looked at me, then looked at the bookcase. And gave an enormous, room-shaking *woof.*

I narrowed my eyes and walked over there. It looked normal enough, just thick wooden shelves and big, leather-bound books. But Rufus didn't bark for no reason. I put my hands on the bookcase—

And felt it move. Only a fraction of an inch, but it probably weighed the same as a small car. It shouldn't move *at all.* I pushed it and it rocked, very slightly. Like it *could* move, but didn't want to at the moment.

All the shelves were crammed full except for one that had a few books missing. I thrust my hand into the gap and felt a hole in the back, hidden by the shadows. And in the hole was a metal handle, worn smooth with age. I pulled and there was a click as the bookcase came loose. I pushed...and the whole bookcase slid smoothly back into the wall. It went back a full six feet, revealing a bare stone floor and a yawning darkness to my right. As my eyes adjusted, I saw stone stairs, leading down.

Rufus shot down them, back on the trail he'd been trying so hard to follow. I was right behind him, bringing the assault rifle up, not knowing what we'd find. We turned a corner and—

The roar of a shotgun, deafening in the confined space, and I felt shotgun pellets tear at one arm. Most of it missed, though: the person holding it had panicked and fired high. But the next shot would get us. I staggered back and tried to find the shooter, but it was almost pitch black and the flash of the shotgun had blinded me—

There was a crash and a cry of pain as Rufus took the shooter down. I finally found the light switch and the whole basement lit up. A man in a suit was flat on his back, coughing and groaning, pinned down by Rufus on his chest. As I walked closer, I recognized the face. The attorney general. The coward must have hidden down here when I arrived.

I was about to ask him where Bethany was when I saw the door. Metal, thick and heavy, like something out of a prison. I pulled the bolts open and then, heart racing, I swung it wide—

A hallway, and along its length were twenty or more doors leading to tiny, six-by-eight rooms. *Cells.* My stomach twisted. Cells to keep women in, until they were needed. But all of the doors were open. All of the cells were empty.

Bethany was gone.

66

BETHANY

I SCREAMED as the floor suddenly lifted under my feet. *Earthquake!* Oh Jesus, and we were in a hidden room in a basement, we'd be buried and no one would ever find us!

The floor twisted and tipped and I went sideways into the wall. I bounced off it and went down on my ass, suddenly glad that everything was padded. Everyone was yelling and panicking, trying to find a handhold on the padded walls.

And then suddenly, there was a jolt, like when you're on a train and it stops moving and you have to fight to keep your balance. Just as I got up, the floor started to slip under my feet, like I'd stepped onto an escalator sideways. I tottered to the side and hit the wall again. *What the hell is going on?!*

Another jolt, and then my stomach shot up into my mouth, like when an elevator starts to descend. And suddenly, my whole perception realigned.

This wasn't an earthquake. The whole room was moving.

And the room wasn't a room. Long, thin, no windows, metal walls beneath the padding: we were in a shipping container! We were being shipped, just cargo in a box. That's what the padding was for: as well as soundproofing, it stopped us from getting hurt when the container was swung around.

There was a final jolt and the container went still. Wait...not *completely* still. I couldn't hear or see any movement but I could feel it. A slow up-and-down that unsettled my stomach. A *bobbing*.

We were on a ship.

They must have loaded us into this thing while we slept and we'd been unconscious for the journey to the port. That whole time when I thought we were still at the mansion, we'd really been sitting on a dockside. Now our container had been loaded onto a ship and the next stop would be Russia.

I hammered on the padded walls. "Help us! Help, we're in here! *Please!*"

But nobody heard.

67

CAL

I COLLECTED UP all the guns and handed them out to the women, then got them to help me hustle all the men, guards and members alike, into the cells in the basement, where we locked them up. The women hugged one another, many of them in tears: they'd been through hell. I was taken by surprise when one of them threw her arms around me. "Thank you," she sobbed into my chest. "Thank you."

I looked down at her in confusion for a second. She was a complete stranger but she wasn't scared of me. I awkwardly patted her on the back, and told her she was safe, now. And then *I* choked up a little, because I felt the crushing weight of the guilt lift, just a little.

What Bethany said was true. I *could* make things right.

None of the women I'd rescued knew anything and the club members weren't any more helpful. But then I thought to ask who was in charge, and everyone pointed me to a guy called Preston Cairns. I pulled him out of his cell and he turned out to be the same guy who'd turned his nose up at me when he opened the door. I threw him on the floor and stood over him. "Where did Ralavich take the women he bought?"

He shook his head and glared up at me, tight-lipped. Even now, with his little empire in ruins around him, he was keeping to some tradition of protecting his member's secrecy. I could beat it out of him, but I didn't have time.

I thought for a second. Then I stepped between his feet and kicked his legs into a wide vee. I whistled and Rufus obediently trotted over, coming to a stop between Cairns's knees. Cairns went pale. I guess he didn't like dogs, especially big ones.

"Ever see a German Shepherd play with a chew toy?" I asked Cairns. And then I looked meaningfully at his balls.

Cairns's face went dead white. "They put them in a shipping container. A red shipping container. And loaded it onto a truck, heading for the port of Seattle. They left early this morning, almost as soon as they came back."

I cursed. Bethany must have left here about the same time I set off from the smallholding. All that time running here had been wasted.

I caught a movement out of the corner of my eye and looked up. One of the women I'd rescued was comforting another, putting a blanket around her bare shoulders. My chest contracted in pity. Okay, maybe not *wasted*. But that didn't change the fact that Bethany was eight or nine hours ahead of me. She could be at the port by now. Even if I jumped in a car right now and drove like a bat out of hell to Seattle, it would take five or six hours. How long did it take to load a ship? Not *that* long. I was going to miss her. She was going to be on some ship and gone. Unless....

I picked up Cairns, tossed him back into his cell, and slammed the door. Then I turned to the women. "Call the cops," I told them. "Local *and* state *and* the FBI." The club might have been able to crush an investigation when it was just the word of a lone witness, describing a mansion she couldn't locate, with nothing to back up her story. But when the cops arrived and found ten women all ready to give statements, a dozen armed guards, a group of wealthy senators, CEOs and the attorney general, automatic weapons and a basement full of cells...not even the club could cover *that* up.

I raced upstairs, then found the mansion's back door and burst out into the gardens, praying I was right. Ralavich had told Alik to call when he'd killed me and he'd send the helicopter to pick him up. Alik had never made that call. So maybe, just maybe—

I rounded a hedge and saw it, and my lungs filled in hope. The helicopter was still there. I ran over, wrenched open the door, and pointed my assault rifle at the pilot.

He threw his hands in the air. He was in his early sixties, with curling white hair and a paunch. "I swear, these assholes just hired me last night to fly them out to the woods. I never would have taken the job if I'd known what was going on out here. But that big Russian guy, he said he'd kill my family if I went to the cops!"

I relaxed and lowered the gun. "You help me," I told him, "and you'll never have to worry about him again. How long to the port of Seattle?"

The pilot pursed his lips. "Two hours. Less, if I push it."

"Push it," I told him, and jumped into the back with Rufus.

Less than two hours later, the helicopter swung in low and touched down beside a warehouse. "Close as I can get you," the pilot told me. "Good luck!"

I thanked him and Rufus and I jumped out. Now, all we had to do was find a red container. We ran around the corner of the warehouse and—

I stumbled to a stop.

The port went on for a couple of square miles. And a huge chunk of it was filled with cargo containers. Thousands of them, stacked five-high to form a sprawling maze. More containers hung from gantries that whirred back and forth on rails, stacking them like building blocks. Still more were being trundled around by huge forklift trucks. And then I turned and saw the ones already sitting on the decks of cargo ships. At least one in five of them was red.

68

BETHANY

THE SOUND of quiet, constant sobbing filled the container. All of us were slumped on the floor, now, our backs against the padded walls. It had been hours since we'd been loaded onto the ship and since then, we'd felt the impact as containers thudded into place either side and then, terrifyingly, on top of ours. We were being buried in a stack. *Is there an air hole, somewhere? What if they've covered it up?* One mistake by the workers loading the ship and we could die in here!

There was a plastic crate in one corner with bottles of water and energy bars and a covered bucket for a toilet. *How long are they going to keep us in here?* The other women didn't know any more than I did. They all had similar stories to me: low-paid jobs, cameras in their workplace, a sudden offer of a job in another city, and then waking up in the mansion. They'd all been drugged a second time before waking up in this room. *Where are we?* I hadn't seen anywhere like this when I was last here, but then I'd only seen a few rooms and the mansion was huge.

And if we did survive the journey, what awaited us in Russia wasn't much better. Rich Russian men, who'd pay to do what those bastards at the club did. Who wanted a woman who couldn't go to the police. My stomach knotted.

I felt something. I couldn't figure out what it was, at first, because there was no sound, just a sensation. A deep, throbbing vibration. There were some crumbs on the floor from when someone had eaten one of the energy bars and they began to dance and shuffle along the padding. I felt my face crumple and I let out a silent *no* of horror as I realized what that meant.

The engines had started. The ship was about to leave.

69

CAL

R UFUS LOOKED expectantly up at me. But I didn't have an answer, didn't have any idea how to find her. I only knew that she was slipping away from us with each passing second. And this place...I'd never felt so out of my element. The city was bad but even a city has trees and parks. This place was nothing but metal and concrete. And after the soft green and brown of the woods, this place was an overwhelming riot of bright primary colors, all mixed chaotically together like a world made of random Legos. Every surface was hard and smooth, reflecting and amplifying the noise as containers banged together and diesel engines roared. I felt like a mouse trapped inside the world's biggest machine.

This wasn't some problem I could solve with a gun, or with brute strength. *What would Bethany do?*

She'd talk to people. She was good at that. I wasn't.

But if I wanted to save her, I had to try.

I hid the assault rifle behind a dumpster and ran to a tall building whose top floor had big, sloping windows that overlooked the dockside—the control room, I hoped.

I burst inside and looked around wildly. It reminded me of the offices on military bases: the ground floor was full of harried staff dealing with questions about pay and assignments. What I needed must be upstairs.

"Hey!" yelled a man in shirt sleeves. "Where's your ID badge? You can't bring a dog in here!"

I had to move fast before I got thrown out. I saw a flight of stairs and pounded up them to the top floor. Behind me, the guy yelled for me to come back.

I burst out of the stairwell into the room with sloping glass windows I'd seen from below. It *was* a control room. People sat at computer screens, their faces lit with reflections of shipping routes, maps of the port, and the glowing, colorful rectangles of thousands of shipping containers. It was quiet and calm.

Until I showed up. As I marched in, my hip knocked against a stack of papers on a desk and the whole thing toppled to the floor and spread out into a wide fan. Rufus bounded in behind me, his tail clearing desks of trinkets and coffee mugs. Everyone looked round.

"Who the hell are you?" a woman's voice demanded.

I turned. She was in her forties, wearing a headset and a trouser suit, and she stood in the very center of the room so that she could see everyone's screen and what was going on outside the windows. I didn't need to look at her ID badge to know she was in charge.

I hurried towards her. A security guard moved to intercept me from the back of the room.

The woman frowned. "Who *are* you?" she asked again. "You can't be in here!"

I stopped right in front of her and now she wasn't mad, she was scared. She backed away from me and the security guard started to run. *Shit.* I was looming. I'd spent so many years looming and scowling and scaring people away, I'd forgotten how to switch it off. I opened my mouth to speak but those cogs and gears were all jammed tight again. This wasn't like talking to Bethany, with her patience and cool, calming voice. Everyone was staring at me, defensive and worried.

I looked down at myself. Bearded and long-haired. Nearly seven feet tall. My clothes were torn and mud-stained from my run through the forest, blood was soaking through one sleeve where a few shotgun pellets had winged me and a big German Shepherd was prowling around my legs. *I'd* be scared of me.

The security guard put his hand on his gun. "Just back away, pal."

I had to talk to this woman. Convince her to help. But she was the first person I'd had to really talk to, other than Bethany, in six years. "I—"

Feet pounded up the stairs. The man in shirt sleeves from downstairs appeared, along with another security guard. "Sorry, Nina, he got past me. C'mon, outta here!"

I stared down into the woman's eyes. She was scared and I didn't know the words to say to put her at ease. "I—"

The security guards each grabbed one of my arms. "Come on, buddy, let's get you downstairs."

I took a deep breath and let it out slowly. I hunkered down, bending my knees until I was at eye level with the woman. And then I forced myself to talk like I did to Bethany. I had to not growl or snarl or grunt. Just *speak.*

"Ma'am," I said, "My name's Cal Whittaker and...I need your help. To save ten women, including the one I love."

The security guards started to pull me towards the stairs. I let them because if I resisted, they'd reach for their guns. I kept my eyes on the woman—Nina, the guy had called her. And I prayed she could see in my face that I was telling the truth.

"Wait," she said.

The guards kept pulling me. The guy in shirt sleeves scowled. "He's just some homeless guy."

"*Wait!*" ordered Nina. Everyone stopped.

Nina walked over to me. She looked down at Rufus, who immediately sat and looked up at her with eyes that would have melted a heart of stone. She looked at me. "What are you talking about?"

"There's a shipping container somewhere on your dock with women inside," I told her.

Nina blinked. "If...that's true then we can get the police involved—"

"There's no time! It got here hours ago, it might already be on a ship!"

Nina debated for a second. "Do you know the container number?"

"No. I know it's red."

The whole office gave a despairing sigh.

"I know it came in by truck a few hours ago and I know the ship's heading to Russia!" I told them.

Nina crossed her arms and frowned at me, trying to figure out if I was a crazy timewaster. I stood there trying to look as sane and sincere as I could. The guy in shirt sleeves shook his head at Nina. She glared at him. Bit her lip....

"Marcus," she asked, without taking her eyes off of me. "Do we have anything heading to Russia today?"

A guy in his twenties tapped at his keyboard and then turned to her, pushing his glasses up his nose. "There is one...the *Charodeyka*. But...that's leaving *now*."

That was all I needed to hear. I threw off the guards and ran for the stairs, Rufus right on my heels. Nina's voice followed me. "*Wait! You can't just—*"

I tore through the office downstairs and out onto the dockside. I stopped for a second, searching. *There!* On the rusting, black-painted stern of a ship a few hundred yards away, I could see the name *Charodeyka*.

And it was moving.

I sprinted down the dock, Rufus racing alongside me. The ship was one of the smaller ones, with maybe twenty containers piled up on its deck instead of the hundreds some of the others carried. But it was still massive. As I pulled alongside it, I could hear the roar of its engines and see the churned-up water at its stern. It wasn't going fast, yet, but it was picking up speed. And they'd already removed the gangplank. *How the hell do I get on board?* There was a good eight feet of water between the dock and the ship, too far to jump.

I looked frantically around and saw a truck parked almost at the water's edge. I climbed up onto the hood and then, ignoring the driver's yells, up onto the roof. That put me a good eight feet above the ship. I took two running steps and *jumped....*

And landed hard on the moving deck, picking up a few new bruises. A second later, Rufus jumped and I turned just in time to catch him in my arms and cushion his fall by going down on my ass.

A man in his fifties marched towards us. His thick black beard was dusted with silver and his face was craggy and weathered from a life spent at sea. "What the *fuck* are you doing on my ship?" he yelled. His Russian accent was as thick as Ralavich's. "You've got no right—"

I grabbed him by the throat and lifted until his feet left the deck. "*Where are the women?*" I snarled.

His expression changed. Only for a second, but I saw it. He knew. "I don't know what you're talking about," he spat. "And you're trespassing on my ship!"

Something was happening on the dockside. Two Port Authority cops were yelling to the crew and I heard the engines stop. *Shit.* I had to find Bethany fast, or they'd arrest me instead of the captain. "*Where are they!*" I yelled into his face. He flinched but didn't break. And now the cops were wrestling the gangplank into place so they could come aboard....

I dropped the captain and ran down the length of the ship, searching. White containers, green ones, blue ones, but no red. Had I got it wrong? I looked back towards the cops and my heart sank. They had the gangplank in place and were running up it. *Shit!*

Then it occurred to me that the containers were stacked in two rows, and I could only see the ones on this side. I raced around the end of the stack and started down the other side—

And there it was. A red container, about halfway along the ship, at the bottom of the stack. I ran to it and got there just as the captain and the two cops arrived from the other direction. "*Freeze!*" yelled the older of the two cops. He was graying and tubby and clearly didn't appreciate being made to run.

I raised my hands in the air, very glad I'd gotten rid of the assault rifle. "There—There's women in there," I panted, nodding at the container.

"This man is trespassing!" snapped the captain. "I want him off my ship!"

No. God, no, not when I'm so close! "Please!" I looked pleadingly at the cops. "Please, arrest me, take me to jail, do whatever you gotta do but just take a look, *please!*"

"He's crazy man," said the captain. "Is potatoes in there!"

The two cops looked at each other uncertainly. I held my breath.

"Maybe you better let us take a look," said the younger cop at last.

I sucked in a huge breath and almost lowered my hands. The older cop made a warning gesture and I raised them again. I didn't care, as long as they opened the container.

Cursing, the captain broke the seals and undid the locks, then pulled the doors wide—

I stared, icy shock sluicing through me. Potatoes piled almost to the ceiling. A few shook free and rolled against our feet.

The older cop sighed. "Sorry, captain. You can get underway." He turned to me. "You, you're under arrest."

He grabbed my shoulder and I let him march me towards the gangplank. It was over. Maybe I'd been wrong about the captain and the container was still on the dock, waiting for a ship. Maybe it *was* on this ship, and Cairns had lied about the color. Or maybe it was on a ship that was already at sea, and the crew had lied about their destination. Whichever it was, Bethany was gone. No one would listen to me now.

When we were almost at the gangplank, I heard, "Get this mutt out of here!"

I looked over my shoulder. The captain was trying to shoo Rufus away from the container, but Rufus had his nose inside, sniffing. Then he started pawing at the potatoes, slowly at first and then faster, as if he was trying to burrow into the pile.

He looked at me and barked.

I drew in my breath and twisted around, shaking the cops off me. Then I was sprinting back down the ship, shoving the captain out of the way, and joining Rufus in front of the open container. I burrowed alongside him, shoving my arms into the pile and tossing huge armfuls of potatoes over my shoulders. I worked frantically, hearing the cops pounding down the deck towards me—

Three feet in, my hands hit metal. I shoved the potatoes aside and found a metal wall...and a door. The captain and the cops arrived just in time to see me wrench it open. The inside was covered in thick, red padding. *"Bethany?"* I yelled.

Running footsteps, muffled by the padding.

And then she shot out of the door and *whumped* into my chest.

A lot happened very quickly.

Rufus went berserk, jumping up and woofing and putting his front paws on Bethany's shoulders and trying to lick her face even as I kissed her.

The other women started scrambling out of the container, blinking in the bright sunlight, some of them sobbing in relief.

The older cop stared in shock at the women climbing out of the container. Then his face darkened and he drew his gun and spun to face the captain, who had started to back away down the deck. *"You! Hands where I can see them!"* he bellowed. The captain reluctantly raised his hands.

And Bethany and me...we just clung to each other. She was hanging onto me like a monkey, arms and legs wrapped around me, and I was crushing her to me and kissing her madly, panting with relief at having her back. She kept saying something between kisses and I couldn't make it out at first, but then I got it. *You're alive,* she was saying. *You're really alive.* I nodded. I was alive and she was safe and I was never letting her go again.

And then, out of the corner of my eye, I saw movement. A man stepping out of a doorway, behind where the cops were handcuffing the captain.

Ralavich.

70

RALAVICH

I WAS IN A FOUL MOOD. Over two weeks since I'd first taken delivery of the little bitch and I hadn't even had a chance to fuck her yet. Now I'd have to do it in a cramped cabin instead of a luxurious room at the mansion. Then I'd heard shouting, and the engines had stopped. I'd grabbed the assault rifle I keep in my cabin for protection and marched upstairs to see what was going on. That's when I saw *him*, that big oaf in the plaid shirt, with his hands all over Bethany, and all my other girls spilling out of the cargo container. *How is he alive?* Then I realized that I hadn't heard from Alik. The big bastard must have killed him.

The rage flashed through me. I pushed open the door and stepped out onto the deck—

That was when I saw the two Port Authority cops handcuffing Vladimir. *Shit.* And then I heard sirens wailing in the distance. I had to get out of here. Losing the girls hurt. Losing one as special as Bethany hurt even more. But it wasn't worth going to jail for. Better to slip away quietly and go back to St. Petersburg. I could find another supplier for my brothels: there was always the Austrian. And once things had calmed down, I could track down Bethany and send someone to kill that big prick and steal her back. But first, I had to get out of here. And to do that, I needed a diversion.

I raised my gun and fired at the Port Authority cops, the gun kicking and spraying wildly. Everyone screamed and ducked for cover, but I kept firing until I saw one of them fall. Then I ran to the gangplank and started down it to the docks.

71

BETHANY

THE FIRST WARNING I had that anything was wrong was when Cal suddenly spun us around. Then gunfire came from behind him and I realized he'd put himself between it and me. I screamed and tensed, waiting for his body to jerk against mine as a bullet hit him. But the impact never came. Then I heard running footsteps and he slowly released me.

When we turned around, we saw the older of the two cops on the deck, his hands to his stomach. Blood was soaking his uniform and slicking his hands. The other cop was kneeling over him, shouting his name, hysterical.

I ran over to them and fell to my knees beside them. I found where the bullet had entered and applied pressure. "Call for an ambulance," I told the other cop, and he nodded and got on his radio.

Cal hunkered down beside me, ready to help if I needed it, but there wasn't much we could do without medical gear. I did my best to slow the bleeding and talked to the cop, reassuring him it was going to be okay.

Cal gently cupped my cheek in one big hand, looking at me, and I saw his shoulders tense and his breathing tighten. For a second, I couldn't figure out what he was looking at. Then I remembered how Ralavich had hit me there. I guess a bruise had formed.

I glanced at the dock. Ralavich was running down the dockside and heading for the maze of containers. Cal saw it too. He turned to the younger cop and pointed to his radio. "Can you get Nina in the control room on that thing?" The cop nodded, switched channel and handed it to Cal. "Nina! It's Cal." He waved in the direction of a building with big, sloping windows. "I got her, I got them all, but the guy who did this is running."

I looked at him, amazed. He was talking to someone! And it sounded like he'd already connected with her.

There was a burst of static and then a woman's voice answered. "I see him. He's heading into the container stacks, but the cops are still a few minutes away."

My guts twisted. "He's going to get away," I thought out loud.

Cal slowly rose, his whole body shaking with rage. "No, he isn't," he said.

72

CAL

He hurt her. I'd already hated him for what he'd tried to do to her, for how he'd treated all those other women. But there was something basic and primal about seeing that bruise on her cheek. I could feel the scalding anger boiling up inside me. *He hurt my Bethany!*

I pounded down the gangplank, Rufus hot on my heels. I saw Ralavich disappear into the maze of cargo containers. It was a sprawling area the size of a few hundred football fields and on the far side of it was the fence that marked the edge of the port. If Ralavich reached that, he could just stroll off into Seattle and we'd never catch him.

I found the dumpster I'd passed by before and I was in luck: no one had found the assault rifle. I realized I was still clutching the cop's radio and shoved it in my shirt pocket, then picked up the rifle and ran into the container maze. As I reached the entrance, I forced myself to breathe slowly, calming myself. Gun up and ready, Rufus pressed tight against my legs, I advanced. Hunting him.

Except I'd never hunted in a place like this. I didn't know the layout of the containers, had no idea when I was heading into a dead-end or when I'd turn a corner and find I was exposed. Ralavich had left no trail to follow: there were no twigs for him to break, no dirt for him to leave fingerprints in. And when I stopped and listened to track him that way, there was nothing: nothing here rustled or snapped and his rubber-soled shoes were silent on the concrete.

This wasn't my world. It was entirely artificial and I didn't know how to hunt in it. If I blundered in there, there was a good chance Ralavich would see me and ambush me. I knew the smart thing to do would be to wait for the cops. But he'd be long gone before they got there. How many more women would be hurt before someone caught him? What if they never did? Bethany would be looking over her shoulder her entire life. She needed to know he was in jail.

I crept deeper into the maze.

73

BETHANY

THE OLDER COP had gone pale and sweaty but was hanging in there. The younger cop and I had been talking to him, trying to keep his mind off the pain. Then I heard footsteps running up the gangplank and paramedics were surrounding us, kneeling down beside us and politely but firmly taking over. I lifted my hands out of the way and stood up.

Police cruisers were arriving at the dock, but they were a long way from the maze of containers where I'd seen Ralavich heading. By now, Cal and Rufus would be in there, too.

A second team of paramedics was coming aboard, now, tending to the other women from the container, checking them for injuries and putting blankets around their shoulders. One of them saw the bruise on my cheek. "Hey," she said gently. "Sit down, let me take a look at you."

I wavered a little on my feet. I was exhausted: I'd been up all night and I'd spent most of it running for my life. The only sleep I'd had was when I was drugged and that had left me nauseous and with a thumping headache. All I wanted to do was sit down and let someone fuss over me.

But not while Cal and Rufus were out there, in danger. "I have to go," I told her, and ran.

I headed for the building Cal had waved to, the one with sloping windows that overlooked the port. I raced inside and then up the stairs to the top floor. From the huge windows, I could see the whole dockside: the ship, with the ambulances pulled up next to the gangplank, the police cars arriving, and the sprawling container maze. Squinting, I could just see Cal and Rufus down there, creeping forwards through the containers. *I have to help them!*

"What the *hell* is with people bursting into my control room today?" asked an aggrieved voice. I turned to see a woman in her forties wearing a headset. Then she frowned, taking in my plaid shirt and muddy jeans. "You're *her*." She glanced at the ship, at the open container, and the other women still on board. "The one he was trying to save."

I recognized the voice. *Nina.* "We have to help him," I told her. There was panic in my voice. Even from all the way up here, I could see Cal's uncertainty in the way he moved. He was used to the wild and the containers were like a freakin' laboratory maze for mice.

"Here," said Nina, and passed me a pair of binoculars. That helped: now I could search the maze and...*there!* I saw the corner of a gray suit jacket peeking out from behind a container. Ralavich was lying in wait for Cal, just a little way ahead. "Tell him to stop!"

Nina spoke into her headset. "Cal! Stop!"

Through the binoculars, I saw Cal stop. He looked down in confusion at his shirt pocket as if he'd forgotten the radio was there.

"Your man is ahead of you in the south-west quadrant," Nina told him. "Take a left." Cal turned. "Your other left!" she told him. "Towards the customs area!"

Cal stopped and fumbled to press the *talk* button on his radio...which meant lowering his rifle. "Where's the customs area?"

"Past the refrigerated containers!"

Cal looked around in confusion. "What do *those* look like?"

Nina cursed. I bit my lip. This was no good: she was doing her best, but she was used to dock workers who knew every nook and cranny of the docks. And every time Cal had to stop and ask something, he had to take his hands off his rifle, which made him vulnerable. It wasn't her fault: she'd never guided anyone who was completely out of their element, before.

But I had. "Please, I need a headset."

Nina motioned to a young, blond-haired guy with glasses and he took off his headset and passed it to me. I settled it onto my head. "Cal?" I said. "It's me. Put the radio in your pocket and I'll guide you, okay?"

Through the binoculars, I saw his shoulders relax. He nodded and put the radio away, readying his rifle.

"Okay, ahead of you there's a wall of containers: blue on the bottom, red on the top. Head straight towards that." He did it. "Good, now turn ninety degrees to your left. There's a big stack of white containers with black fans on the ends. I want you to go past those and keep going until you reach the green container covered in graffiti."

I guided him step by step, just like helping someone on a support call. After a while, I felt Nina move silently in behind me and lay a comforting hand on my shoulder.

I took Cal around Ralavich's ambush and then, when Ralavich realized he wasn't coming and took off again, I guided him down the fastest route to intercept him. The two of them were nearly at the far end of the maze, now, right near the edge of the port. And the cops were still far behind. "You're right on him," I told Cal. "He's moving parallel to you, behind the wall of containers to your left."

And then there was nothing more I could do except watch...and pray.

74

CAL

I CREPT ALONG the container, rolling my feet instead of stepping, making no sound at all. Rufus pressed tight to my side, just as silent. Ahead of us was a rusty fence that marked the edge of the port. It was sagging and ripped and there were holes big enough to squeeze through. Beyond that, there was a patch of marshy wasteland and beyond *that,* the city and a million places where Ralavich could disappear.

I reached the corner of the container and peeked around it—

There was a roar of gunfire and sparks singed my cheek. I whipped back around the corner, hearing the echo of the ricochet rolling around and around the metal walls of the maze. He'd missed my head by an inch.

I'd gotten a look at him, just a fleeting glimpse. There'd been true fear in his eyes: that was why he wasn't taunting or gloating. He knew he was in trouble. But that made him very, very dangerous.

I waited several seconds, the only sound my heart thumping in my chest. Then I edged forward again....

Another blast of gunfire and this time the bullets passed so close, I heard them hiss past my face. I pulled back against the container, poked the assault rifle around the edge, and blind-fired, holding down the trigger for a second, to keep him from coming around the corner. Then I stood there cursing up a storm. He had us pinned down. We were safe as long as we stayed put, but if we stayed put, we couldn't stop him. And at any point, he could just walk away, keeping his gun on us, and escape.

Even as I thought it, he started to do just that. The sun was throwing his shadow on the ground and I could see him backing towards the fence, his gun still pointed at us. *Shit!*

He reached the fence. I heard it rattle as he pushed his way through it. There was the sound of tearing cloth and cursing in Russian. Then he was through and backing away across the wasteland, his shadow getting smaller and smaller.

I checked my rifle and cursed again. I only had one round left.

Ralavich was hurrying, now. He could hear the sirens wailing, just as I could, but it sounded like the cops had only just now arrived at the maze. They still had to thread their way all the way to this end. *He's going to get away!*

I had to step out from the cover, exposing myself, and take the shot.

It might get me killed. But if I let Ralavich escape, he'd hurt more women. And Bethany would never be able to relax, knowing he was out there.

I took two quick breaths and then whipped around the container, bringing the rifle up to my eye.

Time slowed down. It felt as if I was moving through molasses. It took me a second to locate Ralavich, about four hundred yards away, running across the wasteland, checking over his shoulder every few seconds. And I'd emerged just as he did one of his checks. I saw him see me and his eyes narrow with hate. He raised his gun and fired, spraying bullets towards me. Unlike me, he didn't have to aim carefully: he had plenty of rounds to waste.

I heard bullets zip past me, making the metal container ring like a bell. One plucked at my shirt. Then one scored a line along my thigh and I grunted, a shudder rocking my body. My sights wavered and shook.

I gritted my teeth and thought of Bethany. *Do this for her.* I imagined her wrapped around me from behind, her hair brushing my face, her kisses on my neck. My hands steadied. I took a breath, let it out halfway and held it.

I fired my one remaining bullet.

And Ralavich staggered and fell. He went full length in a puddle, sending up a spray of muddy water, and his gun went flying.

I walked over to the fence, staggering a little myself. There was a red slash across my upper thigh, not deep but painful. I found a hole in the fence and ducked through, Rufus right behind me.

We took our time getting to Ralavich. He wasn't going anywhere: I'd put a bullet right through his upper thigh. A body shot would have been easier but that might have killed him and he deserved to rot in prison for the rest of his life.

As we approached, he struggled to get up but then fell back on the ground, groaning and cursing. His expensive suit was ripped, from where he'd struggled through the fence, his pants were soaked with mud and he'd lost one of his handmade leather shoes when he fell.

Just as we reached him, he made a lunge for the gun he'd dropped. I kicked it out of reach. With a howl of fury, he scrambled to his feet one last time and swung his fist at my face.

I dodged backward and gave him a very satisfying punch right in the jaw. He fell back in the mud. Rufus pounced, putting his full weight on Ralavich's chest and snarling into his face. Ralavich went limp, defeated.

I glanced over my shoulder towards the control room: I could feel Bethany watching over us like a protective angel. When I looked at Ralavich again, the anger on his face had been replaced by fear and horrified disbelief. He couldn't believe he'd finally been brought down not by the police, not by the FBI, but by a woman, a man, and a dog.

"Good boy," I told Rufus, ruffling his fur. "*Very good boy.*"

EPILOGUE

Bethany

Three Months Later

"Okay," I called. "Pass the next one up. I got this."

I was ten feet up in the air, straddling a roof beam and swinging my legs in the air, basking in the Colorado sunshine. Cal climbed the ladder step by careful step, his head rising into view from below, a log balanced on his shoulder. I leaned down and kissed him, then helped him maneuver it into place. Then I sat back and grinned. We had a long way to go: we had the floor laid and the walls up but there was no glass in the windows and the roof was just a frame. Slowly, though, our new home was taking shape.

We were building it with thick log walls that would be warm in winter, cool in summer, like the old cabin. But there were going to be modern touches, too. There'd be solar panels on the roof so that we had power, a chest freezer to store the meat Cal brought back from hunting trips, and a modern bathroom with a shower big enough for two. We'd rescued Cal's old metal tub, though—one of the few things to survive the fire—in case we wanted to bathe out under the stars.

Rufus had already moved in. Even though the roof wasn't on yet, he'd dragged his blanket into the middle of what would eventually be the lounge and curled up on it, happy.

Jacques, who had healed up well from his injuries, had taken care of the animals at the smallholding until we could arrange to transport them here. Now Betsy was chewing the cud on her new patch of pasture land, the chickens were clucking happily in their new coop, the pigs were rolling in the mud in their new pen and Hank was helping by eating all of the weeds..and anything else he could get hold of.

We'd already built a barn: Betsy and Hank had gotten a roof over their heads before we did, which might have seemed crazy to some people but we'd wanted to make sure they were safe from predators. And sleeping cuddled up to Cal in a tent for the last few weeks hadn't exactly been a hardship. Now we were working to get the house built and then came the vegetable garden, planting some wheat, a coat of paint for the barn (I was thinking red and white)...there was a lot to do, but I was loving it. We had the advantage that Cal had done all this before. The difference was, this time, he didn't have to do it all on his own.

The first few days after the port had been a blur. There'd been hours of questioning by the police and countless sessions with the FBI to take statement after statement, before we'd finally been allowed to get some sleep at a local motel.

Even now, months later, the investigation was still going on. The other women were all questioned, too, and charges were being brought against Cairns, the attorney general, Ralavich, the guards who worked at the mansion, and all of the members. The club's membership was extensive and went way beyond just the men who'd happened to be in the mansion over those few weeks. The FBI had found computer records at the mansion that led to a broad swathe of arrests across the Senate, the House, industry, and Hollywood. Every day, the press broke a new story about a man who'd thought he was untouchable being led away in handcuffs.

Cal looked up at the cloudless sky. "Doesn't look like it'll rain tonight. You want to ditch the tent, spend our first night indoors?"

I looked down at the half-built house. We'd be even cozier, sheltered by the log walls, and we could fall asleep looking up at the stars through the roof beams. "I'd like that," I told him, and leaned over to kiss him.

We'd stayed in the motel for a while, trying to decide where to live. Cal had claimed that he'd move to Seattle if that was what I wanted. But I knew he'd never be happy in a world of concrete and I'd gotten used to hearing the creak of branches and the whisper of the wind in the leaves. We also had to figure out what to do for money: Cal had spent all his savings on my fake passport and I was up to my eyeballs in debt.

But then two visitors changed everything.

The first showed up during one of our lengthy FBI debriefings. She was in her fifties, with long, ash-blonde hair and a smart suit, and told us she was Carrie Blake, head of the FBI's New York office. She'd come all the way to Idaho to meet the people—and the dog—who'd captured Ralavich. It turned out that he'd been on their most-wanted list for a long time and things had escalated a few years ago when he'd caused chaos in New York. There was a reward for information leading to his capture and, Carrie said with a victorious smile, that we certainly qualified for *that*. I got the impression that this was personal, for her.

When the reward arrived, we had to double-check that we were counting the zeroes correctly. We weren't going to have to worry about money for a very long time. We could buy some land, build a new home, pay off my debts...and the money raised other possibilities, too.

I'd bitten my lip when Cal had first suggested it. "It's a lot of money."

"We *have* a lot of money, now," he'd countered. "And it's what you should be doing."

And so, later that year, I'd be going back to med school. But that still left the question of where we'd live.

A few days later, though, our second visitor showed up. This one arrived at the motel in a black SUV and when I saw it through the window I immediately grabbed Cal's arm, thinking of the club, even though I knew they were all in custody.

But this SUV was different. Red and blue lights flashed from within the front grille. And when the men inside climbed out, they weren't wannabe-military thugs in black combat fatigues. These men had crisp black suits and sunglasses, and earpieces in their ears. The sort of men you see on TV, ushering the president to his car.

Two more men emerged from the rear. One of them was in a smart gray suit, the other in a leather jacket and jeans. But both had the same look: black hair and blue eyes and there was something in their features, in the heavy, dark brows and hard jawline. Something European, something that made me think of cold winds whipping across unyielding dark rock. They could almost have been brothers. Cal, Rufus and I met them at the door.

The one in the suit approached slowly, the other one hanging back. Cal stepped in front of me, silently protective. But Rufus pushed past us, trotted over to the stranger and sniffed at him, then nuzzled his hand, and Cal and I relaxed because that was always a good sign.

"Cal Whittaker?" asked the man. His accent was American but each consonant had been skimmed with a brush dipped in silver. Scottish? No, not quite....

"Who's asking?" rumbled Cal. The man was big but he still had to look up to meet Cal's eyes, and Cal glowered down at him suspiciously. I put my hand on Cal's warm bicep: *Easy.* And Cal gradually relaxed. After so long alone and being intimidating to push people away, it was going to take him a while to master people skills. But he was learning.

"Kian O'Harra," said the man, his voice gentle. I finally locked down his accent. *Irish.* "And I'm not here to cause you any trouble. I just admire what you did and how you handled yourself."

I frowned. "I know you," I said slowly. "I saw you on TV. That thing with the President's daughter."

Cal glanced at me, then looked at Kian, shocked. *That was him?* It had been a huge news story a few years ago. As evidenced by the fact that even Cal had heard about it, even though he only saw a newspaper once every three or four months.

"I've been reading your file," said Kian. "Wilderness survival expert, stealthy, great marksman...I was wondering if you'd be interested in a job."

Cal shook his head. "Don't want to do any more tours." His arm encircled my waist. "I found what I wanted, right here." And my heart lifted and swelled.

"I'm not with the military," said Kian. "This would be an occasional thing: a few days here and there."

Cal's face darkened. "Someone already gave me that speech, Mr. O'Harra. It worked on me back then but it ain't working now. I'm not doing anyone's dirty work for them." And he moved to close the door.

"I understand," said Kian quickly. "I've seen your *whole* file...even the parts that are redacted. I have a pretty good idea what the CIA had you doing. I'm not offering you that. The opposite, in fact. Helping people in trouble. Protecting people who need it. Doing some good. My team'll always know who they're fighting and *why.*"

Cal went quiet, but I saw the way his eyes changed. "I'll think about it," he muttered.

"All I ask," said Kian with a smile. He gave Cal a business card, then turned to me. "Ma'am," he said respectfully. He gave Rufus an expert scratch behind the ears, then strolled back to the SUV. The man in the leather jacket followed: another recruit, I guessed.

Cal stared long and hard at the business card as they drove away. "You're worried he'll use you, like they did?" I asked.

He nodded grimly.

"I don't think he's like that," I said. "I got a good vibe from him. Rufus, too." Cal was silent. "And if you *did* decide to do it, and there was even a hint of it being shady...you'd be out, right?"

"Hell yeah," he said savagely.

I waited, giving him time, because I knew his doubts were only part of it.

He sat down on the bed. "Wouldn't want to be away from you," he murmured.

"He said it'd only be for a few days at a time," I countered.

He looked at the card again, then looked at me, eyebrows raised in a question. My heart lifted. There'd been a hole in his life, ever since he left the Marines: he needed that close-knit group. He needed to serve his country, and to protect. Most of all, he needed to make things right, to do some good. This might be the chance to do that.

But despite all that, he didn't want to do it if I wasn't okay with it.

"You'd have to promise to always come home safe," I told him.

"There's nothing in the world that could stop me coming home to you," he said seriously.

I slipped my hand into his and squeezed it. "Then yes."

Rufus, deciding that he was being left out, pushed his way between us. We gave him simultaneous ear scratches and he pushed his head into our hands, hind leg beating the floor in ecstasy, tail whacking our legs.

After a few long phone calls with Kian, the details were hammered out. Cal would be on a generous retainer, in return for going on a job for a few days once a month or so. The team would be based in a small town in Colorado, where they could train and live in private.

Cal and I looked at each other. *Colorado.* Plenty of wilderness on our doorstep, but a fresh start after everything that had happened in Idaho. It sounded good. And I'd been thinking a lot about what Cal had said about his childhood home, on the very edge of a town: still in the wilds, but close enough for company. A balance.

So that's what we'd done. We'd bought a plot of land right on the edge of the town. We could still walk into the center and it was connected to the roads by a private dirt track, so we could use a pickup if we were taking a long trip. But the cabin would be screened from the road by trees, and there would be nothing behind it but forest. I could go to med school in Boulder and there was even a local hospital where I could try to get a job when I was ready. The air was amazingly fresh and clear and after a few long trips into the forest, Cal reported that the hunting was good. I had a feeling we were going to be happy, here.

I climbed carefully down the ladder. Halfway down, Cal grabbed me by the waist and lifted me the rest of the way to the floor. Then he slid his arms fully around me and drew me to his chest. I pressed my cheek to his pec and we just rocked there quietly for a while. Through the glassless window frames, we could see the sun sinking behind the trees, lighting the forest up orange and gold.

Cal used one big finger to gently lift my chin and turn my head to look at him. I gazed up at that rugged face, at those cornflower blue eyes that looked down at me with such melting intensity, and that silver string inside me pulled so tight that my whole body sang.

He leaned down and I went up on tiptoes and somewhere in the middle, our lips met and I kissed my gentle giant.

The kiss was soft and warm, unhurried and tender. But as our lips moved, an undercurrent began, full of dark promise and raw, animal lust. I heard him growl, low in his throat, and his hands found my ass. I traced the muscles of his back and squeezed his shoulders and he slowed, teasing me. In a few minutes, we might need to distract Rufus with some dog treats and dive into the tent for a while. But for now, the kiss turned tender again. Gentle and loving.

A coyote howled. It would be night, soon, and we didn't yet have windows or even a door. But I knew I'd sleep like a baby. I'd found that safety I'd always searched for, that feeling of being completely, devotedly, ferociously protected. And it came from being in his arms.

The End

Thank you for reading! If you enjoyed *Deep Woods*, please consider leaving a review.

The story of Kian O'Harra and how he fell for the President's daughter is told in *Saving Liberty*. Kian, his brother Bradan and Cal will all return in a forthcoming series. Or if you feel in the mood for tense medical action, blizzards, a shy surgeon and a cocky, gorgeous Irish doctor, you might enjoy *Mount Mercy*.

Stay safe and warm.

Helena Newbury

Made in United States
Orlando, FL
28 September 2023

37368493R00193